CORINTH 2642 AD

CORINTH 2642 AD

BINDIYA SCHAEFER

For my younger self.

TABLE OF CONTENTS

1

I 'D NEVER SEEN A WHITE PERSON
before. Not in real life, anyway. My brothers and I had seen
plenty of old movies and television shows from the Millennial
Era on our parents' Holoscreen. They were aficionados of old
movies and television shows in which most of the actors were
white people. So dinnertime at our household usually meant
cozying up in front of our holographic home theatre with
the lights down, watching an old movie from their extensive
collection. That was my only point of reference for what
Caucasians looked and sounded like.

I had read somewhere that there were only a few thousand
Caucasians still left in the world. Nobody knew where they were
or if they were still alive after all these years in isolation. But now
there was living proof standing in my living room, frowning at
me like I was the strange one.

The first thing that struck me about him was his eyes. His
dark brown irises were wrapped by a light gray-blue circle on
the outer rim—the ultimate sign of bodily decay, my mother
used to say. At first, I thought he was just a really pale person.
It's not that uncommon for people with mixed heritage to have
traditional Caucasian features. Genetics is like rolling dice; you
never know what you'll end up with.

But there was something about the way this old man

carried himself. Maybe it was the haughty disdain on his face that gave it away.

"I'm looking for James Matoo," he said, looking like he'd swallowed a glass of sour milk as soon as I opened my front door.

The old man stood out like a sore thumb, and not just because he was whiter than snow. He looked frail, and the wrinkles on his skin looked closely pinched together. Light from the porch reflected off his thin, silvery hair. Still, there was something rather opulent about him. It was probably his clothes, I decided. The man was dressed immaculately in a three-piece suit and a real silk tie, and his leather shoes were polished perfectly. A gold scale tipped unequally, like the sort Lady Justice carries, was pinned over his lapel. It was the sort of outfit you'd see in a museum. They didn't come cheap, and they weren't easy to find. The closest thing that came to vintage these days was my old 3D printer that took three long days just to create a simple white shirt. Practically a dinosaur considering what the newest models could do.

"You found him," I said, gesturing for him to come inside.

"I hope you don't mind my dropping by your home. I was afraid of drawing unnecessary attention to your office."

Of course I minded. This was my home, my sanctuary. This place was my way of keeping my work separate from my personal life. This was where I'd spent the last few days grieving and coming to terms with the latest tragedy to hit my family.

I started to complain but closed my mouth. There was something frail about this old man, and I needed the clients, anyway. Ever since I'd been kicked out of the SFPD Special

Investigation Unit for punching my commanding officer in the face, I didn't have the luxury of picking and choosing the most exciting cases. Plus, I was desperate for anything—anything to distract me from this searing pain.

"My name is Julius Bull," he introduced himself, inspecting my modest living room like he was afraid to touch anything.

I didn't have much in the way of furniture or décor, and housekeeping wasn't on top of my to-do list recently either, but what this place lacked in interior décor, it more than made up for in character. The bright airy windows, the intricately patterned mosaic tile in the fireplace, and the hardwood floors were original to the building, but most importantly, this was the place my brothers and I had spent most of our summer holidays raising hell. I could practically imagine our younger selves rolling our eyes at Bull's disdain for the place we loved most.

This apartment had belonged to my grandparents back when they lived in San Francisco. Back then they had the most beautiful view of the Golden Gate Bridge and the city. That was before the water levels rose and most of the city went under. Our neighborhood in Telegraph Hill was one of the few places to survive. Some days when the tide was low, I could see the two red towers of the bridge peeking through the water on either side. That was if Karl, the fog, wasn't blinding the city.

"It's nice to meet you, Julius." I closed the front door and offered the stranger my hand. "You can call me Jimmy."

In response, his brown-blue eyes widened in surprise. Bull looked at my outstretched hand like I'd just handed him a bomb. "Oh, I have a cold." He shuddered, straightening his tie instead.

Irritation swirled through my body. "I live in San

Francisco," I insisted and stepped closer to him. "Everything here is covered in germs already."

Whoever he was, he was on my turf. He had sought me out. That look of desperation on his face told me enough: he needed me. Bull's eyes met mine for just a fraction of a second before he relented and slowly stuck his right hand out. I grabbed his wrinkly palm with mine and gave it a firm shake for a good three seconds. When I released his cold palm, he immediately placed it on his chest.

"So what can I do for you?" I asked, motioning for him to join me on the couch.

Bull followed me to the living room. "I need someone discreet, someone with your background and training, to help me with a problem." Bull's reply was quick.

"Uh-huh. And how'd you find me? There are dozens of first-rate private investigators in the city."

A small smile appeared on Bull's face. "Oh, your former colleague Rahul Vera helped me track you down. He agreed you were the best person for the job."

Rahul Vera? My eyebrows knitted together. Vera was the commanding officer whose face had met my fist. It seemed odd that he would recommend me for anything. "He did, huh?"

Bull nodded enthusiastically. "Yes, he told me you might be able to help me with this." That's when he pulled out something small and white from his breast pocket and handed it to me.

I knew as soon as I took it from him that it was a piece of paper. It felt weird against my skin. So smooth and thin. Perfectly opaque. My fingers ran over the razor-sharp edges of the letter. It was not the recycled plastic you'd normally find in online stores. This was *real* paper, made from real wood, that undoubtedly came from an actual notebook. It was even weirder to see the words on it this way. The handwriting on this piece of paper was elegant. It was neat and cursive, written in dark blue ink.

Tuesday, July 11, 2642

Mom, Dad,

Mother Nature is spiteful, isn't she? Always picking and choosing who lives and dies. Sending hurricanes like flying kisses, throwing around earthquakes like basketballs, and for what? Natural selection? Our position as the dominant species of this planet is well-deserved. We were thriving, conquering the solar system, totally indomitable until she went and threw a wrench in our evolution.

Though to be fair, Homo sapiens are still winning the evolutionary race. It's just a certain variety of humans that Nature's jettisoning out of a plane without a parachute.

Do you really wonder why? Have you ever thought about all the things you're forcing me to do? The life you're shoving down my throat? Have you ever stopped to consider that I may not be able to live in this prison? My guess is no. Because if you did, even for just a teeny-tiny second, you wouldn't force this fate on me, nor would you let someone like Hexum bully us.

There are many of us (you'd be surprised how many) in Corinth who do not share your beliefs. And we have no intention of going through life as nothing more than the baby-making machines you'd like us to be. You think we're survivors, but what we really are is stuck.

Stuck in the past — our colonies are frozen in time, and I want to move forward. I need to. My sanity depends on it.

Mom, Dad, whole civilizations have gone extinct — usually at the hands of our ancestors! And, as terrible as it is, I don't believe it's the end of the world. It's just the start of a new one. It's time for you to let go of this ugliness and embrace evolution. Who knows? You might even be happier.

My whole life you raised me to be afraid of everything and everyone outside this colony. All those monsters you told me about? The ones who couldn't wait to get their hands on me? They live here in Corinth. Fear Hexum. Don't waste your life fearing the world outside because the world is not afraid of you. I truly believe that.

The fact that the world outside these walls is different from ours is not a good enough excuse for what you're making me do. I won't do what Isaac did. I just can't.

And that is why I am leaving you, even though it hurts — I know this is the best thing I will ever do for myself. As long as I live here, I'll never be free to be myself, and I will die if I cannot be who I was meant to be.

I desperately wish things were different, that you were different. But I never once wished that I was different.

To my big brother and little sister — wherever I am, wherever I go, I will miss you and think of you every day of my life. All I ask now is that you be brave and stand up for what you believe in.

Love, always and forever,

Cara

I folded the letter back to its original folds and handed it back to the elderly man standing in front of me.

"Who wrote this?" I asked. "Your daughter?"

Bull sighed heavily. "My granddaughter." He grimaced. "She is an exceptionally bright girl but also terribly stupid." He shook his delicate head in disapproval. "About to turn eighteen next week. As you can tell from the note, Mr. Matoo, Cara ran away four days ago."

My chest contracted painfully. Fresh anguish snaked across a briar patch of familiar old wounds, choking my heart all over again. "Did you say four days ago?" *That's a lifetime.*

Bull narrowed his eyes. "Yes, four days ago. Her parents are"—he paused—"distraught. And we need you to find her as quickly as you can and bring her back to us."

"Have you already alerted the local authorities?"

"No, of course not," he scoffed like it was obvious. "Besides, I *am* the local authority." He straightened his jacket and sniffed. "In any case, her fiancé would be most upset. Their wedding is in a week, and I'd like you to find her before he—or anybody else—realizes she's missing."

"And why is that?" I frowned. "I would think you'd want everyone you know to be out there looking for her."

Bull took a seat on the chair across from me and crossed his legs. "I'd rather not get into the politics of it right now. Though I will say that things are a bit complicated on the home front, and I fear Cara's disappearance will only add fuel to the fire."

"Why did you wait so long to ask for help, then?" I asked, trying hard to keep my voice even. "The chance of finding a missing kid dramatically decreases after the first twenty-four hours. She could be anywhere right now. Off-planet, even."

"I doubt Cara is that resourceful. Anyway, we were hoping she would change her mind and return. Teenagers can be so fickle, after all," Bull said, shaking his head slowly. "When she didn't come home the next day, we went looking for her. Discreetly, of course. But," he sighed, "we found nothing."

Cara would not be the first bride in history to get cold feet, but nothing in her letter suggested she had a secret lover. My Auge—a surgically implanted, highly advanced version of the contact lens that did a whole lot more than correct eyesight—pulled up an image I had snapped of Cara's letter before I returned the original to her grandfather.

The text was holographically projected over my irises, and I skimmed through the letter again. There was no mention of a fiancé or anything romantic. Words like *colony*, *monsters*, and *extinct* jumped out at me.

"Tell me about this colony."

Bull gazed out the window—it was another overcast San Francisco day. Shadows as dark as the fog rolling through the city crisscrossed over his pale face. "All right, yes," he said reluctantly. "What I am about to tell you, Mr. Matoo, is strictly confidential. There are few people in your government, and fewer outside it, who know of our existence. Our privacy is what keeps us alive. You understand?"

I shook my head. "No, I can't say that I do."

Bull looked at me with impatience. "Listen to me: the only people in Corinth who know about this letter, about me being here, are my flesh and blood. I can't trust anybody else. If they found out..."

The old man shuddered. "The colonies are our home. There are seven in total, spread across the country, and I am their leader. Cara and her siblings were raised in Corinth, Oregon. It is a place where we are free to be"—Bull hesitated—"us." He shifted, obviously uncomfortable. "You see, a long time ago, when multiethnicity was becoming the norm all over the world, my ancestors knew they needed to safeguard future generations from..."

"Becoming like me?" I could barely hide the disdain in my voice.

Bull looked at me defiantly. "Yes. Yes, from becoming like you. And I make no apologies for it." Bull carefully and deliberately studied my face. His bony features accentuated what could only be described as revulsion. "A long time ago, before you were even a thought, we decided that for our people to flourish and stay true to our roots, we needed to build a home far away from the temptations of this world." Bull leaned forward, resting his elbows on his knees and clenching his palms tightly. "We've had to make a lot of sacrifices to build our colonies over the years, but I believe that in the end, we will prevail. We *have* to."

"So, when you say, 'away from the temptations of your world'..." My voice trailed off.

"My people live a quiet life, Mr. Matoo." Bull's voice was sharp and crisp. "They are kept safe, cared for, and given every comfort in the world. They have no need for anything outside our walls."

The words sank in slowly and painfully. So the rumors were true after all. Bull and his people were the isolationists I'd heard about. They wanted a racially pure world. The way it was centuries ago when people identified themselves by their race and isolated themselves from new cultures and experiences.

Looking at Bull, I couldn't help but wonder why he would ever want to live in a world where somebody else was treated as a minority. Surely, he must know how hard and unfair life could be now that he was on the other side of the fence.

The word *minority* rolled uncomfortably around in my head. The concept was so alien these days when most people could trace their family tree—starting with their grandparents— back to at least four different countries. I couldn't explain how diverse my own family was if I tried.

My dreaded high school history lessons came back in a flash. When globalization was at its peak in the twenty-first century, racial diversity was on the rise across the world. Just before the war broke out, the population of the Earth was divided into neat little clusters. The Caucasians made up for only twenty percent of the global population. That means that there were about the same number of Chinese people as there were white people in the world. But toward the end of the century, India surpassed China to become the most populous nation in the world—meaning Indians, or those of Indian origin, accounted for thirty percent of the population while the Africans took third place with twenty-five percent.

I always had a hard time remembering those numbers, but the next part was the easy bit. Everyone knew that part. After the Millennial War ended, taking millions upon millions of lives with it, there was a massive baby boom—which was normal after any major conflict. But this time, those little babies set the stage for this brave new world Bull and I were living in.

By the time my great-grandparents were born, the metamorphosis of the human race was complete. People no longer identified themselves by ethnicity. We were no longer Black, White, Asian, Hispanic, or biracial. We had become a beautiful multiracial generation. A generation that came to be known as One World.

Bull's hawkish eyes bore into my skull. I flinched. "So you're a modern-day fascist."

Bull stood up abruptly. "How dare you!" he screamed. It was not hard to see the person he had been in his youth—someone full of strength and energy, always ready for a fight. "We are survivors against this disease you call One World!"

That was the first time I've ever heard anyone call us—me—a disease before. I would be lying if I said it didn't sting a little. But I didn't react to Bull's jab. Instead, I just stared at him without blinking. That always made people uncomfortable, and I could see that it was working with him as well.

"Why should I help someone like you?" I asked bluntly. "You have no respect for people like me."

Bull's lips curled upward. I got the feeling he'd been waiting for me to ask just that question. His thin fingers pulled another piece of paper from his jacket pocket and handed it to me. "Oh, I know you're going to help me find Cara," he said confidently. "In fact, I am certain of it."

Curious, I took it from him and unfolded it.

I froze.

I could recognize that face anywhere. Those sharp cheekbones and nose, and that thick brown hair, were so much like mine.

This was my younger brother, Vir.

My dead brother, Vir.

This picture must've been taken the night he died. The same night, I realized, that Cara had run away from her parents' home. The warmth had been sucked out of him. Vir's lean body was covered with blood, and his once-brown eyes were cloudy and gray from livor mortis. Once the initial shock wore off, other things about the photograph stood out. Like the shrapnel wounds in his chest, the burn marks on his face, and the damage to his immediate surroundings.

Vir, a cultural anthropologist from Stanford University, drowned off the coast of Santa Cruz, and his body couldn't be recovered. Or so we were told by the local authorities. But that was clearly not the case. Vir had obviously died from an explosion of some kind.

Countless questions swirled through my mind. Was my brother attacked? Why did Bull have this picture? What really happened the night he died? Where was Vir's body now?

It killed me that this wasn't the first time I'd had to ask these questions about a someone in my family

"Do you really think I would leave the safety of my home if I didn't know for a fact you'd accept this case?" Bull's sharp voice broke my reverie. "You're going to help me."

"I... don't... understand." I struggled to say the words. "What happened to him? Where did you find him?"

"On the outskirts of our town. I believe he died around the same time Cara ran away. Though I couldn't tell you how," he said, without any remorse. "And no, I didn't have anything to do with his death. You know, he was a difficult man to trace and identify, but Vera was most helpful. He was able to find his state ID, and of course, it was all too easy to find you after that."

I finally looked up from the gory image and met Bull's eyes. Maybe he was lying about Vir? It wasn't that hard to create a deepfake image and pass it off as the truth. Anybody could do it. But what could Bull possibly have to gain from tricking me into helping him? If anything, it would probably be easier for him to pay for my services. No, Bull wasn't lying. That much was clear. Vir really had died somewhere on land, but why would we be told otherwise? Unless…it had something to do with Bull's mysterious colony and his missing granddaughter. My brain went into overdrive. I considered the possibility that Cara going missing the same night Vir died was nothing more than a coincidence. The only problem was that I didn't believe in coincidences.

"Was he alone?"

"Yes."

"Where's my brother's body now?"

"Ashes," Bull said simply. "I had him cremated as soon as he was discovered."

I gasped. "You what!"

"Well, of course," he said. "I can't risk anybody finding out about him. We're working very hard to keep Cara's disappearance quiet. Your brother is the first of your kind to wander so close to our borders in decades, borders we go to great lengths to seal. I want answers, and I'm sure you do as well."

I stared at Bull in disbelief. My parents had raised me to respect my elders, but this cocky, arrogant old man had robbed my family of laying my brother to rest. I ought to have socked him in the face. God knows he deserved it, but I resisted with great difficulty.

Bull was right about one thing: I couldn't walk away from this case now.

2

AS I PACKED MY OVERNIGHT BAG, my thoughts focused on Cara. Letter or no letter, she was still a minor and under her parent's guardianship until she turned eighteen next week. And she was more than just a runaway bride. There was real anguish in her letter, even a little anger.

There was also nothing in her note to suggest that she was still in Corinth, but that was the first place to start looking for answers.

Corinth did not show up on any map. My Auge found three cities in the U.S. named Corinth, but none of them were listed in Oregon. There was also no record of a Julius Bull anywhere in any database, nor could I find any reference to the colonies he mentioned. I guessed Bull wasn't kidding when he said his people valued their privacy. He obviously went to the extraordinary length of taking all known records (if they existed at all) of him and his people offline.

Before I saw that picture of Vir, I had seriously considered turning this case down. Cases with missing children always hit me especially hard. Our youngest brother Aric was only nine years old when he was abducted. The police said it had probably happened on his way home from school, but they couldn't be certain.

But I knew exactly what happened. I was supposed to pick him up. I had just switched to a new school a couple of blocks away, and I was late. I don't even remember why, but I was. Aric probably got tired of waiting and decided to walk home himself, but he never made it.

Aric's lifeless, broken body was found less than a mile from our house. Nobody knew how he got there or who was responsible. There just wasn't enough evidence to go on. No eyewitnesses. No suspects. Nothing.

Some days I still expected him to turn up at my parents' house. The same nine-year-old kid wearing his school uniform, annoyed as hell that he had to walk home by himself. I could almost picture him with his tiny hands on his waist and that lopsided frown he always had when he was annoyed, demanding why I kept him waiting.

My parents, Vir, and I spent years trying to figure out what happened to him. We hired countless private investigators and gave interviews every year, but nothing ever turned up. No witnesses. No suspects. Nothing. Just like the police told us all those years ago. A dead end.

It seemed that only Aric could answer our questions.

Just like Vir.

Vir's untimely death had brought all of it back to the surface again. The same feelings of helplessness and desolation. I hadn't been there to help either of my brothers. Now, I had to try and figure out what really happened to Vir. To do that, I first needed to find Cara.

Regardless of Cara's connection to my brother, I couldn't live with myself if something happened to that young girl, even if she left out of her own volition. I needed to know for certain. I needed to give her family a concrete answer and the peace of mind that mine never got. When I decided to go private, I promised myself I would never take money from victims for solving violent crimes and missing persons cases. It just felt gross somehow. Like I was profiting from someone else's misery. I couldn't imagine the sort of bad karma I'd invite into my life if I ever did that.

I *needed* to find Cara and figure out what happened to Vir and how he ended up dead near Bull's territory.

THE STREETS WERE MOSTLY EMPTY, except for a couple of joggers and some people rushing to catch the Hyperloop to work. One of the joggers, a young hybrid man, nodded to me as our paths crossed. Unlike some of the other hybrids I'd met, this man had opted not to cover his scars and new body parts with synthetic skin; the machine side of him complemented the human half. Human-hybrid amalgamations were becoming pretty common, but it was always interesting to see one anyway.

I waited for him to pass before walking over to Bull's antique Tesla. Bull was already sitting in the backseat when I got there. This version still had its charging pod, though I wasn't sure if it was still functional or just a showpiece. The interior of the car had been overhauled entirely. It now had touchscreen navigation on the windshield with a personal virtual reality assistant, similar to my Auge. The center console had a small bar decked with pricey liquor and… were those chocolates?

Bull reached over and helped himself to a couple of bars but didn't offer me any. His teeth gnashed loudly, and he made soft slurping noises. So that's how Bull and Rahul Vera were connected, I realized. Chocolate. Vera had followed through with his plans after all, then…

It was my first big case after the academy, and we were investigating an underground cocoa trafficking ring together. When cocoa went extinct around the time the Millennial War started, it set off a sort of gold rush. The last remaining cocoa beans were suddenly worth a lot of money, and the viable seeds set off a mad race to replicate among the big companies. But it was a lot harder than they expected. Our climate had changed so much that the beans, like many other fruits and vegetables, just didn't take to the soil as easily.

So they pumped in a lot of money to grow the beans, invested in high-quality next-generation fertilizers, and hired the best scientists they could find. But it wasn't long until the beans found their way onto the black market and started sending people to the hospital. Illegal cocoa patches had started popping up all over the state forests in California over the last few years. But there was a new designer strain that could induce unwanted side effects like nausea, seizures, hallucinations, and panic attacks. And it was a lot more addictive than crack cocaine.

It had taken us months, but Rahul and I had finally tracked down the lab where the beans were being grown and processed. There were dozens of boxes, all neatly packed and ready to be shipped. A single bag of these beans would be enough to buy a comfortable floating home somewhere beautiful and retire at sea. And that's precisely what Rahul wanted. Just one bag. He tried hard to convince me, but when I refused to budge, he threatened me. And that's when it happened. The precise moment I broke his nose. The backup team barged in, and it looked like I had just assaulted my superior officer. Which, technically, I did. But it was my word against his. And in the end, he got a promotion, and I got kicked off the team.

Bile and anger mixed together in the pit of my stomach. It was unfair. I hated that people like Bull and Rahul could have their chocolate cake and eat it too while the rest of us peasants made do with mushroom cookies, mushroom cake, mushroom meringue, mushroom panna cotta, mushroom cannoli, mushroom ice cream, mushroom pudding . . .

The Tesla came alive without a sound, and the seatbelts fastened over our chests automatically.

"Nice car," I said as I settled into the backseat with Bull.

"Yes, isn't it? A loaner from Vera."

Before I could react, the virtual assistant's cold and genderless voice boomed through the speakers. This particular voice had been universally adopted a few centuries ago as the face, so to speak, of artificial intelligence tech and digital assistants. Its tone and tenor were as common a fixture as the blue sky above us. "Please enter a destination."

"The airport," Bull answered.

"We're flying?"

Bull nodded. "Obviously. Corinth isn't reachable by any Hyperloops, thank God."

The windshield displayed the route to the airport and

began counting down to the ETA. Seven minutes flashed in bright blue in one corner.

Bull cleared his throat to get my attention and handed me a tablet without saying anything. There was only one folder on the home screen, titled *CARA*. I tapped on one of the sub-folders. There were about a dozen pictures of a stern-faced young blonde girl with Bull's dark brown eyes and light skin. She didn't smile in any of the more recent pictures. Cara looked detached but determined as she grew into adolescence, her jaw clenched in every picture.

Cara's whole life had been documented—everything from her childhood hobbies and interests to her vaccinations and doctors' notes. The folder also had a list of all the names of her friends, teachers, classmates, and people she came into daily contact with.

I always found it unnerving how a person's whole life could be evaluated and compressed into one tiny, computerized folder. I shuddered every time I thought about the kind of information Big Brother had on me.

"I can't believe there isn't at least one person in your seven colonies who could help you find your granddaughter." I turned to look at Bull.

The old man wiped the side of his mouth with his fingers. "There are dozens of capable, intelligent men who would be up to the task, I assure you. But the problem is there are very few people within our colonies I trust—less than a handful, I would say," he began. "My position as Chairman has already been challenged. If my people found out my own granddaughter chose to abandon our ways, I would lose their trust and my authority. Chaos would ensue. I cannot allow that to happen."

"And you trust me?"

Bull laughed. "I trust that you want to get to the bottom of this as much as I do."

We arrived at a small airfield outside San Francisco before I could ask any more questions. There was only one sleek helicopter on the tarmac. I instantly recognized it. It was the Huracan-X in all its glory. Even from this distance, the old warhorse looked intimidating. It was notoriously called the widow-maker in military circles. This one appeared to be the civilian version, without any combat capabilities.

Unlike the Tesla, the helicopter was gloriously loud. Once we had headsets on and the pilot took us into the air, Bull said, "Corinth is unlike anywhere you've ever been before, and I want you to know exactly what to expect once we arrive." Bull tapped his palm. "So I had my AI prepare a little presentation for you."

I had to admit that Bull's colony sounded very intriguing. A mysterious group of Caucasian colonies in the U.S. (with its own subculture) was fascinating. I'm sure Vir would have thought so as well. In fact, I was willing to bet on it. If he had heard the same rumors I had, Vir would've been drawn to studying them too. Even if it meant putting himself at risk. The only question was how far did he go?

Bull's left palm lit up. My eyes fell on his T-Patch. Like the Auge, it was a sleek wearable touchscreen that was embedded under the wearer's skin. Nearly everyone wore a patch these days. It was easier than carrying around a wallet stuffed with credit cards, ID, and whatnot. All you had to do was pull up your ID or digital credit card on the touchscreen, tap it against the point-of-sale machine or ticket counter or whatever, and half a second later you were done.

It definitely made connecting with people easier too. Smartphones and tablets, thankfully, had transformed when nanotech and voice bots went mainstream. It was crazy to think that people used to carry around handheld devices and stare at the screens for hours on end.

The T-Patch could project a tiny hologram of the person or group of people you wanted to talk to, regardless of where in the world they were, and its built-in transceiver routed their voice to the Auge. And voila! You could hear and see the person on the other end like they were standing right next to you.

"Have you tried calling Cara?" I asked Bull.

Bull scoffed. "I would if she had one." His cold eyes met mine. "The colonies have limited access to technology. I'm sure you agree that information corrupts the innocent."

My lips pressed together in disagreement. "Why is it that *you* use technology, then?"

"I use whatever I must to keep my people safe." The answer came promptly. "In any case, they are unaware of the existence of such technology. They would probably find it unbelievable. So I would appreciate it if you didn't bring it up."

From what I could see, Bull's T-Patch appeared to be customized for documentation and tracking paperwork, while mine was connected to my Auge for self-defense purposes. It had seemed like a nifty thing to have in my line of work. But after six months and no incidents, I was wondering if I had thrown money at yet another thing I didn't need.

My Auge displayed an incoming audio message spiel from

Bull over my irises. I blinked the accept code and had the files sent to my aural implant, the same way that I did for calls. The same crisp artificial voice that had spoken to us in the Tesla now addressed me directly.

The AI began, "Many centuries ago, Corinth, Oregon (current population: 1,487, established: 1840 AD), was a vacationer's paradise, a hotbed for anyone in desperate need of a digital detox. Today, it is home to one of the last surviving Caucasian colonies in the world. It has provided a safe haven for countless families and is helping them repopulate this new world in the safety of their own community."

I wondered where this lecture was going.

"Corinth," it continued, "was lucky to escape the material destruction caused by the First Great War of the twenty-first century, also known as World War III or the Millennial War. What started as a small border conflict between India and China escalated quickly into a full-fledged world war. The United States and many European nations came to India's support in its time of need, while Pakistan, North Korea, and Russia (surprising many diplomats and analysts) stood with China. The powerful Arab nations, on the other hand, chose to remain neutral, just like Switzerland.

"Six months into the India–China conflict, the Crown Princess of the United Kingdom was brutally assassinated by a Russian suicide bomber outside Wales. Like Archduke Franz Ferdinand's assassination started WWI, the princess's death set off a rapid chain of events, and what followed was a remorseless showcase of advanced weaponry and arsenal by the British and its European allies as they avenged their beloved princess," the digital assistant droned on.

"Before the war ended, millions of soldiers and civilians were killed, armies utterly decimated, countries crippled, and thousands displaced."

This last part wasn't exactly new information to me. We had a whole history class dedicated to the Millennial War in high school. My grandfather would often tell us the stories he had heard from his grandfather when he was a boy. The drone terror, the pandemic, the cyber blitz, the AI undertaking. That was the reason I joined the force to begin with.

Despite the era's flaws, Vir and I had always thought that the early twenty-first century must have been a spectacular era to be alive. The music, books, technology, and culture of that time was still celebrated. Revered, even. Millennials had been radicals, so devout to equality and mutual respect. They had, despite all their flaws, laid the foundation for a better tomorrow. They championed freedoms that were taken for granted today. Had they not met antipathy with love, trampled sexism with equality, and set a new standard for change, acceptance, and liberation, the world would be a very different place today.

The world truly began to change and evolve when people started to become more interconnected. It was during this period when my ancestors, like so many countless others, began to spread their roots around the world. They left their little city in South India behind to find new opportunities on the other side of the globe, a place that future generations of Matoos would call home. Maybe that's why Vir was so drawn to studying history, human societies, and cultures.

The AI continued without pause, "The war catalyzed what globalization had begun. Millennials unwittingly set humanity on what many would describe as a 'path to course-correction' by simply rejecting the unspoken rules of the past and creating new constructs that worked best for them."

This was something every child and adult around the planet knew by heart. This was how we became One World.

"Those new constructs are rejected in Corinth and its sister colonies. The Survivors, as they prefer to be called, have steadfastly held on to the ideals on which this country was built. Vast resources are dedicated to the growth of our population in the hope of one day regaining our status in the world."

"Fascinating," I muttered to myself when the AI concluded.

Next to me, Bull shifted restlessly in his seat. "Hardly the word I would use to describe it," he replied. "Not when it feels like we're facing our extinction."

I thought about that for a second. "Clearly, your granddaughter feels differently."

"It doesn't matter how she feels, Mr. Matoo," Bull said dryly. "What matters is her commitment to her family and our colonies."

"Right. And how big are these colonies exactly?"

"Corinth is the largest. The other six have less than a thousand residents each," Bull said with a sigh. "But we are doing our best to increase those numbers."

"How exactly have you managed to stay under the radar all these years?"

Bull laughed and pointed below us. The landscape had changed dramatically from bustling cities to swaths of uninhabited wastelands. I couldn't tell from the air if the desolation was caused by wildfires or meteor showers, but whatever the cause, nothing could survive these black and barren lands.

"Corinth is just beyond these wastelands," Bull said. "We've never been discovered because... well, who would come looking for us in the middle of all this destruction?" Bull asked. "It's the perfect camouflage."

But someone had dared to venture through these barren lands. Someone crazy and ambitious enough to track down Bull's mysterious colonies. When my father and I had driven down to Stanford to clean out Vir's office, we hadn't found anything amongst his papers to suggest he was studying these Caucasian colonies. In retrospect, it didn't seem like he was working on anything new at all recently. I wanted to kick myself for missing that. Standing in Vir's office, going through his things, had felt wrong and claustrophobic, but now I wondered what else I had missed in my rush to get the hell out of there. I doubted he was on sabbatical. My brother was a workaholic. Was it possible his research was somewhere else? But what reason could he have had to do that?

My head felt like it was in the eye of a hurricane. "Where did you find my brother?"

Bull pressed his lips together and considered me for a second. Then he leaned forward and said something to the pilot through the comms channel. Next thing I knew, the pilot was changing course slightly and we were landing along an abandoned highway just a few miles away from the desolate lands. It was clear that these roads had not been in use for many decades. There were crater-sized potholes on the lanes, trash and broken beer bottles along the shoulder, and the wilderness had spread unrestrained.

"He was discovered there." Bull pointed to a mile marker

a few feet away from us. "While we were looking for Cara. Thankfully, my son-in-law had the sense to inform me, and we took care of it before anyone else could discover him."

My body felt numb. I walked slowly toward mile marker thirty-three. I knew I wouldn't find Vir's body there, but I couldn't shake the feeling that some part of him was still attached there, waiting and watching as the world passed him by.

The first things I saw were blood stains and shrapnel, probably from the explosion that killed Vir. There weren't any large enough pieces to ascertain what kind of an explosion had killed my brother or its origin. *How on Earth did he get here?* I wondered. If there were any vehicle tracks, the wind had blown them away. The questions were piling on top of each other, but all I felt right then, in that moment, was profound pain. My family had suffered one mindless tragedy after another. It hit me then: I was all my parents had left in this world. And this road I was going down with Bull was a dangerous one. I hoped to hell that I could give them the answers they deserved without them having to bury their only surviving child.

"I'm going to need to talk to your son-in-law," I said as soon as I jumped back into the chopper.

"We're headed there now. Though I would caution you against bringing this up in front of the rest of the family."

I raised my eyebrows at Bull.

"If my daughter found out a colored man was found just outside our borders the same night her daughter disappeared, she would be devastated," Bull said, trying to repress a shudder. "She is already quite distraught, and I would rather not add to her plate. You understand?"

It took a lot of effort to keep a straight face. I would imagine his daughter was already a wreck. What the color of my brother's skin had to do with her fear was beyond me. How could that possibly make things worse?

Besides, after Aric went missing, my mother wanted to know every single, ugly detail. As awful as it was to hear, I knew she would feel so much worse not knowing and wondering.

That familiar claustrophobic feeling returned, and I couldn't help but wonder about this family's priorities.

THE PILOT ANNOUNCED OUR ARRIVAL

in Corinth, and the chopper began making its descent in what appeared to be a cul-de-sac.

Bull hopped out of the chopper and strode toward a Spanish-colonial-style mansion with a driveway larger than any villa I'd seen in San Francisco. Nobody lived in houses like this anymore. At the height of overpopulation, big, luxurious independent homes like this one had been razed to the ground, and skyscrapers with mini apartments had been built in their place to accommodate the post-flood population. That way, everybody could have a roof over their head.

I had no idea houses like this still existed. It looked absolutely beautiful.

"This is your house?"

"No. My daughter Rebecca and her family live here," Bull answered. "I'm on the other side of the city."

Yeah, I wouldn't want to live near him either. Bull led the way up the cobbled path to the front door. A large decorative red flag featuring a blue saltire with white borders and five-pointed white stars fluttered lightly in the wind. I made a mental note to look it up when I got the chance. Once we reached the front door, Bull pulled out an old-timey skeleton key from his front pocket and unlocked the door.

It was a pristine home. Surgically clean, actually. Everything was a shade of white. The furniture was classically minimal. The only non-white object in the living room was a beautiful black grand piano that looked like it had never been played in its entire life.

This was undoubtedly the most unlived-in home I'd ever been in. The photographs on the walls were perfectly aligned and complemented the paintings on the adjacent wall. But there was something not quite right about this home. It took me a few minutes to realize it wasn't a smart home. The house was entirely tech-free, and I doubted if they even had a centralized intelligence system.

Still, it was a charming space, albeit a bit too old-fashioned for my taste. And so goddamn sterile. The only unusual thing that stood out was the chalkboard in the dining room. It seemed like an odd place to put it. I walked over to see what was written on it. The number *1,487* had been scrawled and then underlined several times.

That number was familiar. Where had I heard that? I tried to remember what the AI in the Tesla had said.

"Isn't that the population of this town?" I asked.

"Very astute." Bull looked at the chalkboard and then me. "Yes, it is. And if you don't find my granddaughter soon, it'll be 1,486." Bull shook his head. "And that would be a real shame."

What would be a real shame? Not finding the girl, or becoming one number fewer?

Just then, the patio doors flung open behind us. A smart-looking middle-aged couple, who I presumed were the parents of the missing girl, came rushing in, followed by a teenage girl with hunched shoulders. All three of them wore the same gold lopsided scale pin, identical to Bull's, on their lapels and an even smaller pin of the red flag that hung outside.

The girl bore a strong resemblance to Cara. She was shorter though, and probably no older than fifteen or sixteen. She wore thick glasses. But the resemblance was striking—the same blonde hair, brown eyes, and prominent jawline. The only difference was this girl didn't have the same unhappiness in her eyes as her sister.

"Oh, hi Daddy." The older woman walked up to Bull and kissed him on both cheeks. She was a tall and slender brunette with scattered grey hairs and a low husky voice. "I thought I heard the chopper. What are you doing here?" she whispered. "I thought we were going to meet you at the office?"

Bull glared at her. "Change of plans, dear."

"I told you I didn't want the neighbors to see him here," the woman pouted. "Did you even think of what people will say?"

"If you cared so much about other people's opinions, Rebecca," Bull snapped, "you should've kept a closer watch on your daughter. Otherwise, we would not be in this mess."

Do these people really think I can't hear a word of what they're saying? I cleared my throat loudly.

The woman's face turned bright with irritation. "Ah, yes, you must be the detective we've all heard so much about." She turned as if she'd only just noticed me. She forced a smile, but those big brown eyes gave her away. The way she stared at me reminded me of a frog we dissected in biology. She looked curious and repelled all at once. "James Mathew, isn't it?"

"Mah-tooh," I enunciated my name for her and stretched my right hand out. "Jimmy Matoo."

Like her father, Rebecca hesitated before taking my hand. She looked at Bull, and he nodded okay. Her smile disappeared as she took my hand in hers. The handshake barely lasted a second before she pulled away. Rebecca's reaction to me made me wonder why Bull hadn't warned them that he was bringing me and my dark skin here. It seemed like the kind of thing you'd mention beforehand.

"Rebecca Bull-Smith," she introduced herself. If she was distraught over Cara's disappearance, she didn't let it show. In the days after Aric went missing, my mother had looked like a ghost. She refused to eat or sleep for weeks and weeks. Rebecca, on the other hand, was perfectly coiffed and her clothes—like her father's—were expensive and tailored. "This is my husband, Jonathan Smith," she said, pointing to the man standing next to her, "and our youngest daughter, Florence."

Jonathan was several inches taller than me and rounder around the waist too. His face was round and kindly, and his eyes were red and swollen. "Um. Hello." He smiled and waved at me awkwardly.

I smiled at Florence, but she didn't return it. Instead, the girl just glared at me. I could almost see myself through her icy eyes. An alien with dark features—dark eyes and dark hair—and an almond-ish complexion. *They've probably never met anyone like me until today.*

"Why is your skin that color?" Florence demanded. "Are you sick?"

I pushed the hair out of my face and waited for her parents to reprimand her. But neither Rebecca nor Jonathan said anything. Like their daughter, they waited patiently for an answer. I knew exactly what she was asking, but I pretended not to know what she meant. "Sorry?"

She frowned and pointed at my face. Rude. My parents would have never let my brothers or I get away with that kind of behavior when we were kids.

"You're not like us," she said, looking down at her hands. "What are you?"

My jaws clenched together. "No, I'm not like you at all. But if you really want to know, Florence, I guess I'm mostly of Indian descent," I said, trying to remember my vast and complicated family tree. "My mom is half-Filipino-half-French, and my dad was Indian-American. And I'm pretty sure there's some British in there, as well."

Florence's mouth dropped open. I guessed her family tree was clearly nowhere near as colorful as mine. "Have you never seen anyone else like me?" I asked, my voice hollow.

She shook her head. "Do you need sunscreen?"

Wow. "Everybody needs sunscreen," I answered, starting to feel really ticked off.

Rebecca cleared her throat and put her hand over Florence's shoulder. With just one look, Rebecca had quietly banished her youngest up to her room. I could recognize that look anywhere. My mom had one just like it, and it was enough to put the fear of God in us when we were growing up.

Florence rolled her eyes and acquiesced. As she approached the staircase, she wheeled around and looked me right in the eye.

"You're not going to find her," she said bluntly.

"I'm not?" I asked, taken aback by her forthrightness. "How can you be so sure?"

Rebecca cleared her throat loudly and glared at her youngest daughter before she could answer. "Upstairs. Now."

As soon as Florence was out of earshot, I turned my attention back to her parents. "Your daughter has been missing for four days. Any idea where she might have gone?"

"No," Jonathan answered.

"Have you set up a search party yet?"

"No, we haven't," Jonathan admitted.

"Why not?" I persisted. "Who saw her last? Were there any witnesses?"

Jonathan and Rebecca were both startled by the string of questions and looked at Bull and back to me. Bull didn't answer though. He had his back turned and was busy making himself a drink at the bar.

Jonathan stared at me, wide-eyed. "Um, well—"

"There are no witnesses," Rebecca interrupted. "Because she left in the middle of the night when we were all dead asleep."

"What did she bring with her? Are any of her clothes missing?"

"Just some jackets and a pair of pants," Jonathan said. "We noticed some water bottles were gone too."

I nodded. "Has Cara ever run away before?"

Rebecca and Jonathan instantly shook their heads.

Most people think of teenagers as mature enough to make rational decisions, but the fact is that most runaway youths leave their homes on the spur of the moment. They don't think about where they are going to spend the night or if they have enough money because they simply want to escape a toxic environment. I always thought it was unfair how runaway youth are automatically deemed as troublemakers or kids who can't follow the rules when, in fact, they are probably victims of abuse, unloved, and left feeling unwanted.

Nothing about Cara's case, however, said whim to me. If anything, this was methodically planned and executed.

"Did Cara have any behavioral problems?" I didn't expect an unbiased answer from either Jonathan or Rebecca, but I had to ask.

"None at all." Jonathan shook his head. "She was always so obedient and thoughtful. Always home on time. We never had any reason to worry about her."

"You never argued? Not even once?" I persisted. "Her letter suggests that she questioned the principles of the colony, its goals, and its structure."

Displeasure seeped in between the lines on Rebecca's face. "No."

"Okay, let's move on. How do you know there aren't any witnesses?" I asked. "Did someone canvass the neighborhood?"

"We don't actually have, I believe you call it, police here," Rebecca said. "What we do have is a small group of locals who patrol the city borders, but—"

"But you want to keep her disappearance quiet. Yeah, your father mentioned," I interjected. "Why is that, anyway? It's usually the last thing the parents of a missing child would want. And surely her fiancé would want to help look for her?"

The silence was uncomfortable. Rebecca rubbed her temples with her fingers, and Jonathan looked over at his father-in-law for guidance. When neither of them responded, I said, "Look, I can't find your kid if I don't have all the information. What are you folks hiding?"

That did it. That pushed their buttons.

"Don't you talk to us like that, you chi—" Rebecca started to yell, but Jonathan put a restraining hand on her shoulder.

"We are not hiding anything, Detective," Jonathan retorted. "And I really don't care for your insinuation, either."

"Look here." Rebecca moved slightly in front of her husband as if protecting him. "My family is very private, and we'd rather not air our dirty laundry."

"So, you have dirty laundry?" I raised an eyebrow.

Jonathan's eyes widened, and Rebecca's face flushed red.

"Enough!" Bull sighed loudly, stirring a glass of martini with three olives. He settled on the couch. "Rebecca," he said, "just tell the brown man what he needs to know."

I'd been called a lot of things in my life, but the way Bull said *the brown man* sounded so much worse than any cuss word. I glared at him. His advanced age wasn't an excuse to be an asshole. I expected older people to be wise, as the old saying goes, and act like it. In the ten minutes since I'd arrived, both he and his daughter (not to mention the granddaughter) had thrown racial jabs at me.

Rebecca bit her lip uncertainly. "Fine! Fine." She waved her hands and motioned everyone but me to sit down. "The truth is that our daughter was going to be married soon, and we can't run the risk of the groom's family finding out."

"He knows that part already, you stupid girl!" Bull said impatiently. "Tell him why."

Jonathan straightened his shirt and leaned forward. "I just

want to be sure that you can be"—he looked me up and down—"discreet. I cannot stress that enough."

What made him think I couldn't be discreet? Jonathan must know Bull had picked me for a reason and trust that he had his Cara's best interest at heart.

I took a seat across from them and crossed one leg over the other. Although my attention was now focused on Jonathan, I could see from the corner of my eye that Rebecca's jaw clenched ever so slightly as I made myself comfortable. "Of course." I nodded. "Is it possible she's with her fiancé now? Maybe they eloped?"

"She definitely hasn't eloped," Jonathan said, his eyes tearing up. "Certainly not with her betrothed or anyone else from the colonies. At least we don't think..."

"Why are you so certain?"

"Because she was against having an arranged marriage."

An arranged marriage? I raised my eyebrows again.

"She didn't believe in..." Rebecca cleared her throat. "Well, our beliefs."

"Arranged marriages have been a part of our tradition since"—Bull took a sip of his martini—"since the war. Since ...you know." He waved at me as though it were my fault. "Everything."

As a man of Indian descent, I was well aware of the old custom. Arranged marriages had been a way of life once upon a time; parents and close family members would come together in the name of tradition to find the perfect match for their son or daughter.

For generations, Indian families had been built on anonymity. Young brides and grooms had been rushed to the altar by their families, having never even met each other or given a say in the matter. The criteria for holy matrimony in those days had been dependent on family background, the size of the homes they owned, and the cars they drove. But the most paramount requirement of all was having fair skin.

I liked to think that had I been born in another era, another place, my parents might have trusted and respected me enough to allow me the freedom to choose—for better or for worse—the person with whom I would spend the rest of my life. But in many ways, I was a product of that old custom. If it hadn't been for centuries of arranged marriages, my family tree would look very different. My grandfather might have never been born. Neither would my dad nor my brothers or me.

Still, it was disconcerting to hear those words here in this context. An arranged marriage in this century seemed so foreign and unreasonable. I struggled to remind myself that I wasn't here to pass judgment on these people and shifted my immediate concern back to the missing girl.

"When did your daughter first express these concerns?"

"That's the thing, Detective," Jonathan said, taking his wife's hand. "She never did. Not even once. If anything, she seemed acquiescent. This letter she left behind is the first time we're hearing this."

I thought about Cara's letter again. Sitting here with her parents, I realized how much that letter had already told me about her as a person: she was thoughtful, intelligent, well-read, and someone who clearly did not share her parents' ideology.

Cara's note also told me something else besides her disapproval of her parents' lifestyle. "There have been other runaways in Corinth," I concluded.

"Yes. Over the years we've lost dozens," Bull said. "We've done everything to keep them in, but somehow, they keep getting out!" He huffed. "With every disappearance, we've increased border security, used guard dogs, and had residents patrol their neighborhoods. You'd never know it, but we are guarded like a fortress."

"I'm surprised you didn't tag them," I said, half-joking.

"Oh, trust me, I've tried," Bull said ruefully, the sarcasm completely lost on him. "We don't know how they're getting out of the city without being spotted. They must be disabling their trackers, but I couldn't tell you how."

My chest tightened. The idea of microchipping human beings like dogs and tracking their every move was heinous. Cara was right. Corinth was a stifling place to live. "So that's how you know she hadn't had contact with anyone on the outside?"

"Exactly. Cara has never been anywhere she shouldn't have been. Neither have the other kids," Jonathan said.

"Is her microchip still active?"

Bull grimaced. "No, the last time it was active was the night she disappeared."

"What I want to know is why anyone would even want to go out there," Rebecca cried. "I can't imagine living out there with all those people."

Beside her, Jonathan nodded in agreement.

"Did Cara know any of them? The other runaways?" I asked, trying to keep my voice even.

"Yes, of course!" Rebecca rolled her eyes. "Everyone knows everyone here, Mr. Mathew. This is a tiny town." She talked to me like I was a kid.

What is her problem? "Mah-tooh. Matoo," I enunciated slowly. "I'll need a list of all the runaways—names, dates, that sort of thing. They all left notes?"

"Some, yes. Others just... disappeared." Bull looked unsympathetic. "I'll have all that information transferred to your virtual assistant."

"What about home security? Street cameras? You must have—"

"We try to limit our use of technology here. We only have what we need. As you can imagine, we try not to send up flares telling your people where to find us," Jonathan explained.

"My people?" I repeated.

"Mm-hmm. The whole point of our colonies is to ensure our bloodlines thrive without being contaminated by your kind."

Bile rose in my throat. "Right," I said. "That totally explains the fancy helicopters and cars."

"Well, we're not simpletons," Rebecca piped up in her high-strung voice. "We just believe in moderation. Besides, I wouldn't want to be fused to a machine like you people are."

The hypocrisy of it all made me want to laugh in her face. While the rest of us took the Hyperloop, Bull and his family were being ferried around in unmanned Teslas and state-of-the-art helicopters. Surely, somebody noticed their supreme leader wearing a T-Patch?

Before I could retort, Jonathan cleared his throat loudly. "Maybe you'd like to see Cara's room?" He smiled at me apologetically and gestured to the staircase.

I stood up and nodded. "Lead the way."

3

THE STAIRCASE LEADING UP TO
Cara's bedroom was wide and carpeted. On the walls were
old-fashioned black-and-white photos of the family—Rebecca
and Jonathan on their wedding day, a young Bull and a woman
(presumably his wife) with two little children standing in front of
a house, and another of Rebecca beaming down at a newborn.
The pictures hadn't been updated since the Bull-Smith children
were toddlers.

I followed Jonathan to the end of the corridor. He pushed
the door open and let me through. "I'll be downstairs when
you're done," he said and turned to leave.

"Before you go, I'd like to talk to you about the night you
found my brother."

Jonathan shifted nervously and looked down the hallway.
"Um, I'm not sure I should. Julius would be very upset with
me."

"Could you live without knowing where your daughter is
or why she left?"

That did it. Jonathan's eyes teared up, and he shook his
head.

"All right, then. When you found Vir, was there anything
else in the vicinity that struck you as odd?" I asked.

"Well, that was my first time venturing so far out of

our borders, Detective. I honestly wouldn't know if there was anything there that shouldn't have been."

"How about vehicle tracks? Anything to indicate how he got there?"

"No, there was nothing there besides the drone." Jonathan clapped his palm around his mouth.

"What drone?"

"Oh gosh," Jonathan cried. "I wasn't supposed to say anything about that. Julius is going to be so angry with me. Please don't tell him I told you anything."

I folded my arms and met his eyes. "Listen, Jonathan, I won't tell him you said anything. You have my word. Now, my brother is dead. Your daughter is missing. If you want answers, you're going to have to start talking."

Jonathan fidgeted with the buttons on his shirt. "Okay, yes. There *was* a drone close to where I found your brother, but it was in pretty bad condition. Julius tried to access the memory disk, but it looked pretty fried to me."

My heart expanded uncomfortably. "Where is it now?"

"Probably his home. He'd never leave anything that important in his office."

"Why not?" I wondered. "Wouldn't his office be safer?"

Jonathan shook his head. "Julius has a lot of enemies. He was paranoid before but now ...he thinks he's got a mole in the office. I wouldn't be surprised if it were true. He wouldn't risk bringing something he couldn't explain into his office."

I needed to find this drone. If the back-up memory disk had survived, I could see exactly what happened that night—if Vir had launched the drone himself, or if a remote pilot was following him, and more importantly, if my brother was attacked. I hadn't ruled out the possibility that it might have been an accident of some sort, but my gut told me it was deliberate. Someone in Corinth was responsible for his death. It was the why and who that eluded me. Was he killed for discovering this place? Had he gotten too close to something or somebody here and been silenced for it? Was Bull responsible for this death? I hadn't ruled Bull out as a suspect. He might have come to me for help, but that didn't mean he wasn't guilty.

"I'm really sorry about your brother." Jonathan's voice broke through my thoughts.

"Thank you. I appreciate that," I said, and meant it too.

After Jonathan left, I took a minute to collect my thoughts and focus my attention back on Cara.

Like the rest of the house, Cara's bedroom was neat and organized. The three walls surrounding the bed were painted in a soft, dull pink while the other side had a contrasting wallpaper with maroon rosebuds and dark green leaves.

A few feet above the bedpost was a brown floating shelf with some houseplants and picture frames. I recognized nearly every face in the black-and-white pictures except for one: a young woman with dark almond-shaped eyes and long dark hair. In the picture, Cara and the mystery woman were locked in a tight embrace, and their faces were bright with laughter. I made a mental note to figure out who she was and see if she might have any information.

Cara had put a lot of thought into her reading nook. The bookshelf stood tall and proud with little trinkets and baubles on the shelves, while the books themselves were organized by size and color. A rocking chair with some pillows, soft toys, and throw blankets sat next to it. Beside the bookshelf was a desk facing the window. I could almost picture her sitting here, looking out the window and writing the letter she'd left her parents.

I tried to put myself in Cara's shoes and imagine where I would have hidden something I didn't want to be found. Although I didn't expect to find anything under the bed or amongst the books, I decided to check them anyway just to be on the safe side. Most of the titles, I was surprised to see, were about feminine health, childbirth, and (even more surprising) how to be a good wife. These titles did not match the environment Cara had created around the warm and inviting reading nook. I could not picture her sitting here before bed, cozying up to one of these ridiculous books.

Rather than pull each book out and flip through the pages, I studied each shelf so I could see the books from the spine down. If Cara had stuffed anything between the pages, there would be a small crevasse between the pages. I started with the bottom-most shelf and worked my way up. I was nearly ready to give up when I found it on the penultimate shelf.

Wedged in the center was a book with a large gap. I pulled it out and studied the front cover. I rolled my eyes at the title: *Training Your Wife in Ten Simple Steps*   . I flipped the book open to where the crevasse was. Several pieces of paper were folded carefully inside. The first one looked like a child's painting, but I realized after a couple of seconds that it was a pamphlet Cara had drawn on.

She had disfigured the man's face by giving him horns,

thick facial hair, and blood-red eyes. Could this be the mysterious Hexum? Whoever he was, I would never recognize him in this state. Under his face the words "A woman is only as good as the children she bears!" were printed in a large, bold font. If I were Cara, I would've trashed this leaflet too. The other pamphlets had fewer scribbles on them. Corinth's leadership was calling for each family to produce at least four children in total. The families who could deliver those numbers would be handsomely rewarded.

Whoever came up with this program had clearly snoozed through their history lessons. Overpopulation nearly destroyed our planet once before. And we were still facing the consequences of it. It seemed foolish to encourage four kids per couple, even if the colonies wanted to increase their population count.

The last piece of paper was not a pamphlet. It was written in some sort of cypher, but it wasn't in Cara's handwriting. This had come from someone else. I instinctively activated my Auge by blinking the correct sequence. A thin clear-blue screen materialized over my right eye, scanned the message, and added it to its translation queue. My digital assistant would be able to crack the code in a couple of hours, if not sooner.

Once I crossed the bookshelf off my list, I stepped gingerly on the floorboards. No creaks. Not even a whimper. Next, I opened the closet door. What I found made me smile. The level of chaos and disorganization here could only have been caused by a teenager. In my mind's eye, I pictured her dumping everything in here to disobey her parents' orders to keep her room clean.

Organized chaos is how I used to describe my own

bedroom to my mom. I could always find what I was looking for, no matter how messy my room got. I also had my hiding spots—tiny spaces nobody else would think to go through. Not that I hid much stuff in my room anyway. Most of my secrets (a porn collection) were safely tucked away in the cloud, only accessible by my Auge.

But where, I asked myself, would I hide things I didn't want my parents finding if I didn't have an Auge? I took a step back and looked around Cara's bedroom again. My focus drifted across each corner until it finally settled on the coats hanging in her closet. I rummaged through each piece of clothing and checked the pockets until my fingers finally found something other than fabric. A small leather notebook the size of my palm was tucked away in a snowboard jacket. I pulled it out and flipped through the pages carefully.

"Clever girl," I whispered appreciatively. To most people, Cara's notebook would be gibberish. What it was, really, was encoded.

Cara had gone to great lengths to keep her thoughts private, and yet she had left this diary where somebody could easily find it. Why would she do such a thing? If it were me, I'd have burned it and scattered the ashes somewhere far away for good measure.

None of the symbols and elliptical figures in here made sense—not to me, anyway. I activated my Auge and let it scan through a couple of pages.

I flipped through a few more pages until I reached the very last one. A simple drawing, nothing more than a scribble, of some sort of mechanism facing the moon and a few stars caught my attention. The image looked oddly familiar, but I couldn't quite place it. My mind wandered, trying to connect the dots. What on Earth could Cara have been thinking when she drew this?

The answer came swiftly and unceremoniously. *Peregrinus*. The drawing may have been childlike, but there was no denying it. Cara had, indeed, drawn something deeply connected to my world—to One World—as it were.

Project Peregrinus was Earth's do-or-die endeavor to save humanity. It had taken 147 nations over fifty-two long, gruesome years to build a large assortment of spacecraft, of various sizes and uses, that would soon transport mankind into the farthest corners of the universe in search of a new home before Earth turned into a wasteland. It was an incredible feat.

The project had many detractors and setbacks from the start. In fact, people were taking bets on whether or not Peregrinus would ever leave Earth's orbit. Flanked by a dozen or so Stella-class spacecraft, Peregrinus wasn't just carrying precious humans and DNA; it was carrying humanity's last hope for survival.

The flagship, Peregrinus itself, was 1,788 meters in length and had four faster-than-light engines, a doomsday vault containing the seeds of nearly seven thousand plant species, the DNA of five million animals, mammals, and reptiles, and countless more human sperm and egg samples. I'd seen the footage of the lift-off countless times, and I got goosebumps each time. It was almost as iconic as the first time Neil Armstrong walked on the moon.

On our way to Corinth, Bull had made a point to inform

me of the evils of technology. *Corrupts the innocent*, that was the phrase he'd used. I very much doubted Cara or any other person in Corinth kept up to date with the latest news updates from beyond their walls.

Unless someone somewhere in Corinth knew about Peregrinus and had told Cara about it. Or someone outside Corinth was feeding them this information. A million questions swirled in my mind. One thing was certain, though: this same someone, I was convinced, had helped her and (probably all the others) escape. But was that person my brother or someone else entirely?

I stuffed Cara's notebook in my breast pocket and turned my attention back to the rest of the bedroom. If there were other hiding spots, I needed to find them. I checked the usual hidey-holes: drawers, shelves, and even shoes. Just as I expected, there was nothing to be found. I got on my hands and knees and checked the other most obvious spots—under the bed, the underside of the drawers, jewelry boxes, between the mattress and pillows. The only things under the bed were dust bunnies and tennis balls. Dozens and dozens of little yellow balls were littered underneath the space. Curious, I reached in and pulled one out.

Tennis wasn't my favorite sport in the world, but I knew tennis balls were supposed to be firm. This one felt soft and hollow to the touch. Puzzled, my fingers ran over the rim in the center until I discovered it had been slashed neatly and sewed back together. The thread holding the ball together came undone easily after a couple of hearty tugs.

What I found inside had me do a double take. Pills of all shapes, sizes, and colors were stuffed inside. "What on Earth?" I said. I grabbed a couple more tennis balls and ripped them open too. These were also stuffed with the same pills.

The dossier on Cara that Bull had given to me did not mention anything about any medication she might've been on. And I couldn't imagine why a young girl her age would be taking so much medication. Judging from the amount hidden here, I guessed this was at least a year's worth—if not longer.

Cara's choice of cache was intriguing. If it were me, I'd flush unwanted medication down the toilet and then pretend to have taken them. Everything she had done so far told me how careful a planner she was. So why risk hiding something in a place her parents could easily find?

The answer came to me like a jolt of lightning. Cara wanted this stockpile and the diary to be found. She wanted her parents to know how she had been quietly rebelling against them, without their knowledge. She wanted them to know who she really was underneath the persona she had created.

I couldn't help but laugh at her deviousness. "Very clever girl."

I emptied one of the tennis balls and put the pills in my jacket pocket. Maybe her parents would be able to shed some light on what they were meant for.

"ANY LUCK?" JONATHAN ASKED AS soon as I joined him, Rebecca, and Bull in the living room.

I dropped the pills on the coffee table and nodded. "Can

you tell me what these are?"

Bull's face was unreadable, but Jonathan and Rebecca seemed genuinely surprised. Rebecca scooted in front of the table and touched the pills gently with her fingers. "Where did you find these?" she managed to ask.

"In your daughter's room," I explained. "What are they?"

Jonathan and Rebecca shared a concerned look, then turned to Bull as though seeking guidance. But his face remained impassive.

"Just vitamins," Jonathan answered.

There was nothing in Cara's dossier to indicate she was ill. "Was your daughter sick?"

"No! Of course not! She was healthy as a horse," Rebecca scoffed. "They're just prenatal vitamins. Florence takes them too."

Prenatal vitamins? Why on Earth would a teenage girl need prenatal vitamins? "Why would a doctor prescribe them?"

"To help them conceive quickly, of course," Rebecca answered matter-of-factly. "Cara's going to be married soon, and we expect a grandchild immediately."

Rebecca made procreation sound like a business transaction. Almost as if her daughter owed her a grandchild in exchange for her getting married. An involuntary shudder passed through my body.

"Apparently, Cara had other ideas." I gestured to the prenatal vitamins. "I'm starting to think she's wanted out for a long time. Did any of her friends express a similar sentiment?"

"She's a girl!" Bull laughed. "Women don't know what they want!" He waved a hand. "If she had a good, strong male presence at home to tell her what to think, we wouldn't be in this mess."

Jonathan flushed, then turned back to me. "Not that we know of."

I wasn't surprised. If Cara had gone through the trouble of playing along to their expectations and keeping a secret diary, then it was safe to assume the other kids had too.

"I need to meet this Hexum person she mentioned in her letter," I said, more to myself than to them.

Jonathan and Rebecca gasped simultaneously in response. Their faces registered shock and fear.

"Impossible!" Bull's impassive façade finally cracked. His wrinkled fingers pointed at me accusingly. "I won't allow it."

I took a deep breath. Arguing wasn't going to get me anywhere. I needed to take a more tactical approach. "Who is this guy, exactly? And why was Cara so afraid of him?"

"Hexum is my enemy." Bull gritted his teeth. "An animal. And if he found out someone like *you* was here, in our homes, he would raise hell and then send us all there."

I frowned. "Then why risk bringing me here?"

"It was not my first choice, I'll tell you that much." Bull sighed and looked at his daughter. "If Hexum found out that Cara had left us, it would ruin the entire family. Florence would be without prospects, and I can't imagine what would happen to the rest of us."

Clearly, Bull wasn't going to give me a straight answer, and I didn't want to waste my time hearing half-truths. "Well, sooner or later, someone is going to notice me walking around this town. What then?"

"Then you're on your own. We will not acknowledge ever meeting or knowing you."

I scoffed. Bull was even more cold-hearted than I expected. He knew I wouldn't leave Corinth without finding out what happened to Vir, and I could only do that by finding Cara. Any dangers I faced along the way were no concern of his, so long as his family saved face.

"So, where can I find this Hexum?"

"Please, whatever you do, stay away from Hexum!" Rebecca cried. "If he found out about Cara . . ." She shuddered.

"Listen to me carefully." Bull's voice became sinister. "Hexum *cannot* know about Cara. Nobody can know. You have no idea what he is capable of. Trust me on that."

Bull's fear seemed excessive, but I wasn't going to waste time arguing with him. For now, I just nodded and let it be. Later I would do what was needed to find Cara and bring her home. And if Hexum or anyone else discovered Bull's secret and my presence along the way, then so be it.

"Are the women here forced to have children?" I asked, struggling not to add *against their will* in the end.

Jonathan gasped. "Good God."

"Of course not!" Rebecca clutched her chest dramatically. "Whatever gave you that idea?"

Just about everything I've learned so far, I wanted to say. I bit my tongue and instead pointed at the prenatal vitamins in front of us.

"That's just a little something to help her get pregnant easier," Rebecca said. "Though I can't speak for every household on how their children are conceived."

"And nor do we care," Bull chimed in. "At the end of the

day, a woman must do her duty to the colonies. Children are, after all, the future."

Anger rose through my insides. Bull's lack of empathy and his desire to grow the population at any cost was disturbing. As was his lack of respect for women. Why should women have to bear the brunt of procreating when men had an equal part to play? I could see now what Cara meant about becoming a *baby-making machine* in her letter. To Bull, a woman's worth was tied to her reproductive gifts. I shuddered to think about what life would be like in Corinth if those gifts were to fail.

"There's a picture of a woman hugging Cara on one of the shelves," I said. "Who is she?"

"Cara has lots of friends." Rebecca rolled her eyes. "I assure you none will speak with you."

"Maybe this one will," I said.

Rebecca let out an exasperated sigh. "Cara's friends will tell you nothing we haven't already."

"I would like to at least try," I insisted. "Teenagers aren't exactly famous for confiding in their parents, you know. Her friends most likely know more about her life than you do."

Rebecca's face turned bright red, but before she could answer, Jonathan interrupted. "Did you find anything else?"

"No," I lied. "Nothing else."

The diary and its mysterious contents were safe within my jacket. Cara's parents hadn't exactly been forthcoming, and their reluctance to introduce me to this friend of hers just cemented my instinct to protect whatever few clues I had found so far. Especially if decoding this diary might be the key to figuring out where Cara went and what Vir had to do with it.

4

AFTER LEAVING THE BULL-SMITH residence, I walked around their quiet neighborhood for a bit, trying to get a sense of everything I had learned. Whatever their skewed ideologies about survival might be, I refused to believe that their lives were as technologically deficient as they claimed.

Or worse, the people here honestly did not know the extent to which they were being monitored by the colony's topmost echelon or that he even had this level of technology. Bull's dossier documenting his granddaughter's life had been precise and thorough, and the probability it was compiled by a little old secretary was pretty slim.

Until I could figure out what else Bull was keeping from me, finding his granddaughter without eyewitnesses or security footage would be almost impossible. For now, I would have to try to put myself in her shoes and do my best to retrace her steps the night she left home.

Alone with my thoughts, I activated my Auge. There was an unread message from Bull, another from my parents, some random reminders, and one medical alert that cautioned me my glucose levels were dangerously low.

Corinth was a quiet city. The usual signs of life were missing here—there was no hubbub of families, traffic noises, or pets scurrying along. Even the wind was discreet. The silence was stifling. Even though I'd only been gone a couple of hours, I missed San Francisco. I missed its lively, upbeat energy, music, and the chatter that could always drown out my loneliness.

The last time I'd been somewhere so quiet was during the asteroid attack of '47 in Mexico City. The residents who'd chosen to stay—volunteers like myself and the national guard— had taken shelter in the underground bunkers while everything above ground burned. Over a hundred people had been crammed in the bunker in silence, just waiting for it to come to an end.

The stillness in Corinth brought back those terrible days. My palms felt clammy, and tiny beads of sweat started to roll down the side of my head despite the cool weather. There was no tranquility in the quiet here. The only sound I could hear as I walked was my own erratic heartbeat.

If it weren't for the clean air, I would probably feel even more suffocated. The air in this city felt different here somehow—I could almost taste how unprocessed and fresh it was. There were dozens of air recycling units in Corinth, at least three on each block, as far as I could see.

Most cities had one on every street corner, on the roof of tall buildings, and even portable ones on trees. The air quality had taken a beating over the last couple of centuries. Even aggressive reforestation measures hadn't been enough to weed out the dark, unhealthy smog that clung to the sky in the big cities. The forest fires along the West Coast had been raging nonstop for three years now, and the extreme drought didn't help air quality either. The Earth just wasn't recovering—not fast enough, anyway.

Besides the Bull-Smiths' residence, there were a couple of houses that looked nice and well-maintained, but for the most part, the rest of the town looked unkempt and grimy. The uncollected garbage was out of control and spilled onto the potholed streets, its odors spewing into the air.

Most buildings were shorter than three stories, and a majority of them seemed abandoned and shuttered. The façades must've once been brightly colored, but now they were worn out and dark from years of sun damage and heavy rainfall. Some corners were especially black and greasy from dumpster fires.

Posters with unequal gold scales (like the one Bull was wearing) were plastered on the windows and doors. Except there were people on the scales in this version—a white couple on the top one and dozens of people of other ethnicities on the lower one. It was a subtle call to One World and their perceived unequal status in the world.

Someone had spray-painted the words "we're not dead yet" in bright red under the posters—another call to the injustice of being on the other side of the aisle, no doubt.

There were others, more racially charged ones, that called for the *beaners to suffocate in their own shit* and for the *chonkies* (which my Auge told me were people of Asian heritage and Caucasian qualities) to *choke on bananas*.

The very last one on the other end of the wall caught my attention as I walked along the street. It was more political in nature. A caricature of a young man in a leather jacket said, "I will beat the infertility out of the colonies" while a Bull caricature sat crying in the corner, holding dead white babies.

I shuddered. Racism had always felt like an intangible

concept for those of us born after the advent of One World. It was always something I'd only thought of in theoretical and philosophical terms—until now. These images were blatant in their hatred for people like me.

No, it was more than hatred. The intent behind the "art" was clear—the colonies did not just want to equalize the scale, they wanted to tip the balance back in their favor.

The same red flag with blue saltire and white stars that I'd seen at the Bull-Smiths was painted over these walls next to the faces of people I didn't recognize. I blinked my Auge on and scanned the flag for its origin.

My digital assistant found an exact match within a couple of seconds: it was called the Stainless Steel banner—aka the Confederate flag—an ancient symbol from the American Civil War in the 1800s.

A cold shiver ran through me as I read about the fight to free enslaved black people. So much had happened since the Millennial War that the 1800s was considered ancient history now. But standing on the streets of Corinth, staring down an emblem of the white man's superiority over the inferior colored people, I felt a surge of fear.

My arms and legs felt wobbly, and my palms were cold and clammy. I looked over my shoulders to see if I was being watched or, worse, followed. My paranoia went from healthy to petrified in a matter of seconds.

I wasn't safe here.

Suddenly, my body was alive with adrenaline. In the distance, I thought I heard a howl. It was far enough away for me to dismiss it as a case of bad nerves and yet sinister enough to stop me in my tracks. I couldn't remember if there were coyotes or wild dogs in this part of Oregon, but whatever animal it was, it seemed to have passed.

Everything about this city was terrifying, but I had to get a hold of myself. I stepped away from the flag and forced myself to calm down. It was just a flag, I told myself. I wished Vir was there with me. I could almost picture him walking down the street, excitedly explaining in anthropological terms the significance of the "artwork" and how closed-off societies like this one functioned. After Aric's death, we had grown apart. Both of us grieved for our younger brother in very different ways. While I had thrown myself into police work, he had buried himself in schoolwork. We rarely talked. The only time we saw each other was at family gatherings and Christmas. Even then, we never really connected. He was a mystery to me.

I wished so desperately now I had made more of an effort to get to know my brother and his work. Maybe if we had been closer or if he had trusted me, I would've known what had driven him to come find this place. I might have even come with him.

My guilt over Vir's death coupled with Aric's bubbled back up to the surface. Regret and anger blurred my vision, and I desperately wished I could turn back time. God, what I wouldn't give to have both my brothers alive and well with me today. I was the oldest of the three of us. Looking out for them was part of the job description, and I had failed so miserably. But I was determined not to fail again. I couldn't live with myself if I did.

I wiped the edge of my eyes and carried on. It was hard to know which way I was going, but I figured that in a small town like Corinth, I'd eventually end up where I started. My stomach rumbled louder than my thumping heart. I'd been walking around aimlessly for over an hour, and I needed to recharge before I did anything else.

My other emotions had drowned out the fears, and I no longer cared who saw me. Vir had been brave enough to study this town—maybe he had even snuck through the borders a couple of times (I wouldn't be surprised if he had)—and the least I could do was show an ounce of the mettle he had.

There's got to be at least one goddamn restaurant somewhere in this town. I turned around and refocused my attention on finding something to eat. The fear hadn't subsided, but I hoped the food would help calm me. I heard slow jazz music and muffled voices of men laughing. I bet this was the right way—this part of the city seemed a bit more alive, and the streets were better lit.

It occurred to me as I walked that I was probably the first person of color to be here since the late twenty-first century. It was not a comforting thought. Dread and anxiety bubbled up from my stomach again. I knew it wouldn't help, but I pulled up the collar of my jacket and tucked my chin under to feel less conspicuous.

I walked into the first bar I saw with an *OPEN* sign in the window. It was called the Hercules, and it was a cozy little place; the jukebox in the corner was playing an old Christian rock tune, and the lighting was subtle. The exposed brick walls were a nice touch. So were the classic bar signs I always found amusing.

Though when I looked closer at the signs, I realized these were not your typical one-liners. One sign read *White Lives Matter.* Another said, *Make America White Again*, and the worst one was a sign with a picture of a black man with the words, *Your face when it's Halloween.*

A bitter taste crept into my mouth. If I had seen signs like this anywhere else, I would be throwing a fit, but here in Corinth, I had no power to express my opinions. They were as unwelcome as I was.

I clenched my fist and looked away from the signs.

The bar was empty except for a young couple sitting by the window, drinking beer and snuggling. They stopped talking as soon as I walked in. This, I realized, was exactly what Bull and his family had warned me about.

The man was heavily tattooed. As far as I could tell, both his arms and neck were covered in black ink, like the sort gangbangers had, except these were Bible verses, a crucifix, and a couple of skulls. The girl with mousy brown hair and big shoulders looked alarmed by my presence. The man glared at me, his body alert. I recognized the tension on his face. I'd seen it many times when my team and I were preparing for a raid.

I smiled as politely as I could when I walked past them. They, too, were wearing the same gold scale pin and what I now recognized as the Confederate flag. The couple stayed rooted to their table. They looked away when my eye caught theirs and went back to staring intensely into each other's eyes.

The bartender, a muscular young man with a mop of brown hair and a sharp nose, hadn't noticed my arrival yet. Or maybe he was ignoring me? I wasn't sure. He was standing behind the half-open kitchen door, polishing silverware absently, his face completely blank. I had to clear my throat several times before he took notice.

"Yeah," he yelled without looking up, "be with you in a minute. Sit anywhere you'd like!"

I decided it was best to sit at the empty bar and use the mirrored wall in front of me to keep an eye on the place. Even with my back to the door, I could see the young couple was staring and pointing at me again. The man with the tattoos leaned over and whispered something to the girl, who squealed with laughter. Encouraged by her response, the man imitated a monkey and started screeching like one.

That did it. "Seriously?" I turned around in my seat and called out to the couple. "Seriously?"

Taken aback by the outburst, the couple stopped laughing instantly. The man stood up and scowled at me. "Yeah, seriously," he said. "Have you seen your face? It's seriously ugly."

The girl screeched with laughter again. "Like a monkey!"

I considered my options. I could say something and start a fight less than six hours after arriving in Corinth, or I could just let it go and focus on why I was really here. The latter was really hard to do after a day of swallowing my pride, but starting a fight with this guy wasn't going to help me find Cara.

"All right, that's enough," a stern voice called from behind me. "I won't have you idiots fighting in my bar."

The young bartender was carrying a small piece of paper that read *Hercules' Specials + Wine and Beer List*. He placed the menu on the table unceremoniously, without even looking at me, and motioned the other guests to sit down. "I'll handle this," he said. "Just sit down, Hank." The bartender held up a hand to the heavily tattooed man. "You too." He pointed at the girl. "I mean it."

As I turned my seat back around, I found the bartender staring at me, his eyes wide and unblinking. I frowned and checked my reflection in the mirror to see if I had something on my face. It occurred to me then that it was actually my face that had drawn this reaction.

It was apparent he had never met another human being who looked so different from him before. There was nothing funny about the situation, but I couldn't help but laugh at the bartender's bemused look.

My fingers, still unused to the feeling of paper, gripped the menu tight. "It's all right," I assured him. "I don't bite."

"What the hell are you doing here?" the barman demanded. "No one told me you were coming here!"

What on Earth? I looked at the bartender more closely—his face looked familiar, but I couldn't really place him.

It was my turn to frown. The tone in his voice was off-putting, and I had just about had it with everyone. "Dinner," I said. "I'm happy to go somewhere else if this is going to be a problem."

The barman was still staring at me. His blue eyes were wide with curiosity and irritation. The look on his face brought back a long-lost memory from the time our parents had brought Aric and me to the zoo in San Diego one summer. We had walked around for hours pressing our little noses up against the glass panes, studying animals and making fun of their smelly furs and dank surroundings.

"So it's just a coincidence that of the three bars in this city, you walked into mine?" He sounded flustered.

"Yes?" I smiled a bit, hoping the gesture would put him a little bit at ease.

The barman cursed under his breath. "Fine. But you're

paying. My grandfather mentioned he'd be bringing someone from..." He filled my water glass too full. "My grandfather said he'd be bringing you, I mean." His jaw tightened. "So, have you had any luck finding my sister yet?"

Ah! So this was the brother from Cara's note. Bull's dossier only had childhood pictures of the Bull-Smith kids, and this guy looked to be in his early twenties. "I just got here a couple of hours ago. The only people I've talked to so far are your parents and Florence." I shrugged. "So, no."

I remembered Florence's impetuous remark about my skin at that moment and wondered if he would make some off-color remarks like his little sister. His behavior so far had given me no reason to think he wouldn't, and the fact that he stopped the weird couple from harassing me probably had more to do with protecting his property than upholding common decency.

"Oh," He raised an eyebrow. "So. Did they send you here to talk to me?"

"No, I just told you it was a coincidence," I said, barely able to contain my exasperation. "Your parents didn't even mention you. I can go somewhere else. Really."

A shadow passed over his face. "Nothing else is open right now." He hesitated. "Anyway, it would be un-Christian of me to turn you away hungry. You can stay. It's fine." He said it to himself more than me. "I'm Isaac Bull-Smith, by the way."

I kept my right hand to myself this time—I was not in the mood to do this little dance with yet another member of the Bull-Smith family. Instead, I nodded and lifted the cold glass of water to my lips and took a tiny sip. Isaac looked like he could barely hide his displeasure of serving me.

My Auge quickly scanned the files Bull had shared for extended information on the family. Usually, it would glow and change the color of my irises from brown to electric blue when I had it on, but I wasn't ready for that conversation until I had eaten. I looked down, pretending to read the menu, and used my Auge discreetly.

Isaac turned out to be the bar owner. He was twenty-four and the oldest of Jonathan and Rebecca Bull-Smith's three children. His wife of five years was Clarissa Evans. They were both so young when they got married! There was no picture here, but according to the file, Clarissa was a schoolteacher and native of the Arizona colony.

"I'm Jimmy—"

"Mathis. From San Francisco," he interjected. "Yeah, I know who you are. I've never met a colored person in real life before. You're not as dark as I expected. Is that normal or is it just you?"

And there it was. Unfiltered bigotry wrapped up in ignorance and served with a racist cherry on top. "Mah-tooh," I said slowly. "Matoo."

I could feel the chagrin emanating from my body. Isaac didn't seem to care that he wasn't making the best first impression here, but he moved on from this line of questioning when I didn't answer his question. "Anyway, we're thrilled you could come out here on such short notice," he said. "I know my parents feel better knowing you're looking for Cara."

Isaac was saying all the right things, but there was something in his tone that made me think he wasn't all that thrilled. If he was such a concerned brother, why hadn't he met me earlier at his parent's home? In my experience, families tended to unite during times of crisis and offer support even in the smallest ways. But here he was, tending to his bar instead of looking for his sister.

Why wasn't there a search party out there looking for Cara right now? The question gnawed at me. When Aric didn't come home that fateful day, our relatives from India, Canada, and Europe had descended on Fremont within the first twenty-four hours. They helped us with door-to-door interviews, canvassed the streets, and did everything they could to look for him. I hadn't appreciated it at the time, but if it hadn't been for them and their support, we wouldn't have survived. And for that, I'd always felt so grateful.

"I'm not sure how much I can do," I answered honestly. "If I'd gotten here within the first forty-eight hours, we might have had a better chance, but it's been nearly five days. She could be anywhere by now."

Isaac forced a smile—a cold, disingenuous one. "Well, you're here now."

Curiosity battled my hunger and won. I took a sip from my glass and leaned forward, hoping that the backdrop of the bar might be enough for Isaac to lower his guard. "Why did your parents wait so long to call someone, anyway?"

Isaac's face went blank. "Don't ask me," he snapped. "Ask them."

"I did," I responded smoothly. "But I want to hear it from you as well. Unless you have something to hide?"

It felt like everyone in Bull's family had something to hide. The wheels in Isaac's head were turning furiously. I could see it in his eyes. "I don't have to answer your questions."

I nodded. "That is true. You don't," I said. "But when I find Cara—and I will—I'll be sure to remember you refused to cooperate. And I'll be especially sure to pass my assessment of you to the authorities if she's found hurt or worse."

"I don't know what you're accusing me of," Isaac said sharply. "But I'm innocent."

"Nobody is innocent when a kid is missing," I responded, equally sharp. "Especially people who don't lift a finger to find their family members."

Isaac narrowed his eyes, carefully thinking through his next steps. "It's a bit complicated."

"In what way?" I prodded, shifting in my seat.

Isaac grimaced and looked around the bar to make sure no one was listening. "My parents are mostly worried about being embarrassed if the town found out. And then there's her fiancé's family... they're not the most understanding people in the world. If they found out, they'd be furious."

I made a mental note to ask Bull for the fiancé's contact info. "You mean worried," I corrected.

"No, I mean furious," Isaac repeated quietly. "Cara's future mother-in-law is from a prominent family from the Arizona colony, and my parents wouldn't want to burn any bridges now that..." He hesitated like he was trying to decide whether or not to tell me. "Now that someone is challenging my grandfather's leadership."

There it was again, I thought. The most baffling thing about Cara's disappearance was the complete lack of concern for her safety. If anything, her family seemed to want her back not out of concern for her well-being, but to save themselves from the potential embarrassment and fallout her disappearance might bring on them.

"What does her disappearance have to do with your grandfather's hold over this place?"

Even though Isaac was having a hard time maintaining eye contact with me, I noticed that he was watching me closely when he thought I wasn't looking. Almost like he was studying me just as Florence had earlier this evening. It was an uncomfortable feeling, and I tried to ignore it, but the image of zoo animals kept popping up.

Isaac squinted at me, his eyebrows raised ever so slightly. "Our family is supposed to set an example for everyone here, okay?" he said. "And if my grandpa can't even get his own granddaughter to live by the rules he created, then why should anybody else?"

Something from Cara's note flitted into my mind. "And the person challenging your grandfather is..." I ventured a guess. "Hexum?"

Isaac didn't answer, but I knew I had guessed correctly from the look on his face. His face flooded with fear, and his shoulders tensed in response. "Look, do you want to eat something or not? I can't stand here all night answering your questions."

I was tempted to ask if he had something better to do. The Hercules might as well have been a graveyard. I turned my attention back to the menu and ordered myself a cold beer. While Isaac poured my drink, my mouth began salivating from a delicious aroma that had suddenly engulfed the bar.

"What is that smell?" I asked, sniffing the air.

"What smell?" Isaac wondered, looking around the bar. "Oh, do you mean the steak? That couple over there just had their order served."

My stomach rumbled again. "My God, that smells incredible!"

"Yeah, it just went on the grill. Everything here is organic and grass-fed; no antibiotics either," Isaac said.

Organic and grass-fed? That couldn't be right—unless... "Hang on," I asked slowly. "When you say steak... do you mean actual real meat from an animal?"

"Um... yeah." Isaac raised an eyebrow. "What else is there?"

"Not some lab-grown, vegan mushroom thing?"

"Um, no, like a cow with four legs, goes by the name Bessie," he answered, looking very confused. "You don't have meat in San Francisco?"

"We don't have real meat anywhere!" I laughed almost hysterically. "I mean, we do, but the real stuff is incredibly rare and way too expensive."

"Well, the food is free for residents here, but I'm gonna have to charge you for it," Isaac said flatly. "It's gonna be 275 DAI. Can you afford that?"

Isaac's tone was so condescending that I would have agreed to pay two thousand DAI for the meal just to wipe that smug look off his face. I tossed a few hundred DAI on the table in response and watched Isaac's eyes widen as the plastic currency teetered in front of him. I knew my rainy day funds would come in handy someday. Mom always said I was a fool to put my savings in plastic but I didn't trust the digital savings protocol.

Twenty minutes later, Isaac came back with the most beautiful piece of steak I had ever seen in my life. It looked exactly like the pictures in my mother's cookbooks—perfectly cut, juicy, marbled. My mother collected recipes in the hope that maybe someday it might be possible to cook a real meat dinner for our family.

It had been decades since raising animals for meat became infeasible. Global warming had reached such a malevolent peak in the early 2200s that environmental disasters, like extreme droughts and floods, had become commonplace and food shortages severe. By 2212, the world had unanimously voted for and adopted the clean meat policy, making plant-based and cultured meats the new normal.

Surprisingly, it had only taken one generation to adjust to the new plant-based diet. Positive impacts had been slow to follow, but at the very least, it had given Peregrinus enough time to find us a new Earth-like planet to settle on. The doomsday vault on Peregrinus wasn't much by scientific standards, but it was just enough for what remained on our planet to survive and, hopefully, thrive on New Earth.

I looked down at my plate and wondered what kind of food the astronauts ate aboard Peregrinus. Whatever it was, I was certain it wasn't half as good as the meal in front of me. The last time I had such a wonderful dinner we were celebrating Grandpa's 105th birthday, and Mom had gone all out. She had even sprung for the expensive plant-based meat and farmed salmon. Looking back, it had been such a great meal, but it did not hold a light to Isaac's steak. I tried to savor every bite and let the juices wash over my mouth, but I wolfed it down.

"That was amazing; thank you!" I said, after polishing off the last morsels.

Isaac took the compliment without so much as a smile. The edge in his voice was gone, but now he seemed to have taken on a more derisive tone. "The food out there is really bad, huh?"

"Actually, the food is pretty damn amazing," I said, taking the opportunity to explain to Isaac how 4D printing technology was adapted nearly two centuries ago to print edible, nutritious food during the Wheat Crisis. After waiting over an hour for a single piece of steak, my appreciation of the tech we had (and took for granted) grew tenfold. "Anyone can now have a Michelin-quality meal at home. It's just not as"—I hesitated, looking for the right word—"fresh."

I wasn't sure how much of that Isaac really understood, but he nodded along anyway. He reminded me of myself back when I was in high school. I used to nod along just like that while the teacher droned on and on about some mindless topic that I pretended to care about, my mind occupied with other, more exciting things.

"Where do you get your produce from?" I asked.

"We have a greenhouse here," Isaac said absently, cleaning the counter. "Almost all the fresh produce comes from there. We also have a pretty large farm on the outskirts."

This was the opportunity I'd been waiting for. "Did you know that every Peregrinus spacecraft has a greenhouse onboard?"

A blank look washed over Isaac when I mentioned Peregrinus. The baffled expression on his face confirmed my suspicion. He had no idea what I was talking about. There was someone in Corinth, someone intimately familiar with life beyond the colonies, using their knowledge to convince a select few people like Cara (and undoubtedly the other runaways) to think for themselves.

It was time to switch topics. "Listen, Isaac, I really do want to find your sister and bring her home safe and sound. But for me to do that, I need to understand Corinth better," I said, hoping to appeal to his brotherly instincts. "So, can I ask you a couple of questions? For real this time?"

Isaac gave me a long hard look before nodding back. No doubt he was wondering how much (if at all) he ought to share with me.

I decided to start small. "Tell me about your colony. There are six others, just like Corinth?"

"Yep, besides Corinth, there's one in Arizona—where my wife's from—one in New York, in Nebraska, South Dakota, Texas, and Idaho." Isaac counted on his fingers, reciting like he was reading it off of a list. "Ours is pretty small, though, compared to the colonies in Russia and Europe." Isaac shrugged. "We used to mingle with them... actually, there was a running joke in Corinth that if you didn't have at least one Nordic grandparent, you weren't truly one of us," Isaac went on. "Anyway, that was a long time ago. There was a falling-out a few decades ago. Don't know why, but now we don't have anything to do with them." His voice flattened again. "In fact, we don't even know what their condition is."

An uneasy feeling stirred in my chest. The idea of more such colonies all over the world was a hard pill to swallow. If they existed, were they as bad as Corinth? Did the kids there feel as stifled and caged as Cara had? I just couldn't help but wonder how many other helpless kids from the other six colonies had run away over the years. Did they make it out safely? I hoped so.

What killed me was the fact that this was the first time an investigative authority had been called in. The first time they cared enough about a missing person. I knew why, of course. It was because none of the other kids had Bull for a grandparent. I wasn't sure if that helped Cara, though. After having only been here a couple of hours, I couldn't say that I blamed her for leaving.

"Before I forget, how can I get to your grandfather's house?" I asked, hoping he wouldn't see through my bluff. "I'm meeting with him tomorrow morning but forgot to ask where it was."

Isaac stopped what he was doing and raised his eyebrows. "You are?" he asked. "Well, it's a bit of a walk and someone might see you."

"Someone already saw me today. Anyway, he said he'd rather meet with me at his house than his office," I lied smoothly.

Isaac thought about it for a second before reluctantly agreeing. He drew me a rough map to Bull's place on the back of a paper napkin. I tucked the map into my jacket pocket and thanked Isaac for his help. Now all I had to do was wait for the opportune moment and hope that Isaac and Bull didn't exchange notes until after I'd gotten what I needed.

I stepped off the barstool and yawned loudly. This day had taken its toll on me. I had planned to walk around until I found a motel or a hostel-type situation, but now that I thought about it more clearly, it seemed unlikely there were any motels here. It would have been kind of Bull to make some sort of arrangement—or at the very least, suggestions—for me while I was in Corinth. I tried not to overthink it. Bull was probably just overwhelmed by his granddaughter's disappearance, I told myself. Though somewhere deep in my heart, I knew that was probably untrue. I was not a guest here. I was the help. And a man like Bull did not concern himself with the well-being of the help.

"Is there somewhere—like a motel—where I could stay?" I asked.

"You're welcome to stay in the studio I keep upstairs. It's pretty small but comfortable," Isaac offered after informing me what I had already guessed—no hotels or motels in town. Something in his eyes told me that this wasn't just a gesture of goodwill, either; Isaac was keeping his friends close and his enemies closer. Ever since I'd walked into the Hercules, Isaac had been rude, sullen, and unfriendly. He probably would've liked nothing more than to have tossed my butt on the streets and slammed the door shut. This sudden shift roused my suspicion even more, and I raised an eyebrow.

"I usually stay there when I need to get away from the wife." Isaac shrugged with a smirk.

I shook my head. Goodwill, regardless of meaning or significance, tended to muddy investigations. With a young girl's life on the line, I did not want to owe Isaac or anyone else in Corinth any favors.

My protests fell on deaf ears. "I insist." Isaac raised his palms to his chest. "Unless you prefer to sleep on the street."

5

I T WAS ALMOST MIDNIGHT WHEN ISAAC finally closed the bar. When all the lights were turned off and the coast was clear, I slowly snuck back downstairs.

The smell of lemony disinfectant and surface cleaner was overwhelming. All the tables had been wiped clean and the chairs stacked neatly on top of each other. I peeped through the storefront windows to make sure nobody was lurking around on the streets, but it was all completely empty. There was enough light coming in through the windows, so I pulled the directions to Bull's home out of my pocket and tried to map out the route mentally. If I jogged, it would take me thirty minutes or so to get there, and hopefully Bull would already be fast asleep when I arrived. But more than anything, I hoped finding the drone wouldn't be too hard.

I walked back over to the end of the bar and pushed the door to the kitchen open. The steel utensils glimmered in the darkness, and I could hear the rumble of the dishwasher somewhere in the kitchen. I headed over to the back where the lighted exit sign glowered at me. I had fully expected to jimmy the lock, maybe even break it, but luckily it was one of those doors that locked from the outside but opened from the inside. Before I stepped out, I grabbed a small pot from the counter.

Holding the door open from the outside, I wedged the pot between the door and the threshold. The open space was small enough that in the darkness it still seemed like it was closed shut. I hoped it would hold until I got back from Bull's. Otherwise, I would be sleeping on the street after all.

The first few minutes of my run to Bull's were mostly uneventful. I felt cagey and my footsteps sounded loud. The air was heavy with the stench of wet dogs, and there were no streetlights in the vicinity, which I counted as a blessing. The chances of someone seeing me out and about were pretty low now. I was *mostly* sure I was headed in the right direction. Isaac's map was pretty detailed. Of course, I would have preferred to use my Auge rather than just blindly try to find my way, but Corinth wasn't exactly mapped out. It was good to challenge myself every now and then anyway. Who knows, there might even come a time in my life when I couldn't rely on my Auge and I would have to make do without it.

There were a few men, a group of two or three, walking the streets. Some of them carried batons and flashlights, and a few smoked cigarettes. This was probably the patrol Bull had mentioned. I stopped and hid in the shadows, waiting for them to pass.

"Did you hear about the ruckus near the valley?" I heard one of the men say.

"Sure did," another chuckled. "Boy, Hexum's gonna make a show of it tomorrow, isn't he?"

"When doesn't he?"

Both men laughed at that.

"God, you'd think these fools would've learned their

lesson by now, but guess you can't beat the stupid out of everybody."

My fists curled instinctively. I had no idea what they were talking about, but the schadenfreude in their tone was unmistakable. It was also hard to ignore the way they said Hexum's name—so full of reverence and fear. Without warning, the image of Vir dead on the outskirts popped into my head again, only this time my imagination was taking me down a dark road. In my mind's eye, I saw my brother lying dead on the ground with men standing over him, full of glee at having killed him.

I pressed my head against the cold brick wall and counted to ten, forcing myself to calm down. When I peeped out of the shadows, it didn't seem like they were walking anymore. So, I walked over to the other end of the side street and looked over to make sure nobody was around. If these men only patrolled certain streets at certain times, then I figured I had a short window of opportunity to ditch them, even though that meant taking a slightly longer route. I had initially expected to arrive at Bull's in thirty minutes, but with this long stop, it was probably going to be an hour or later now.

When I finally arrived at Bull's, I was lightheaded and breathless, but there was no time to waste. The lights were off, but I could see that the exterior of the house was very similar in style to Rebecca and Jonathan's, though twice as large. I cursed under my breath. The size of this mansion would make finding his home office much harder. I also had no idea who else might be in his household. But it was a risk I was willing to take. I made my way through the dead shrubs and trees to the backdoor. I didn't even bother checking to see if the door was open. I went straight to the first window I saw and pulled it up. It worked. You could always count on people to diligently bolt their doors shut and forget all about the windows.

It had been some time since I crawled through a window in the dead of night, and my feet hit the ground a lot louder than I expected. I waited and looked around the room to see if I had set off any alarms or sensors, but nobody came rushing in.

Relieved, I had my Auge set a timer for ten minutes, which is usually how much time the average thief spends ransacking a house. If I had had the time to case the place, learn Bull's routine, and count his household staff, I would feel comfortable taking my time, but there were too many variables, and I couldn't risk getting caught. How would I explain that to Bull?

I wasn't sure what room I was in. There were cardboard boxes everywhere, some stacked on top of each other, and the furniture was covered in white sheets. I carefully tiptoed out of there and opened the door to the hallway.

Bull was an old man, and I doubted he climbed up and down the stairs to get to his living space and office. By that logic, his office was probably somewhere on the ground floor. There were still a lot of rooms though. Maybe I could streamline my search further? Assuming that his office had a fair bit of tech, maybe even a couple of private servers, I could use my Auge to identify and connect to those signals and then narrow down the vicinity they were coming from, which would then lead me to the correct room. I blinked my Auge on and input the search parameters. Within seconds it had found a quantum computer down the hall.

The door was ajar. I poked my head through and sighed with relief. The hallway was empty. Bull's home office was a lot smaller than I had expected it to be. Matching cabinets lined the wall behind his large antique wood desk. On the other side of the room were screens that were currently turned off, and the only window in the room was boarded up.

I needed to find that drone. According to my Auge, I'd already spent four of my ten minutes. I needed to hurry. The first place I searched was the cabinets, but no luck. The only things in there were old documents and books. Nothing I had time to study right now. Next, I tried the desk cabinets. I started at the very bottom and worked my way to the top as fast as I could. I was starting to worry that Jonathan had been wrong about the drone—maybe Bull had brought it to his office after all—when I saw it in the top drawer.

A miniature pilotless aircraft.

It had taken quite a beating, all right. Only one of the four rotors was still attached, and the chassis was heavily dented and scarred. This type of drone was mostly used as a target decoy and for combat missions, research and development, and supervision. If it was remotely piloted, that meant Vir hadn't been entirely alone that night. Someone had been monitoring him from a secure location.

Did Vir have a partner? I felt nauseous. If he brought backup, he must've known he was putting himself in a dangerous situation. And if that was indeed the case, why didn't his partner come for him? Maybe something happened to them? Maybe whoever it was wasn't in a position to help?

I steadied myself against the cabinet. I couldn't afford

to break down here and now. It was stupid. *I* was being stupid. Knowing that Vir came here with someone didn't make me feel better at all. Instead, my chest felt like it had been stung by a thousand bees. My brother didn't just keep me in the dark. It was clear he didn't hold an ounce of trust toward me. How could he, anyway? It was my fault our youngest brother had died. I wouldn't trust me either.

Distressed, I tried to ignore my thoughts and focused on the drone. I flipped it on its back and pressed the power button. These things could fly up to twelve hours without having to recharge, so I hoped for the best—which, in this case, would be undamaged audio and video with GPS.

Next, I reactivated my Auge and directed it to launch a brute force attack on the drone's memory banks. Should be easy enough.

While my Auge worked on downloading whatever information the drone had recorded, I kept checking the clock. I was still okay for time, but I couldn't risk staying here any longer than necessary.

The content was eighty percent downloaded when I heard muffled footsteps behind the door. At first, I thought maybe I was imagining it, that the adrenaline was making me paranoid, but then the door handle turned quietly.

My heart rate accelerated tenfold. I could practically hear it thumping like a drumbeat. My options were fight or flight, and I only had a split second to decide which way to go. So I carefully placed the drone back in its drawer and crawled under the desk. It was, by far, the worst place I'd ever hidden in, but my options were sorely limited. I could only hope that Bull wouldn't peek under the desk.

The door creaked shut, and I heard two distinct sets of feet shuffle in. I didn't dare breathe.

"Is this the one?" a male voice whispered urgently.

I would have gasped if I could have. This was unbelievable. Somebody else was breaking and entering into Bull's house on the same night as me. The footsteps approached the desk. I leaned as far back as I could. One of them walked over to where I'd just been standing a few moments ago and immediately opened the drawer with the drone. It was too dark to see anything except for the man's dirty sneakers.

"Yes! Damn, woman, you were right. It's right here."

They were after the drone! Somebody inside Bull's trusted circle must've talked. To this Hexum? Or maybe to somebody else altogether? It was all I could do to sit still and not bust them for doing the same thing I was. God knows I wanted to, but the chances of that turning into a full-fledged fight were pretty good, and I'd still rather Bull not know I had broken into his home while he slept.

"Great, now grab it and let's go!" a soft female voice whispered.

The man grabbed the drone and shut the drawer. Seconds later they were gone. I stayed under the desk a few minutes longer before leaving the house the same way I got in. There was no sign of anybody else when I left Bull's estate, and I ran as fast as my feet could carry me.

The first thing I did when I was back at the Hercules was check the video. My Auge had salvaged only ten seconds' worth, and even that was pretty grainy. Still, it was something. I took a deep breath before playing the video. Suddenly, I was deeply aware that these were the last images of my brother before he died. I felt numb and nervous at the same time. I would finally know how he died—if someone had hurt him—but a part of me just wasn't ready yet. Despite everything Bull and Jonathan had told me about Vir's death, a tiny part of me was still hoping it wasn't true. Maybe they had lied, maybe he was still alive, maybe, maybe, maybe...

"All right, let's do this," I told myself.

The quality was worse than I expected, and the night vision didn't help either. The video showed the drone hovering at least twenty feet directly above Vir's head. It started with him waving to somebody off-camera behind him. Seconds later he began jogging ahead and helped someone who'd fallen down. *Is that Cara?* I couldn't be sure. They were wearing a thick hoodie over their head, and their face wasn't visible. The video blurred, but I saw him motioning for them to run. And that's when it happened. A small grenade or maybe a dirty bomb, I couldn't be sure, landed near them, and he pushed the stranger away with force. And then the video went blank.

I replayed the video again.

Judging from the angle, the strike had probably come from a small grenade launcher that was set up far away enough that the attackers weren't caught on video. *A surprise attack.* Vir and his companion on the ground had clearly been caught by surprise; maybe that's why the drone pilot couldn't send help soon enough?

There was one thing I knew for certain, though: Vir had died saving someone.

No, I corrected myself.

Someone had killed Vir and would've done the same to the mystery hoodie if it hadn't been for my brother.

Anger washed over me. Anger at whoever was responsible. Anger at the authorities for covering it up. Anger at myself for not being there. And at Bull for using my brother's death to lure me here.

I felt nothing but a white-hot rage. This entire time his death had felt vague and abstract, but now the proof was undeniable. My brother hadn't just died in some stupid accident. It wasn't a mistake. Vir had been killed in cold blood. Someone fired at him, knowing full well the damage it would cause. Whoever had done this to my brother was going to answer for their crime.

6

DAYLIGHT WAS SEEPING INTO ISAAC'S loft above the Hercules, but I wasn't ready to face Corinth just yet. The images of my brother being blown to pieces kept coming back to me. All I wanted to do was stay in bed and tuck myself under the warm comforter and cry, but that wasn't going to help Cara. And it certainly wasn't going to help me find whoever was responsible for Vir's death.

I sat up in bed and mentally went over everything that had happened yesterday.

The last fifteen hours or so felt dreamlike. I never imagined I would find myself in a secret all-white community, or that I would be here trying to figure out how my brother died, or that I would ever have to worry about racial discord ever. Corinth was a big change from my life in California, and I hated that I stuck out like a sore thumb here. It had occurred to me last night that this city was probably the most dangerous place in the world for someone like me to be wandering around in. I was a walking target.

I couldn't stop thinking about the couple at the restaurant last night—the way they had heckled me and called me names. The shock and revulsion in their eyes. I had come very close to a bar fight last night—and for no reason other than the fact that my skin was a different color. To them, I might as well have been an alien, some tiny green reptilian creature that had just landed on their planet. I guess in some ways, I was. I was as strange to them as they were to me. I wondered what my face must've looked like when I saw them.

At the Bull-Smith home, I had done my best to appear impersonal and detached during my meeting with Bull and his family members. I pretended not to notice their sly glances when they thought I wasn't looking, the way they studied my dark, wavy hair or stared at my deep caramel skin. Even Bull, despite his superficial politeness, had barely managed to hide his feelings. Not that he even really tried. It irked me now thinking about how he had first refused to shake my hand.

They could stare all they wanted. It was probably a nice change to see someone so good-looking anyway. I clenched my jaw tight. I was determined not to give Bull or anyone else in Corinth the satisfaction of knowing they had gotten to me.

Agitated, I jumped off of the edge of the bed. The floor was unexpectedly cold and relaxing. I wiggled my toes and tried to bring myself back to the here and now.

Isaac's small studio had turned out to be a cozy seven-hundred-square-foot loft with hardwood floors, airy windows, and a tiny balcony that overlooked Corinth's Hvalsey Mountains.

And the studio had character, I had to admit. His art and camera equipment took up most of the coffee table, stunning black-and-white pictures hung on the walls, and there were books everywhere—on shelves, the coffee table, and the floor next to colorful throw pillows. One picture stood out in particular. I recognized it from Cara's bedroom. It was the one of her and the mystery friend, whom Rebecca had refused to identify.

I picked up the first book within my reach. I just couldn't resist the temptation to touch, open, and smell a real book. When I'd seen the books in Cara's bedroom yesterday, I had approached them empirically and without emotion. Those books were evidence. They didn't evoke the same response today. This was a totally different experience.

My fingers slowly caressed the binding and traced the golden embossed words on the cover. It was heavier than I expected. I took a moment and let it sink in—this was the first time I had ever held a whole, undamaged book in my hands. That crap from Cara's bedroom didn't count as real books either. These were actual novels. Stories written by people from a bygone era.

I flipped the front page open carefully and smelled it, taking in the glorious, divine scent that new books emit. It felt incredible to feel the paper between my fingers, hear the crisp sound the pages made when I turned them.

The abundance of books and reading material in Corinth was astonishing. Where and how did these people get their books? I wanted to know. Toward the end of the twenty-first century, the digital age hammered the final nail in the coffin for print publishing, and the only place anyone could buy an actual paper book nowadays was at expensive antique stores.

I had skimmed through some of the titles before bed last night and realized two things. One was that there wasn't a single book here that had been written after 2050. And two, all the authors on the shelf here were white and male.

I didn't recognize any of these titles. But my Auge ran a quick analysis of the authors and titles and found that over ninety-eight percent of the books on these shelves were written by conservative pundits, right-wing extremists, and neo-Nazis. These writers were ultra-nationalist, anti-Semitic, sexist, anti-immigrant thugs who believed that Auschwitz was a good thing.

This shouldn't have come as a surprise, but it did. Corinth's commitment to its roots was even more problematic than I had originally thought.

Looking at these books in Isaac's loft, it hit me that Bull didn't just want to revive the Caucasian community, but to reestablish the dominance his people once had over the world. By excluding writers of color, Bull was telling his people that writers of color were not good enough to share the space with white authors—on the shelf and otherwise.

A familiar, unsettling feeling poked through my skin. There had been numerous disappearances over the years, and no formal investigation had been launched to find any of the missing children. It had taken a high-profile missing person for Bull to care enough to bring in someone like me.

How could nobody have made an effort to find the others? I rarely went a single day without thinking about Aric. And now Vir. Losing a loved one was bad enough without adding the pain of not knowing what happened to them. Parents, good or bad, don't sleep at night not knowing where and what condition their children might be in.

Obviously, I was missing something, but I knew just where to start looking for the answers I needed. I activated my Auge and began sifting through the documents Bull had transferred to me last night. There were scores of farewell notes just like

Cara's, from other kids and even a few adults, going back several years. I picked one at random and began reading it.

A sixteen-year-old girl named Iris Gruger had written to her parents last year: "Just because I'm infertile doesn't mean I'm worthless. I would rather die than become one of Hexum's useless concubines."

Another girl named Martine Fox wrote, "You're going to hate me for saying this, but I don't care anymore: I don't want to be a mother. I don't even like children. I don't want to spend the next fifteen years popping out babies like some sort of machine. That's what you expect, isn't it? For me to have a kid every year? You know, there's only so much my body can take. I can't go through the hormone treatments and tests every month. I'm done letting you tell me what to do with my body."

There was a note in here from a woman whose name wasn't included. "I'm pregnant. But I'll die before I let this innocent child be born in this miserable hellhole."

I read scores of similar notes until I found one from a young boy called Max. "I'm so, so sorry I disappointed you guys. I know how much you wanted me to have children and help our colony survive... I swear I did everything the doctor suggested to increase my sperm count but... my body failed me. I know what you'll do to me if I stay here. I don't think I could survive it."

Another young kid named Beto Fischer, only seventeen years old when he left Corinth, wrote to his parents, "I told you guys over and over and over again that I won't go through this. But you just wouldn't listen. You wouldn't trust that I knew what was best for me. You thought you could force me down the aisle no matter what I said or did, but you thought wrong. I have a mind and heart of my own, and I will do what is best for me."

Each note was more heartbreaking than the one before. There was so much sadness and pain between these lines. All of them were unique and yet so similar. By the time I'd read all of the letters, my own heart was shattered. How could Bull not see the agony he was inflicting upon these people by forcing them to live a life they didn't want? How could the parents have missed it?

After I regained my composure, I checked to see if my digital assistant had cracked the code while I'd slept. It had, indeed, deciphered the pages I'd scanned, but the most surprising thing was the result itself. According to my assistant, Cara had used a pretty ancient form of taking notes called shorthand. It was popular in the late 1800s and early 1900s but had gone out of style with the invention of the personal computer. No doubt she had learned it from the same person educating her on matters outside this town.

A bitter taste crept into my mouth as I read Cara's note. It was shorter than I expected and gut-wrenching.

Corinth is hell, my personal hell. Today I found out that we're all microchipped. This is how Grandpa always knows where everyone is, but Raptor says that there's a way to get it out safely. We're going to do it when I go into the clinic for my mandatory monthly check-in. Really hate going there, but it has to be done. Can't risk being tracked. There's just no privacy anymore. I don't like having to report when my monthly cycle starts and ends to Dr. Shaw. My uterus is my business. Wish I was gone already.

There was no date for this entry, but I had to assume

they were recent recordings of her thoughts. Who was Raptor? I wondered if it was a code name for the mysterious person or group I needed to find. Either way, Raptor was somehow connected to Vir. The people who broke into Bull's office had known exactly what they were looking for.

There was another, equally alarming entry under the first one. Overheard Mom and Dad talking today. They say fertility rates are down again this year. So they want to up our hormone shots. My body is so tired and confused by these treatments already. Don't think I could survive a higher dose. Counting down the days to freedom.

Poor kid.

My Auge had also decoded the sole slip of paper I'd found between the pages of Cara's book. Like the diary, this one was also written in shorthand. "Rendezvous point and final group confirmed. Destination to be shared en route. Pack necessary items only."

Cryptic but interesting, I noted. If I read this note correctly, Cara was not alone the night she escaped. She either left with other runaway youths or she had a guide of some sort. But wouldn't Bull have told me if other kids had gone missing the same night as Cara? I dreaded the answer.

Though I had the impression from Bull and his family that they believed the string of disappearances were unconnected, it seemed highly unlikely, given the amount of planning and preparation that had gone into Cara's escape. In fact, I was becoming more and more convinced that Corinth (and possibly the other colonies) had some sort of an underground resistance.

So who in Corinth would have the means and connections

to smuggle dozens of people out of a heavily guarded border without being detected?

With a heavy heart, I went over the files Bull had sent. My digital assistant brought an anomaly to my attention: there had been a steeper increase in disappearances over the last six years than at any other time in Corinth's secluded history. More worryingly, over sixty percent of the missing persons were female and under the age of twenty-five.

Another concerning aspect was that in the rare instances that a missing person had been found, he or she was always discovered deceased. I had expected their deaths to be attributed to natural causes, like exposure or starvation, but the images in Bull's files told another story.

In one shocking instance, a boy (only seventeen years old at the time of his death) was found on the street stark naked and bloody only a few months ago. That boy, according to this file, was Beto Fischer. The same kid whose note I'd just read. The quality of the pictures made identifying the cause of his death extremely difficult, but from what I could see, the boy had been beaten to death.

Just like Fischer's unexplained death, there were dozens of similar cases dating back ten years or so. Since the records only went back to that period, I knew there were a lot more deaths than just the ones on Bull's file. It was even more concerning to me that there were no autopsy reports for any of the cases listed. The photographs of Fischer were clearly taken inside Corinth; it was not hard to recognize the rundown red buildings I'd seen yesterday. *If he didn't make it out safely, did that mean the others didn't either?*

A wave of anger washed over me. These murders had taken place inside the city, not somewhere beyond these borders. And yet Bull had washed his hands clean of these deaths.

Could it be that he was directly involved in their killings? Or perhaps he was covering up for whoever was responsible? I leaned more toward the latter. Bull was cold, ruthless, and a driven egomaniac, but I couldn't see him killing anyone. His whole purpose in life was to increase the population of his colonies. He couldn't do that if he kept killing his own people.

That was probably why the Bull-Smiths were so desperate to keep Cara's disappearance quiet. Clearly, they were terrified she might end up sharing Beto Fischer or Iris Gruger's fate. That only threw up more questions, though—who in Corinth could be responsible for such violence? And why would Bull, who was so anguished over their declining population, stand by and let innocent kids die like this?

Another pattern emerged as I perused through the files: nearly eighty-nine percent of the runaways were between the ages of sixteen and twenty while the others averaged between twenty-five and forty years. The data was as sad as it was fascinating. I couldn't help but wonder why the older demographic had waited as long as they did to make a break for it. Were they simply unable to leave and didn't know how, or had something happened for them to break away from Bull's propaganda? The other odd thing they had in common was the fact that they were all unmarried and without progeny. What were the chances of that?

It was nearly eight a.m. when I was done going over the data from Bull's files. With more questions than answers, I was impatient to get on with this investigation. And I intended to start by getting some real answers from the Bull-Smiths.

7

I T WAS STILL TOO EARLY IN THE DAY FOR the Hercules to be open, but I could hear a faint voice calling out Isaac's name in the restaurant below. Whoever was down there was making their way up to the studio.

I scrambled to put some clothes on before they came up here looking for him, but the creaking in the staircase retreated—they were going back down. Relief washed over me.

Quietly, I pushed the bedroom door open and tiptoed to the edge of the staircase where I couldn't be seen. Downstairs, the restaurant's front door creaked open and heavy footsteps shuffled in.

Someone wolf whistled.

"You knocked up yet?" a grating male voice boomed through the bar downstairs.

I did not have to meet this person to know I already disliked him. The tenor in his voice was reminiscent of the scumbags I was used to dealing with in San Francisco.

"If your husband isn't up to the job, I'd be happy to put a baby in that little belly of yours," another voice roared.

My fingers balled into a tight fist as I prepared to head down to put an end to whatever this was. I had barely taken a step when I heard a loud wallop. Whoever the men were talking down to had responded with their fist. "Go ahead and say something else," a female voice, sharp as a bell, shouted. "I dare you."

Neither of the two men responded.

"What are you idiots doing here anyway?" she demanded. "Shouldn't you be out somewhere torturing someone?"

The first man with the grating voice answered. "We heard a stranger was here last night," he snorted. "Talking to your husband."

I froze. The stranger they were looking for was clearly me, and I was pretty sure from their tone it wasn't to say howdy, either.

"A lot of people come in here, Clayton." She sounded tired and exasperated. "It's a bar."

"This man wasn't from here, you stupid monkey," he growled. "He's brown-skinned. Does that sound like someone who's here?"

The woman laughed. "You're joking, right?" I could almost imagine her crossing her arms in front of her chest as she said it.

"She obviously doesn't know a thing, Clayton," the other man scoffed. "She's just a woman."

The man named Clayton whispered something I couldn't quite make out, but the woman responded by calling him an asshole.

Just then, somebody else stomped into the Hercules.

"Ah-ha! Just the man we were looking for." Clayton clapped loudly. "Or should I say the other man?"

It was frustrating not being able to see exactly what was happening down there, but my instincts commanded me to stay put.

"Um, what's going on?" I heard Isaac's confusion reverberate through the room.

The floorboards shifted against someone's weight. One of the men, I figured, had taken a couple of steps toward Isaac. "We heard from a reliable source that you've been entertaining a colored fella," Clayton's unnamed companion said. "Hexum sent us over to find out what the hell is going on."

There was a loud thunk. Isaac, I presumed, had just dropped something heavy on the bar counter because when he responded he was out of breath. "You heard wrong," he said.

"Don't lie to me, now," Clayton snarled. "Hexum knows your grandfather is up to something. If a colored man is walking these streets, it's because he allowed it."

Isaac sighed. "Then why doesn't Hexum just go ask him instead of sending you to harass me?"

"You know, that's not a bad idea," Clayton said, dragging his feet toward the exit. "I'm gonna go do just that." The Hercules' only door creaked open. "Say, how's the blushing bride doing?" he asked Isaac. "Haven't seen her in a few days. She excited to marry my baby brother or what?"

"She is. Of course, she is," Isaac said quickly. "You know how girls are before a big event . . ."

"She better be," Clayton warned. "We wouldn't watch another barren bitch like you walking around."

"That's enough," the woman snapped. "You needn't concern yourself with Cara."

When the door slammed shut, I heard the mystery woman take a deep breath and lock the door after the men. "Where have you been?" she cried. "I was worried sick!"

This piqued my interest even more. The conversation downstairs had quickly gone from unpleasant to intimate.

The woman's voice was strained and full of concern. Her tone suggested a deep familiarity, one I assumed borne from marriage.

Isaac didn't respond, but I was sure he heard her as loud and clear as I did from up here.

"We're too old to give each other the cold shoulder, Isaac." She was starting to sound ticked off. God knows I would be too if someone ignored me like he did her. "We're going to have to talk about this sooner or later."

"I thought..." Isaac's voice broke. "I thought you loved me."

I could hear him sigh, and I didn't dare move from my spot now. The slightest sound could give me away, and I hated the idea of either of them finding out I was eavesdropping on a very private conversation. Well, actually, I hated the idea of getting caught. Eavesdropping on conversations was practically half my job as a PI.

"I do!" the woman said tenderly. "You know I do."

"What I know is that you've been lying to me since the day we got married," he choked. "Christ! I'm such an idiot!" There was a loud bang, like a fist pounding the wall, "I knew I should've listened to my mom when she told me to let you go! It's my own damn fault for sticking up for you!"

The woman's high heels clicked softly. "You don't mean that."

"I do," Isaac spat. "I wish I had never met you!"

He sounded like he meant it too. The next thing I heard was the door slamming. Someone—I couldn't tell if it was the woman or Isaac—had walked out of the conversation. I stood in my clandestine spot, debating if I ought to go downstairs and face whoever was still there. Whoever it was, I figured catching them in a vulnerable moment might be to my advantage. So, I stepped down the narrow staircase and pushed the thin curtain separating the bar and the upstairs studio aside.

The woman immediately spun around. Tears were streaming down her face, her cheeks flushed red. "Isaac?"

I recognized her as soon as I saw her. She was the mystery woman in the picture in Cara's bedroom. The photograph didn't do her justice, though. She was gorgeous in person. Her almond-shaped brown eyes were exactly the same color as her long, wavy hair and perfectly complemented her tanned skin. She was dressed in monochrome dark green pants and a polo neck sweater.

She was not a very tall woman, but she carried herself gracefully. And she looked nothing at all like any of the women I'd seen in Corinth so far. I couldn't quite put a finger on it, but even though she was Caucasian in appearance, her features were just uncommon enough (at least for Corinth) to stand out.

Her eyes narrowed at me in recognition, and she took two effortless swoops forward. I was close enough to her now to see the dark shadows under her puffy eyes. "Hi, I'm Clarissa, Isaac's wife." She held out her right hand without hesitation.

It was my turn to be surprised by the gesture. Since meeting Bull and his clan yesterday, I was prepared for her to recoil just like them. When Isaac had mentioned his wife last night, my first thought had been that he was too young to be married, but now I realized that it was his wife who was the young one.

"You can call me Evie—everyone does." She shrugged. "Don't ask me why. It's short for Evans, I guess." Clarissa—Evie—smirked. "And you're obviously Jimmy Matoo. I've heard a lot about you." She gave my palm a hearty squeeze. I expected her to have one of those soft, dainty hands that felt like cotton. Instead, I was met with a strong, blistered palm.

"Oh yeah, from whom?"

Evie's face suddenly became mask-like. Her expression was a cross between confusion and embarrassment. "What, now?"

"I didn't mean to eavesdrop, but I heard you talking to those men," I said.

"Ah, well, from Isaac's grandfather of course." She flashed me a smooth smile. "We've been expecting you."

"Right. Well, I was going to come by your home later and introduce myself," I tried to smile back at her. "But since we're both here now, do you mind if I ask you a couple of questions?"

Evie inhaled sharply before answering. "All right."

"First of all, who were those men?"

Evie snorted in response. "Didn't anyone tell you?" she asked. "They're Hexum's men."

That name again. Hexum. Isaac had dodged my question about this Hexum person last night. "This Hexum person—is he Bull's right-hand man?"

An involuntary shudder passed through Evie's body. "Was," Evie corrected. "Hex is his own man now. Leland Hexum is the leader of the Federate Army," she whispered. "The man challenging Grandfather's leadership."

I knew the last part, but what I didn't understand was the fear associated with Hexum's name. "Cara called Hexum a bully in the note she left her parents," I said. "And Isaac all but avoided me when I mentioned his name last night. Why is that?"

Evie straightened her back and looked around to make sure we weren't being eavesdropped on. "Hexum is the devil," she said. "He's vile and crazy. You wouldn't think by looking at him, but if he had his way, he'd have the entire city worshipping him and the ground he walked on."

I listened to her impassively. The fear associated with Hexum was unmistakable. Before I could ask Evie any more questions, she announced it was time for her to leave. "School starts in a few minutes, and I can't be late." Her carefully crafted veneer returned. According to the bio I'd read last night, Evie was a substitute teacher at the local high school, and she sometimes volunteered at Corinth's only clinic. "Meet me at the library at noon. We'll talk then."

She turned around and walked out of the Hercules before I could even respond.

WITH HEXUM'S MEN ON THE LOOKOUT FOR

me, I decided I needed to blend in if I was going to walk around Corinth asking people about Cara. There wasn't much in my overnight bag that would work as effective camouflage, but there was a pile of Isaac's freshly laundered shirts that might just do the trick.

I pulled one of his dark-blue flannel shirts over my old t-shirt and threw on a baseball cap with the uneven gold scale pin for good measure. It wasn't much, but it would do if I kept my head down.

There was a soft knock against the half-open door, and Isaac poked his head in tentatively. He looked even grumpier than last night. His face was gaunt, and his eyes had heavy bags underneath them. "How much of that did you hear?" Isaac shoved the bedroom door open and walked in uninvited.

"Enough to know I'm really not welcome here," I said, buttoning up the shirt.

Isaac walked past me and over to the open balcony door and closed it shut. After securing the latches, he pulled the curtains close together. "Yeah, you've only been here one day, and I already have those goons breathing down my neck," he said angrily. "My grandfather made a mistake bringing you here. You need to leave! Go back to San Francisco and forget about this place."

If my lips hadn't been pressed so tightly together, I'm certain my jaw would have hit the floor. This was the last thing I was expecting to hear. In fact, I'd hoped Isaac would have a change of heart. That he might see me more as an ally here to help and maybe even offer to help me look for Cara. I was so off the mark with that one.

"What about Cara?" I managed to ask when I regained my composure.

Isaac was unperturbed. "What about her?" he shrugged, shifting from one foot to another. "She knew what she was doing. The fact that we haven't found her yet tells me she's long gone."

Isaac's logic made zero sense to me. "This town is surrounded by wasteland. There's nothing alive at all for a hundred miles. The fact you haven't found her doesn't mean she made it out safely. If I were you, I'd be extremely concerned,"

I protested. His blasé attitude toward his sister's safety was infuriating. How anyone could stand idly by when a member of their family was missing was beyond me. My parents still couldn't get through the day without checking in with the police about Aric's disappearance, if there was a lead on his killer. It was a long shot, but they wouldn't stop until his killer was brought to justice. "Isaac, your sister might be lying dead in a ditch somewhere, or worse. How can you be so indifferent?"

"I'm sure she's fine," Isaac said brusquely. "Anyway, I really don't want to waste my time looking for someone who doesn't want to be found."

All I could see now was my two dead brothers' faces. The pain of losing them returned full force. I tried to shun the awful memories, but they were morphing into something else. Something deeply unpleasant. Having seen firsthand how Cara's disappearance was being handled by her family, one thing became crystal clear: I was no longer interested in finding just Cara Bull-Smith. I was intent on finding every single person from Bull's missing person file. Nothing and nobody, in Corinth or elsewhere, was going to keep me from finding out what happened to these missing teenagers.

"That is unacceptable!" I said, barely containing my anger. "And I'm not leaving until I find her—dead or alive."

"She knew what she was doing when she chose to leave us," Isaac said coldly. "She knew the consequences!"

The word *consequence* was starting to sound like a bad word to me, worse than any curse word I knew. The way Bull and Isaac said it made my insides squirm. "And just what are those 'consequences' exactly?" My arms automatically folded against my chest.

Isaac shook his head and laughed humorlessly. "You wouldn't understand. Why would you? You're the reason we're forced to live this way. You and your people."

He had one thing right at least: I didn't understand. Not even a little bit. "Then explain it to me!" I demanded. "You can treat me like the enemy all you want, but I'm the only person here trying to help your family."

Wearily, Isaac slumped on the couch and stared up at the ceiling. "Help? Your presence here is enough to start a riot!" he cried. "I could be lashed for letting you sleep here."

A riot? Isaac lashed? That sounded a bit melodramatic, even to me. If Isaac's grandfather was the man in charge, then surely his family must benefit from his position. Their pristine homes and vehicles were a stark contrast to the dwindling condition of the rest of the city. The Bull-Smiths wouldn't be the first political family in the world to lap up a bit of nepotism, and they certainly wouldn't be the last.

I inclined my head toward Isaac. "I'm sure your grandfather took this into consideration when he brought me here."

"You're so clueless it's not even funny," he said roughly. "My grandfather is barely holding onto his office. There are a lot of people here who believe he ought to step down and let someone else, someone young, someone with a vision take over."

"Someone like Hexum?"

Isaac looked at me sourly. "Someone *exactly* like Hexum. My grandfather was the one who plucked Hexum out of obscurity to lead his precious Federate Army. He thought he was choosing the person least likely to succeed at the job. A yes-man, someone who could follow orders, someone dispensable, ask-no-questions-and-lie-through-his-teeth-for-you   infertile man Friday."

An interesting reference, I noted. "Obviously, not anymore."

"Obviously." Isaac rolled his eyes. "And now my family is one of two things Hexum truly hates. I'll let you guess what the second one is."

He regarded me with revulsion. His face twisted and his jaw clenched together as if he'd just been hit in the face with something stomach-turning. I wondered what my own face must look like as I stared back at him. Could Isaac see the anger and disbelief radiating from me?

"Anyway, Hexum's become suspicious—about you, about Cara. He's probably already guessed about her." Isaac looked around the room, breaking eye contact with me. "They've set up mandatory curfews, and I'm sure they'll begin door-to-door check-ins soon to make sure people are where they're supposed to be."

I sighed. It didn't surprise me that Hexum knew about me already. I would've bet anything that the Hercules' patrons had gone around telling the entire town. In fact, I was surprised they hadn't come looking for me yet. They probably couldn't wait to make a spectacle of me.

A lightbulb went off in my head. Those horrifying pictures of Beto Fisher lying in a pool of his own blood were still fresh in my head. Bull had deliberately shared half-truths with me. He manipulated the evidence to make it seem like the deaths were unsolved. Like they were random, unexplained acts of violence. When in reality their deaths were probably some form of punishment. Punishment executed by Hexum and his men.

Nothing else would explain the inexplicable fear everyone in Corinth seemed to have for Hexum. "And when he does find out, it'll be like Beto Fischer all over again."

Isaac's eyes bloomed in surprise. Evidently, he had not expected me to know that name or what had happened. "How do you know about that?"

How I knew hardly mattered now. I was in uncharted territory, and the laws I had vowed to defend did not apply here. If only Bull had been honest with me from the beginning, I might have prepared myself. Now I understood why Cara's family had been so insistent on keeping her disappearance quiet—the man they feared so terribly had just become my prime suspect.

8

TALKING TO ISAAC HAD BEEN DRAINING. The little energy I'd amassed from last night's sleep had evaporated by the time I left the little studio.

The pleasant 109°F heat felt rejuvenating, and I let it melt away the frostiness I'd encountered since coming here. Centuries ago, weather like this would have been unbearable for most people, but after passing the irreversible point of climate change, 109°F was basically fall.

With a muffin that I'd grabbed from the Hercules on my way out in hand, I ventured back out into the streets of Corinth, unsure of what awaited me. I stood rooted there on the sidewalk for several minutes, trying to remember which way Rebecca and Jonathan's place was when the sounds of barking dogs and loud voices broke my reverie. They were so thunderous, they could only be coming from loudspeakers.

The commotion had a magnetic effect on me. My instincts were trained to run toward danger, not away from it. I pulled the hoodie over my head and tugged down on the sleeves so my fingers could clench them. It was hardly what I'd call incognito, but something was happening a few blocks away, and I needed to check it out.

I realized as I got closer that it was a rally of some sort. This was probably the city center. At least a hundred people were facing a makeshift stage, where a middle-aged man with closely cropped blonde hair and light blue eyes stood facing them from behind a podium. The skin all over his face and neck was covered with dark sunspots and looked like well-creased leather, and his thick beard and premature grey hairs gave him the appearance of an overworked high school teacher.

Maybe it was the way he stood there with two large black wolfish dogs, staring down at everyone, or maybe it was the way everyone watched him—the fear and respect were unmistakable. This man, I was willing to bet my meager life savings on, was Hexum. The mysterious man I knew so little about.

I activated my Auge. This time, I wanted it to record everything just the way I was seeing it. For those of us who didn't have a photographic memory, it was a handy feature that allowed us to revisit memories and study them later for anything we missed. It was an expensive feature, too, and I didn't use it unless I really needed to, but I figured I could afford it since I'd only used two of my five memory units for this year. Each unit could store up to six hours' worth of recordings, though I never recorded any event for longer than two hours.

My eyes searched the crowd for familiar faces, but there wasn't anybody I recognized. I hunched my shoulders and lowered my head as much as I possibly could. The congregation was packed together like sardines and was chanting "BULL MUST GO" in unison. A small group of men threw empty beer bottles at Bull's picture. "Bullseye!" they screamed every time a bottle struck Bull's face. From here I could make out a few signs that floated above people's heads. "White is Might," screamed one sign. "Make babies, not monkeys," said another.

The hostility and anger seeping out of this crowd were palpable, as was the collective lack of hygiene. The malodor emanating from the crowd made my nose crinkle in self-defense. It was all I could do to keep from barfing. I wondered if the people who broke into Bull's house last night were here right now. Everywhere I looked, there was a sea of unkempt and gangly white people, a few with swollen bellies, some barefoot and shirtless, waving the old Confederate and Nazi flags. A few in the crowd wore the flags as t-shirts or bandanas, and others had the same tattoo, that I now recognized as the Nazi swastika, as the man from the bar last night.

"What's happening?" I overheard a woman standing a few feet ahead of me asking the heavily tattooed man standing next to her.

"Haven't you heard the rumors? They're sayi—" The man never had the chance to finish. A low, sinister howl pierced through the crowds from Hexum's direction. I looked over people's shoulders to get a closer look at the two large animals Hexum had leashed beside him.

The black dogs (if you could call them that) bared their unnaturally large, sharp teeth, uneven like a baby shark's, as they snarled at the crowd. Their most terrifying feature wasn't their teeth, however—it was their scarlet eyes and the way they watched everyone closely, scrutinizing our every move, ready to pounce. There was a deep bloodlust in those red orbs, a visceral hunger that didn't belong among the living.

I shuddered. These were not run-of-the-mill domesticated puppers. Hexum's pets were some sort of a wolf-dog-demon hybrid. There were rumors, a few years ago, in certain circles that a covert government agency was experimenting on animals, dogs in particular. They were meant to be a next-gen hybrid hunter-weapon for soldiers, but I doubted the goal had been to turn man's best friend into man's worst nightmare.

Guess there was more truth to the rumors, after all. But the real mystery was how they had ended up in this remote part of Oregon. Were the colonies breeding them? I couldn't imagine the government would ever approve these animals to be used as a policing tool. I shuddered. The only logical answer that came to mind was that they had been acquired on the black market or using some back channels.

"Why does he have to bring those things out?" the woman groaned.

From his podium, Hexum raised his right palm in front of his chest, and the crowd immediately fell into a hush. "I don't know about the rest of you, but I am sick—sick and so goddamn tired," Hexum spoke in a cold and steady voice, "of Julius Bull and his lies! We are dying!" Hexum smacked the podium. "Look around and tell me how many pregnant bellies you see." He pointed. "Not enough, I'll tell you that! Our fertility rates are falling fast. And we might have a better chance at surviving as a clan if so many boys and girls didn't give us the slip and run outta town."

Hexum let that sink in. "Hell yeah!" someone whooped in the crowd. Some people nodded their heads, and others clapped loudly in agreement. The signs seemed to rise higher up in the air.

"And what is our fearless leader doing about it? Nothing!" Hexum's voice thundered across the square. "Where is the medical equipment he promised? The fertility treatments? Empty promises from an empty shell of a man! The only thing he's done so far is to bring a colored man into our town."

Shock buzzed through my body. Hexum was using me as a rallying cry against Bull and his authority over the town. A hush fell on the crowd. People exchanged startled looks. I pushed the cap I was wearing even lower and wished I were invisible right now.

"That's right!" Hexum cried. "Even as we speak there is vermin—honest-to-God colored vermin—roaming our streets! Why? I ask why! For that, Bull will answer!"

A deafening roar erupted from the crowds. "Bull must answer" chants took over.

"If I had a child that defected right from under my nose, I would be ashamed," Hexum spat into the microphone when the chants subsided. "Ashamed to have raised a child that did not understand the importance of what we are trying to achieve here! Ashamed to face my neighbors." He paused. "Ashamed to be alive."

A sense of foreboding came over the crowd. They were now looking at each other accusingly, wondering who among them had a child who had defected. From the way Hexum appeared to be challenging Bull, another thing was certain—there was nothing democratic in the way leaders were elected in the colonies. Hexum could overthrow Bull without due process and get away with it too.

Hexum paced across the stage, pretending to be deep in thought. "Now, here is someone who should feel shame." He gestured to someone off-stage. "Send her up."

A palpable tension passed through the crowd. Someone in the front gasped loudly. I craned my neck to see who they were bringing up, but all I could see was a blonde head bobbing toward the podium. Could it be Cara? I prayed it wasn't her. I had pinned all my hopes of learning what happened to Vir on finding Cara and talking to her. My sanity depended on her safety now. My fists clenched together. If they had, indeed, found Cara and were putting her dissidence up on display, I knew I had to act.

A delicate figure stumbled onto the platform where Hexum waited. Her long blonde hair covered her face, and she had her arms crossed tightly across her chest. She seemed almost afraid to breathe. Her pale body was angled away from the crowd, so it took me a second to realize she was completely naked.

The crowd watched patiently as Hexum walked over to her and grabbed her by the hair, forcing her to face them. "Look at them," he said, viciously shaking her head. "Look at all the people you've let down."

The girl wouldn't give into Hexum's command, though. No matter how hard Hexum shook her head around, the girl kept her eyes tightly shut. I didn't recognize her, but I guessed she must be about the same age as Cara.

"LOOK. AT. THEM."

The girl cried out in pain and tried to free herself from Hexum's hands, but her skinny arms were no match for his. Still, she kept her eyes closed. Even in her vulnerable state, she wasn't going to let Hexum make her do anything she didn't want to.

Some of the men wolf-whistled at her exposed breasts.

Others catcalled. And some threw trash at her.

"Not so brave now, are you?" Hexum mocked her. "We found her by the valley last night, sneaking out of town like a thief. How are we going to survive if children, like this ungrateful cow, don't understand what's at stake? Do you think your life is greater than our collective existence? Do you?"

The girl whimpered but didn't answer. I knew from reading Bull's file that this was how dissidents were punished, but seeing it happen firsthand was another thing entirely. *Where on Earth are her parents?* She must have someone in her life who cared enough about her to stand up for her. I looked around, hoping to see if someone might stand up for her, but this crowd just looked way too pleased with Hexum. It was probably for the best that she kept her eyes closed. Sometimes not knowing was a blessing. I would never want to know if my family had just stood there and watched, without even lifting a finger to help, while I was broken and humiliated in public. That would have killed me.

"Make her pay, Hex!"

The crowd cheered. Even the animals growled in approval. I knew what was coming next. The files from Bull hadn't left much to the imagination. I couldn't just stand by and watch an innocent kid be tortured and whipped to death. I took a deep breath and started to make my way to the front.

If I were a betting man, I'd put all my money on that whip making a mark (or several) on my back. There was no way I was walking away from this in one piece—this was going to be a crowd-pleaser.

A cold hand grabbed my elbow.

Startled by the unexpected touch, I wheeled around,

expecting to find myself face-to-face with one of Hexum's men, but instead, I was greeted by a wide-eyed blonde girl. Surprise registered on Florence's face.   She had probably expected to find her brother, given that I was wearing his shirt and cap, and instead found me. Confused, she looked me up and down, clearly waiting for some kind of an explanation. Instead, I blinked my eyelids rapidly, turning off the recording function.

"What are you doing here?" we whispered simultaneously.

"Why are you wearing my brother's clothes?" Florence demanded. "Did you steal them?"

Over my shoulder, I could hear the animals growling slowly and Hexum saying something about teaching the girl a lesson. Even under all the layers I was wearing, I could feel goosebumps poking through my skin.

Somebody handed Hexum a pail. At first, I thought it was ice-cold water, but when he dumped the contents over her head, Florence and I gasped. "You want so much to be a part of them, now you are!" he announced. Black paint covered every inch of her, like a second skin. The crowd erupted.

Florence's fingers dug into my hand. "Let's go!" I could barely hear her over the shouting and clapping.

"No, she needs help! You stay here."

I shrugged Florence's hand off mine and started making my way to the podium. I saw Hexum pull something small out of his back pocket. At first, I was relieved. It wasn't a whip. He wasn't going to beat her to death.

But the relief quickly dissipated. I had barely taken a single step forward when he slid his hand, quickly and expertly, past her throat. It was hard to see what exactly he had done with all that black paint covering her. She didn't scream, or at least it seemed like she couldn't. When she opened her mouth, no sound came out. Her eyelids finally popped open, and all we could see was the whites of her eyes, terrified and in pain. Her hands moved hysterically to her neck, but it was no use. Blood gushed out of her delicate neck. Seconds later, she was dead. Hexum finally released her hair and threw her lifeless body on the ground, sending a drizzle of black paint mixed with thick blood into the air.

"And that's what we do to traitors in Corinth!" he laughed.

Florence pulled me through the crowd and out the back, leading me down the street and turning onto a new one. The cheers and whoops began to fade in the distance.

I felt nauseous and angry. Logically, I knew that it was over the second Hexum slit her throat, and I knew that if I had intervened there was no guarantee for the girl's safety. I might have even made things worse. But that didn't make it right. I should have done something, anything. Vir wouldn't want me to sacrifice my morals, my humanity, for his sake.

"I don't understand," I said, trying to choke back tears. "Why did he kill her?"

Florence looked up at me, her eyes like slits. "She tried to run away. So he punished her," she said matter-of-factly. "Only runaway girls who can still have babies are allowed to live."

"But if she couldn't have babies then why not let her leave?"

"Because everyone here has a responsibility to the colonies. If you can't have babies, there are other things you can do to help."

Like what? I wanted to ask. Set an example by dying? Knowing what I knew about Corinth now, I was starting to think Vir probably had done more than observe the colonies. He couldn't have just stood by, like I just had, and watched helpless young people suffer. He would've wanted to help. He probably did. I was certain he did. And I didn't need Cara to confirm that. I knew my brother well enough to know that.

Beside me, Florence walked with purpose, her head held high and her blonde ponytail swaying from side-to-side. If she was fazed by what we just witnessed, she didn't let it show. "I'm late for my class," she said, picking up speed.

"I'll walk you there," I said, hoping the school and the library were somewhat close to each other. "I'm sorry you had to see that. Things like that happen often, don't they?" I was having a mind–body disconnect. The scene at Hexum's rally was surreal to me, but clearly to the people here, it was probably just another day. I just couldn't wrap my head around it.

Florence shrugged. "Only if they're caught. Anyway, you get used to it."

"So, if the fertile girls aren't beaten to death, what happens to them?"

"Usually, only the boys get beatings. The girls are given away to their grooms. As long as they can have babies, they're safe. This is the first time an infertile girl has been caught in a while."

My chest ached. The price these women paid for having a functioning womb was unfair. Everything from their mental and emotional well-being to their individual freedoms took a backseat to their child-rearing abilities. It made me physically sick.

I looked over at Florence. Her lack of empathy was

disturbing. She seemed unaffected by what we had just witnessed. Apathetic, even. It had taken me a long time to separate my personal feelings from my work. When I first joined the force, every incident, trauma, and death would take me right back to Aric's disappearance. I felt for the victims' families like I did for my own. I was emotionally stretched thin until I got to a point where it didn't affect me as much as it used to. I don't know what the tipping point was; maybe I'd just seen so much death and carnage that it all started to blur together. Eventually, I could distance their pain from mine. It was oddly liberating. Maybe it was the same for Florence. Maybe she had learned to distance herself, without even knowing it, from the horrors of Corinth to protect herself and her sanity.

I still had an hour or so before I rendezvoused with Isaac's wife and figured I might as well take this opportunity to speak privately with the youngest child of Rebecca Bull and Jonathan Smith. "How are you holding up?" I asked as I trailed after her.

My adolescent years had been entirely consumed with coming to terms with my brother's death. I never did, of course, but looking back all I could see was a befuddled, lost teenager who couldn't really connect with anyone. Florence was probably on a rollercoaster of emotions—controlling parents, an independent older sister, an aloof older brother, not to mention the responsibilities that probably came with being a descendant of Julius Bull.

"Fine," she replied promptly, keeping her eyes straight ahead. "Hexum's men came by the house today, but Daddy managed to send them away."

So Isaac was right. Not only did the Federate Army suspect

Cara's disappearance, they *knew* she was gone. That conversation I'd overheard between the Federate Army and Isaac was most likely a precursor. Those men were tugging on random strings to see which one would come undone first.

"Daddy said I was rude to you yesterday," she said matter-of-factly. We came to a halt and considered each other for a moment.

If there was any remorse behind Florence's dull brown eyes, I couldn't see it. "You were," I said.

She shrugged. "Okay."

Okay, then. "Tell me about your sister," I said, readjusting the cap over my head. The streets were just as quiet during the daytime as they were at night, but every now and again we heard muffled voices from behind the windows we passed by. "What made her decide to leave?"

Florence looked at me uncomfortably. "Mom says I'm not allowed to talk to you."

This did not surprise me. Rebecca, it seemed to me, was the sort of woman who liked to control the flow of information. She liked to put her best foot forward at all times, even during moments of crisis. For instance, last night she and her family had elected to share only a tiny morsel of information, even though I would normally need a lot more info to conduct a decent investigation. "You're already talking to me, though." I grinned at Florence. "So you might as well keep at it. Were you and Cara close?"

Florence considered the logic and me. We walked in silence for a bit. Like her brother, Florence could barely conceal her aversion toward me. Her dull eyes darted all over my face, studying the apparent differences between the two of us. It was fascinating to me that given everything going on in Corinth, *I* was the one who brought the yuck factor.

"Yeah, we were," she finally said. "Not as close as she and Evie were, though."

"Evie?"

"Yeah, Isaac's wife."

"Oh, that's right," I murmured. "Clarissa is Evie."

Florence stared at me.

"I met her this morning." I shrugged.

She just nodded in response and stepped off the curb without looking left-right-left. Instinctively, my arms instantly lurched forward. I caught Florence by the arm and pulled her back on the curb. I hadn't seen a single motor vehicle besides Bull's. Not even a bicycle. But crossing the street without the customary left-right-left shoulder look was a no-no.

The second our skin made contact, Florence pulled away sharply. Revulsion and horror shadowed her pale face. Shocked by the response, I released her immediately and took a few steps back. Her other hand traced the spot I had touched as if making sure my hand was really gone.

"You okay?" I asked.

Still frowning, Florence nodded and turned to cross the street again. This time I let her go without saying anything.

The neighborhood was unfamiliar, but I recognized the usual signs of poverty. Used needles and garbage littered the sidewalk, and there was an overwhelming stench of putrefaction. The buildings on either side of the street were vandalized with the same style of graffiti I'd seen yesterday, except these were even more disturbing.

America: No Country for Coolies, *Back crawlers destroyed this country*, and *Black lives don't matter*, were some of the more polite posters. Another depicted a group of white soldiers whipping monkeys. On the other end of the spectrum were images of dark-skinned people crawling through a fence as cherubic angels peed over them from atop the fence. Apart from these were weather-beaten campaign posters promoting Bull as the only leader Corinth needed, and a few posters of Hexum challenging Bull's authority.

Instinctively, I moved closer to Florence, though not close enough to repulse   her. The idea of an impressionable young kid walking past such offensive signs made my blood boil. The last thing we needed in the world was hate and disparity.

It struck me then that in the colonies race, culture, and heritage all meant the same thing. I could see it clearly now. To the seven colonies, the advent of One World wasn't just a world free of racial disparity, it also meant one absolved of cultures.

But to anyone with a drop of diversity in their blood, race and culture were not mutually exclusive. Our genetic make-up did not change how we honored religion or culture or even our homelands. If anything, all that became so much more revered than before. People took immense pride in their national identity; religion still played a vital role in modern society. So did gender politics and culture.

In the early days of One World, the demographics of European nations whose Caucasian population was offset by massive waves of immigration were the first to be affected. Parts of the Middle East and small Asian countries like Japan, Sri Lanka, and Indonesia that already had small native populations faced similar population and identity crises. And today those same countries were thriving culturally, economically, and religiously.

Ramadan was still marked as fervently as it was before the war. So were Samhain, Chanukah, Día de Los Muertos, Obon, Christmas, and Diwali, among all others.

Race did not equal culture in One World. One only enhanced the other.

Florence had put a little more distance between us. She strode down the street without saying anything more. She simply gave me a side-eye and waited for me to say something else.

"Florence, your sister might be in terrible danger." I tried to imbue a sense of urgency in our conversation. We walked past a man with long gray hair and black teeth preaching the word of God to an invisible flock. His hands wildly gestured to the sky, and he barely even reacted to our presence. "You don't want Cara to get hurt, do you?"

"No, of course not!" she snapped. "You don't know my sister. Cara was strong enough to leave this stupid town and smart enough not to get caught. If she could do that, she can do anything!"

It dawned on me then that the only reasonable explanation for Isaac's relaxed attitude and Florence's unwavering conviction toward their sister's disappearance was that they had both had prior knowledge of her plans. Perhaps they had even helped her escape to some degree. "You knew Cara was running away, didn't you?"

Florence's face distorted wildly in anger and irritation. "Of course I did!" she screamed at me. "She'd been begging me to go with her for months, but I didn't want to hike and camp in the woods or go somewhere they might harvest my skin and bones! I was scared, okay? And getting caught is so much worse!"

This was not the first time an interviewee had released an onslaught of emotion at me, but it was the first time I'd been screamed at by a girl since high school. Her diatribe told me a great many things, but the first one I latched onto was the part about harvesting skin and bones.

My stomach twisted into knots. "Hang on, did you just say harvest?" I came to a stop, wishing we could be sitting for this conversation instead.

Florence nodded at me like I ought to already know what she meant. "Yeah, you know because my ...our skin and bones are precious. Some people"—she looked pointedly at me— "think it might have magical powers."

I burst out laughing before I could stop myself. The knots turned into a million little needles. What a horrifying thought. Ridiculous too. Was this what children were taught here?

"Who's being rude now?" Florence snapped at me.

"You're right. Sorry," I apologized. "It's just ...that's the most absurd thing I've ever heard!"

Back when I was in school, we learned about how albinos from Africa were hunted by witch doctors who believed their skin and bones were special and how their limbs were chopped off to make medicine for everything from the common cold to erectile dysfunction. Florence had regurgitated a version of ancient history that, thankfully, was very much in the past.

Her mannerisms and the way she talked reminded me very

much of her mother. If Florence had inherited her mother's mean streak and Cara her father's easy-going nature, I couldn't help but wonder which way Isaac truly leaned.

I looked at the girl in front of me with pity. Kids her age in One World were already graduating university, traveling to the moon, and even developing the next generation of technology. Here, Florence and her peers were learning values from a time so long gone it was ancient history to us. It broke my heart that children were learning from an early age that the world outside Corinth was dangerous and leaving would mean certain death. No wonder she and her brother looked at me like some kind of monster. They probably thought I wanted to harvest their body parts. It would take years and certified therapists to undo this sort of brainwashing.

Beside me, Florence scowled. She kept looking up at me like she was waiting for an apology.

Instead, I raised my eyebrows. "Hang on, what do you mean they hiked?" It should have occurred to me sooner—of course, the Hvalsey Mountains! The Hvalsey Mountains would be the perfect escape route. The mountain range ended just a few miles away from where Vir had been killed.

More than two centuries ago, it was famous for its abundant wildlife; throngs of deer, rabbits, birds, and wildcats inhabited the woods. Today, it was a dry and desolate landscape that was unable to support any life. Its harsh terrain would make it nearly impossible to follow and track anyone. In fact, making it through the mountain itself was a tough task. It would take a lot of guts and desperation—both of which the dissidents clearly had plenty of.

"Florence, is that how everyone has been able to get away

without being found? Does your grandfather know this?"

Florence bit her lips. Guilt and embarrassment replaced the anger on her face. She had revealed too much, and I knew it.

"Do you know where she went after the mountain?" I prodded, mentally expanding the search radius.

"I—I—" She shook her head wildly. "I don't know! I really don't."

"Florence, someone must have helped your sister. Do you know who?" My voice came out sterner than I had meant it to be.

"No. Cara never told me."

"How about Raptor?" I asked. "Have you ever heard that name before?"

Florence shook her head.

Why hadn't Cara confided in her younger sister, especially if the plan was for them both to leave?

I glanced away from her for a moment, which is when I realized we had reached the school. The library sat beside the campus.

"I have to go." Without a second look, Florence walked at a brisk pace through the campus gates. I continued on toward the library, astounded to discover that it was bustling with activity.

Unlike the empty and lifeless streets of Corinth, everywhere I looked people were milling about. A group of small children huddled in a corner, listening to a man who enthusiastically read aloud to them. A couple of librarians shuffled past pushing carts with books, and readers were forming lines at the check-out counter.

My Auge scanned the faces around me, but Evie wasn't there yet. With a few minutes to spare, I walked around the atrium, looking for a quiet corner where I could wait and discreetly watch the newcomers when I heard an audible gasp from the counter next to me. A round-faced librarian with a messy bob and a pink scarf around her neck was watching me with her mouth half-open. I recognized that look instantly, of course; Isaac had worn a similar expression when he'd met me for the first time last night.

The old phrase *the black sheep of the family* kept turning over in my mind. Wherever Cara was now, she was the black sheep. Somewhere, someone was studying and judging her features, skin, and body the way everyone in Corinth was examining mine.

Shit. "Um, hello." I waved awkwardly. I felt like I was walking on pins and needles just waiting for the librarian to scream bloody murder. After witnessing Hexum's little demonstration, I was on edge and knew this was not the smartest idea in the world.

Without waiting for a response, I turned to the closest door and walked straight to the aisle marked *Satire*.

The library reminded me of a hay maze my parents used to bring the family to every year just before Halloween. The shelves were as tall and winding as the stacks of hay, but at least my allergies were dormant among the pages.

I was beginning to think this was a bad idea. There were too many people here, and any one of them could be a member of the Federate Army. Maybe Evie was playing some sort of joke on me. It would be a cruel thing to do, but I wouldn't put it past anyone who lived here.

Until I knew for certain where everyone's loyalties lay, I needed to treat them with healthy suspicion. I was just about to retrace my steps back to the atrium and head out to find Bull when I saw Evie sitting on a little bench between two rows, her nose practically one with the book.

"Oh, there you are." Evie slammed the book shut as soon as she heard me approach. She was wearing a little more makeup now. Her dark circles were gone and her sharp cheekbones bronzed.

"Here I am." I flashed her my most charming smile, but she didn't reciprocate. Despite her serene appearance, her mood was just as foul now as it had been this morning. "Thanks for meeting me here."

Evie leaned against the shelf and pushed her long hair out of her face. "Of course." She nodded. "Did anybody see you?"

I told her about the librarian who'd caught my eye, and Evie swore under her breath. "Well, let's just hope she doesn't rat you out." Evie shifted nervously.

I realized what a huge risk she was taking by talking to me here. Maybe being Bull's granddaughter-in-law gave her some privileges? Her appearance seemed to suggest so. So far everyone I'd seen looked down-trodden and unhealthy, unlike Bull's immediate family members, all of whom looked to be hale and hearty. "You said you have some questions?" she prodded.

Normally I would just tread slowly, maybe start with some small talk, but after the rally and seeing Hexum in person, I was more than ready to get some answers. I was going to have to face him eventually, and I needed to know as much as I could about him. "Let's start with Hexum and why he killed those kids."

Evie crossed her feet and put the book in her lap. "I want

to be clear that I am only telling you this because I think you have a right to know what you've gotten yourself into," she said earnestly. "This place is dangerous for someone like you." Evie lowered her voice. "Cara is long gone, but if you still want to stay and try to find her, at least do it with both eyes open."

The warning was appreciated, and I made a mental note to add Evie to the list of people who didn't believe Cara could be found.

"Let's start with the Federate Army. Do you know how they came to be?" she asked.

I shook my head.

"No, of course you don't," she mumbled. "A few years ago, when the birth rate was spiraling, Grandfather and the rest of his council decided to test for infertility as a way of ensuring the most success for survival."

A light bulb went off in my head. That would certainly explain why the colonies were so hell-bent on arranged marriages. These people, or at least most of them, wanted to keep their bloodline pure and untainted. And, from their perspective, people like me were an abomination. They didn't just hate the color of our skin; they hated the fact that we didn't have their fertility issues.

"So, only two people capable of having children are allowed to marry?" I asked.

"Bingo!" Evie said tartly. "Well, two infertile people could marry if they wanted to, but there's a gender imbalance in the colonies..." Evie frowned.

Christ, the pressure to procreate must be unbearable in Corinth. That would at least explain why kids were married off when they turned eighteen. If the fertility rate was as bad as everyone said it was, then the powers that be would want couples to start popping out babies as soon as possible. Still, the average birth rate seemed to be two-and-a-half children per couple. Comparatively low when you considered how young they were at the time of their weddings.

"A gender imbalance..." My voice trailed off.

"Yeah, the men outnumber the women," she said. "Anyway, the program was pretty effective. Lots of couples were able to have children, and the population grew. But it also left them with a large number of infertile men and women."

Shocked, I sat down on the floor facing her. If I understood Evie correctly, it meant that Corinth also stifled sexuality. Both fertile and infertile people were forced to either marry someone from the opposite sex (regardless of their sexuality) or not at all.

The thought of forcing two people to marry was a hard pill to swallow. But forcing people to live solitary lives because they couldn't reproduce was an equally hard one. It was certainly one thing to be single now at my age, but I couldn't imagine spending my whole life alone without the love, support, and companionship of a partner. Nobody deserved to live like that. Not even the members of the Federate Army. "What happened to those people? The ones who couldn't have kids?" I asked, trying to ignore the bitter taste in my mouth.

Evie sighed sadly. "Those people became the Federate Army. They're basically a street gang, but that's what they call themselves. Grandfather initially suggested culling them. If they couldn't serve a purpose, they had no reason for being here. But someone in his council thought finding a proper use for them might be easier than, you know..." her voice wavered a bit. "They were split into two groups—border patrol and farming. Suddenly they had a renewed sense of purpose, and they took their responsibilities very seriously."

I could almost picture it—as dissent became more frequent, the punishments became harsher.

"So seriously that they took it upon themselves to police the city in whatever manner they saw fit," I concluded.

"And now they exist solely to keep us inside," Evie said miserably. "We are required to report runaways immediately, but we've been telling people that Cara is visiting her cousins."

A piece of the puzzle fell into place now. Finally, I understood the intense need for secrecy. I remembered what Isaac told me about Hexum, but something didn't quite make sense.

My mind raced. "Listen, I think he already knows. Maybe not for certain, but he knows something is up," I said, glancing over my shoulders every few seconds. I told her about the young girl Hexum had covered in black paint and just murdered in front of everyone.

"I know it's hard to stand by and watch, but you were right not to intervene. They would've only taken it out on her. Trust me," she said, wiping the corner of her eyes. "And you would've been outnumbered anyway."

"There must be someth—"

"There really isn't at this point," Evie interrupted. "I don't even know who she is. I could find out though. I volunteer at the hospital sometimes and that's usually where they bring the kids after... you know." Her voice choked and her eyes welled up.

"Oh God, this is awful. This town is awful."

"Then why do you stay? Why does anybody?"

Evie blinked. She hadn't meant to say that out loud. We both knew it. "I have my reasons. The children stay because they're raised to think there's nothing outside this city except death. When you grow up believing a lie, it becomes your truth. We're all told about One World when we turn eleven years old, and even then, it's not the whole truth."

I grimaced. "But clearly not everyone buys the party line."

Footsteps shuffled behind our aisle. I hoped to God we hadn't been overheard. We sat there unmoving and alert for several minutes before the person on the other side moved along. Evie peeked through the space between books to make sure we were alone. When the coast was clear, we resumed where we left off.

"Evie, there's something I need to know," I said more urgently. "Has anybody... um, anybody like me ever been to Corinth? Have you heard any rumors or seen anybody unusual around here?"

Evie shook her head sadly. "Your brother has never been inside Corinth."

Surprised didn't begin to cover the effect her words had on me. "How did you—"

"Julius mentioned it," she said, flustered a bit. "I'm sorry for your loss. I know how hard it is to lose someone."

"Thank you." I nodded. "So, how did Hexum become the almighty one?"

"Hexum had us all fooled. Everyone thought he was a joke, but he was just biding his time . . ." Evie trailed off. "Those men—the ones who serve him—they know that if it hadn't been for Hexum that they would be dead. They owe it all to Hexum. Their lives, their blood, their sweat. Everything. They swore obedience and loyalty to the man who pulled them out of the trenches."

Finding Cara was starting to feel like a race—both time and the odds of finding her were starting to feel slim. I took a deep breath and stood up. Hiding from Hexum and his men wasn't going to make this job any easier. If I wanted to find Cara, I needed to face all the players in Corinth.

9

THE LIBRARY PLAZA WAS A LOT MORE crowded than before. All of Corinth, or at least it seemed like it, was out enjoying the sunny afternoon. Parents scrambled after their little ones, giddy teenagers huddled near the fountain, some dipped their toes in the water, and a small group gathered around a busker playing the harmonica. The wholesomeness of this scene outside seemed out of place in Corinth. I would have never imagined happy families spending the day laughing and socializing just blocks away from Hexum's little gathering.

"Finally, some life," I muttered to myself. After everything I'd seen in Corinth, this was a welcome change. Still, most of the people here were wearing the gold lopsided scale and confederate flag pins, and a few others wore t-shirts with the same slogans I'd seen graffitied on the walls on the way here. But not all. In retrospect, I realized, neither Isaac nor Evie wore them.

Dozens of curious eyes bored into me from every direction. I doubted if it would have made any difference if Evie (or anyone else for that matter) had been walking beside me. I hated the idea of calling unnecessary attention to myself, but hiding was no longer an option. Sooner or later, I was going to be found out, and I wanted to get ahead of it and surprise Hexum by making the first move.

I pulled the cap off my head and walked straight, wading through scrutinizing whispers and pointing fingers. I wondered how long it would take before someone said something to me. Or maybe they would skip the trash talk and jump straight to throwing shoes at me. My imagination went to a dark place again, weaving together the worst-case scenarios.

I disregarded the attention as best I could and continued down the plaza, eager to head back to the Bull-Smith home. Bull had a lot to answer for. Everything I'd learned from Evie should have come from him before bringing me to Corinth. He had thrown me into the lion's den without any sort of warning, consideration, or forethought for my safety.

As I made my way through the plaza, I felt a prickle on the back of my neck. Someone was watching me. I could feel it. My feet slowed to a stop. From the corner of my eye, I picked up the imminent danger: two deeply scarred men with deep circles under their eyes and matching black jackets were walking toward me from the other side of the square. One of them carried a baton. The look on their faces said it all: *you're dead.*

The last time I was in a street fight, I was seventeen and my friend's honor needed defending. I wasn't much of a fighter back then, and I ended up with two cracked ribs and a black eye. But those days were long gone. After that incident, I spent years learning the fine art of self-defense.

My lips curved up in a smirk, and I planted my feet on the ground. I kept my arms at my sides just in case this wasn't a fight. A part of me hoped it was, though. I really needed to punch something today.

As I watched the two men, a dark shadow loomed in front of my own: a tall, hefty figure was approaching from behind. A surprise attack. The shadow had its right arm raised and was aiming for my skull.

I ducked at precisely the right moment and swerved out of the way. As I did so, a thick fist wearing a brass knuckle-duster swept a couple of inches past my face.

The attacker was massive. His biceps were bigger than his face. Luckily, the unexpected blooper had distracted the big guy. Now, I had an advantage over him. Without any hesitation whatsoever, I launched the side of my right palm against his Adam's apple with just enough force to neutralize him. The attacker hit the ground in pain, gasping desperately for air.

With one immobilized, I wheeled around to face the other two. They looked torn between attacking me and helping their friend. I followed their gaze to the big guy on the ground, who was gesturing violently in my direction as if to say: *get him, get him!*

I felt like a matador in a bullfight. They charged at me. I was able to deflect a punch from the shorter man with curly white-blonde hair but couldn't stop the red-headed attacker with surprisingly feminine features from striking me over the shoulder with his baton. The blow echoed through my bones, but I stayed on my feet. So far, so good.

Now, it was time to test the hand-to-hand combat techniques I'd learned at the academy. The crowd from the plaza gathered to watch. Nobody intervened, though. They just stood there. Typical mob mentality. I cursed, taking my first punch in the gut.

The first attacker had recovered from my throat punch. From the corner of my eye, I saw him sit up, his face white with shock and fury. While he came back to his senses, I fended off the other two men with relative ease. We turned to look at each other at the same time. He was on his feet now. Our eyes locked, and he cocked his shoulder and arms.

"Is that all you've got, blackie?" he croaked painfully. His voice instantly stirred something in my memory. I recognized it. He was the man who'd tried to bully Evie this morning. My eyes fell on the pins I'd come to recognize as a symbol of Corinth's racist propaganda. Whoever this guy was, he was a member of the Federate Army.

As he came closer to me, he slowly pulled out a long black whip from his back pocket that I hadn't noticed before. The crowd shuddered at the sight of it and instinctively took a few steps back. I wished I could do the same. That thing made my insides squirm.

His tattooed fingers caressed the whip, slowly and lovingly, before he swung it in the air, sending an ear-splitting sonic boom through the air. I whirled around looking for the effect of the explosion, expecting to see fire and chaos, but there was none of that. The unexpected detonation had thrown me off-guard, and it was all my attackers needed. Someone out of my line of sight kicked me in the knees and jabbed me in the face. With my ears ringing painfully, I was on the ground for only a few seconds before someone dragged me over to the big guy wielding the whip.

My heart thumped erratically. The sight of the whip conjured up the image of Beto Fischer lying dead in a pool of his own blood. The pictures from Bull's file had showcased the boy's prominent and painful wounds. I was looking at Beto's murder weapon. I was sure of it.

One of the two men holding me up smacked the side of

my face with a baton. "Guess he's black and dumb," he chuckled.

"Technically, I'm, uh, brown," I said sarcastically. The taste of blood enveloped my tongue. The adrenaline was masking the pain, and I wondered where else I was bleeding.

"You think you're funny?" the man with the whip asked, clearly incensed by my cavalier attitude.

"Well... I think it's funny you're picking on a guy you've only just met." I spat blood out onto the ground. "Or is this how you usually welcome people here?"

Sunlight illuminated his sweaty face, exposing his one brown eye and one blue eye. "You won't be laughing when I'm done with you, boy!" he bellowed, cracking the whip in the air again.

My laughter intertwined with the last embers of the sonic boom. It felt strange to laugh right now, but it was better than crying. They were expecting me to be afraid, to beg for mercy, to plead for my life (which, believe me, I wanted to), but I knew I had a better chance of getting out of this in one piece if I turned the tables on them and reacted in the least expected way possible. "What god-awful movie did you steal that line from?" I scoffed.

At his signal, one of the men struck my back with the baton again. God, that really hurt. "Look, if you're going to beat the crap out of me, you might at least want to tell me why!" I tried to reason.

"You know why! Don't pretend you don't know!" he screamed. "You think you can just walk around here like you're one of us?"

"You mean like people?" I asked. "Then yes, I did think I could walk around here like I was one of you."

"Don't be a wise-ass," he yelled, signaling for the man on my right to smack me. "We know what the Bull girl has done! Does she think she can just ditch my baby bro at the altar?" He spat on the ground. "That bitch."

I groaned. Did they think I had something to do with Cara's disappearance? The timing of my appearance and their discovery would explain why they might think I was responsible. On the other hand, they couldn't possibly think anybody would be stupid enough to hang out at the scene of the crime after kidnapping a teenage girl. Or could they? "Okay, I really have no idea what you're talking about." Even I could hear how exasperated I sounded. "Is it possible you're confusing me with someone else?"

Fat chance.

"Don't play games with me, you little piece of crap," he threatened, his voice dangerously low.

"Okay, that's offensive," I warned him. "I'm not little."

Someone in the crowd chuckled. In all my years at force, I never once imagined I would be on the receiving end of such an interrogation, but I did know that there was nothing more frustrating than an interviewee who would not cooperate. Or worse, one with a smart mouth.

I planned to deflect the questions long enough to find the perfect moment—ideally before the whip made contact with my body—to launch my counterattack.

It wasn't the best plan, and I was painfully outnumbered, but I would have to make do. The bystanders were definitely not on my side, either. Would they turn on me if I managed to immobilize these three men? Almost certainly, but I was trained for this. It wouldn't be easy, but I knew I could get them to yield in a fight.

"We know it was you," the attacker with the delicate features snarled in my right ear. He was so close it sent a cold shudder down my spine.

"Me, what?"

"Helping the kids escape, you moron," the curly-haired attacker screamed. "Where did you take them? Where did you take Bull's granddaughter, huh? Answer me!"

This was worse than I expected. Much, much worse. These guys didn't just suspect me of kidnapping Cara—they were accusing me of helping all the runaways escape Corinth. The fact that they had reached this conclusion only bolstered my belief that there was indeed some sort of underground resistance, but if I fought their accusation now, then I could be dooming the people who might actually need my help.

My options were terribly limited. I could take the fall and falsely admit it, or I could play dumb. Either way, I was not getting out of this easily.

"Listen, why don't we all go down to Chairman Bull's office and talk about things calmly?" I suggested. "I'm sure we can figure it out."

"That old fool is in enough trouble as it is. Don't expect him to come rescue your black ass," my accuser snapped. "He's going to pay for what he's done!"

"And what exactly has Bull done?" I asked politely.

"What's he done?" he repeated angrily. "That old bastard has done nothing—*nothing!*—to save our colonies. Look how he's violated our home instead." He pointed up and down at me.

The anger that resonated from the attackers at the mere mention of Bull's name was worrisome. If these hoodlums could unabashedly attack, in broad daylight, a former officer of the law, I couldn't imagine what they might do to a defenseless old man like Bull.

He had to have known bringing me here wouldn't win him any friends. But did he know how much of a risk? Did he think he could control these men? Or maybe I was dispensable, and he just wanted to find Cara through any means necessary?

The man in front was still waiting for an answer. "Last chance, blackie. Where are they?" he repeated.

Behind him, I saw Evie squeezing through the crowd. There was an edge in her eyes—anger. Her fists were balled. She was coming to my defense. When our eyes met, I gave her a very subtle nod to indicate that I was fine. That stopped her in her tracks. I hoped she would know better than to intervene when she saw what came next.

I sighed loudly. "Again, it's brown." The baton met my back with renewed wrath. "You can ask me that until you're hoarse. You can beat me all day, if you like." I clenched my fist. "But I'll never say because I. Don't. Know."

"I can make you tell me," he threatened.

Somebody in the crowd clapped loudly and whooped in response. My head jerked to the side looking for the source, but all I saw was a cluster of emotionless faces studying me like a lab rat. I could tell from the look in their eyes that I was the most alien thing they had ever seen. I had expected the onlookers to be surprised or concerned by the scene that was unfolding in front of their eyes, but they seemed more entertained than anything else.

"No, you really can't," I goaded him. Retributive justice

was the norm here, I reminded myself. These people were used to seeing their friends and family members dragged into the streets and tortured to prove a point. I felt a surge of respect for the dissidents. They spent their entire lives here feeling suffocated and caged, unable to speak their mind. No amount of steak and chocolate could ever make up for the freedoms forfeited in Corinth. Cara's life had been so stifling that she (and so many like her) chose to venture out into the unknown and risk death rather than suffer silently in this old forgotten city.

This was the moment I was waiting for. The attackers were getting complacent. The two men holding me were starting to loosen their grip. They no longer thought of me as a full-blown threat.

In one swift moment, I arched my back, locked my captor's knees with my inner elbows, and pulled my arms forward with enough force to trip them. When they landed, I reached forward and grabbed their ankles. The time had finally come to put my T-Patch to use. I used my Auge to activate it. Instantly, a thin blue line encircled both my wrists. Just like in the ads, the blue lines multiplied and blanketed my palms like a glove and, at my command, sent electric pulses through my attackers' bodies.

Screams echoed through the plaza while the onlookers watched, horrified. The bodies of the two attackers, temporarily paralyzed by the low-charge vibration, fell stiff against the cold concrete.

Now it was time to face the last attacker. The fight with him would set the stage for the rest of my time here, and I needed to make sure I had the upper hand. My Auge ran a deep search and managed to uncover some pretty old agreements from decades ago. "First of all, you're in violation of the treaty between the United States and the seven colonies." I walked toward him. "Your attack on me is—"

"Nothing you can prove!" he screeched. "You think these people are your witnesses? They're nothing—"

I raised my hand to silence him. "I don't need witnesses. I have something better."

My T-Patch was still glowing. It shifted and twirled like a snake and came to a rest in the middle of my palm. I held my palm in front of me for everyone to see. A tiny holographic video recorded from my point of view popped up. The crowd gasped. Even I was impressed. The hologram began with me leaving the library, the moment I first caught sight of the two attackers who were now lying unconscious on the ground.

"I've been documenting everything and everyone since I got here," I said, summoning my most polite voice. This wasn't entirely true, but they didn't need to know that. "You're probably thinking that killing me will make it all go away. But that's only going to make it so much worse. You probably don't know what 22G internet and a satellite can do. But my partner"—another white lie—"already has a copy of the attack—he probably even saw it in real-time—and knows just where to look for you and your pals here."

The attacker's dual-colored eyes widened in alarm. Even the crowd was visibly disturbed. Low murmurs and whispers flooded through the crowd, and the circle around me widened. This type of technology, that I took for granted every day, probably seemed like magic to these people. They may have been born into the twenty-seventh century, but they might as well have been cavemen. If I had known my T-Patch would have this effect on them, I could've saved myself some pain.

Before my attacker could respond or accuse me of witchcraft, I continued. "Oh, and since you're probably not up to date on the current laws of this country—you know, on account of living under a rock and everything—the law does not discriminate." I grinned.

The man stared at me slack-jawed. "I'm gonna—"

"What, kill me? Sure, you can, but one way or another you're going to answer for your crimes," I added. "And the color of your skin will not exempt you from paying for your crimes either."

"Lies!" he called out to the crowds. "It's all lies! Don't believe a word of it."

While he was still distracted, I leaped forward and knocked him unconscious with one single punch. "Idiot."

As soon as his body thudded to the ground, I turned around and walked away, making sure to look straight ahead and avoid eye contact with the bystanders.

The crowd parted like the Dead Sea and let me through without another incident. I'd only gotten a few feet when both Evie and Isaac rushed to me.

"Oh my God! Are you okay?" Evie was the first to ask.

The fact that I had just endured the first racially charged attack of the century had not yet sunk in. Hate crimes belonged in textbooks and fiction; at the police academy, cadets dissected and analyzed thousands of case studies on twenty-first century hate violence and speech as part of their training. Lessons in civility were just as, if not more than, valuable as criminology or police science.

The adrenaline was disappearing from my bloodstream and taking the numbness with it. I touched my busted lip gingerly. "Ouch," I said, realizing that my right cheek hurt just as much. But my back and head had taken the worst of it. I knew I should've just stayed in bed this morning. Actually, I should've just stayed in San Francisco. "Yeah, I'll be fine. I take it that was the welcoming committee?"

Husband and wife shared a meaningful look. One of those secret, subtle glances that only a better half could decode. It was the first time I'd actually seen them together. Whatever they had argued about this morning was clearly still not over. Isaac could barely look at Evie, and when he did, it was with disdain and contempt. Well, at least she and I had that in common.

"This is my wife, Evie, by the way," Isaac said curtly.

I was about to say that we had already met but Evie interrupted, "It's nice to meet you."

Confused, I nodded back. I couldn't fathom why she would want to keep our meeting from her husband a secret, but at this moment I didn't care enough to worry about it. I figured she had her reasons and would tell me when she got a chance. Right now, we had bigger problems.

"You should get out of here before they wake up," Evie said, looking nervously over her shoulders. Some of the crowd was still lingering, pointing and smirking at me.

The worst part of it was seeing the disgust and hate for me in the eyes of the kids. You expect grown-ups to be jerks, but when children look down on you with a sense of superiority it feels like a slap in the face of innocence and everything still good in the world. How did these kids turn out so differently from the likes of Cara and the other runaways? In cult-like scenarios, children tended to be extremely docile and timid. They wouldn't even dare to think for themselves, and yet so many had exhibited independent and free-thinking attitudes. The idea of those voices being stifled and punished was so much more painful than the beating I'd just gotten.

I turned to face Evie and Isaac again. "We shouldn't be seen together," I said. "Especially now that they think I had something to do with Cara's escape."

Isaac flinched when I used that word—escape—but didn't correct me. Instead, he folded his arms and stared at me sullenly.

"I don't understand why they think you had anything to do with Cara running away." Evie shook her head.

"Or all the others," Isaac added. "I mean, you just got here."

I wanted to laugh. Maybe I was in shock, or maybe it was grief hitting me again. I don't know, but it was all I could do to stop myself. Vir's bloody face kept flashing before my eyes. I was angry with him for dying, for keeping his life a secret from me, for coming to this God-awful town. I was just so mad. My brother deserved more than to die in a place where we were reduced to the color of our skin. The last twenty-four hours had been an education. A steep learning curve in hatred and racism. It all made me so mad I wanted to laugh and cry at the same time.

"I have to head out to the clinic," Evie announced. She gave me a short but meaningful glance before walking away.

"Welcome to Corinth," Isaac said as soon as she was out of earshot.

At first, I thought he meant Evie but realized, of course, he was talking about the Federate hooligans. "Your grandfather should've warned me about them." My nostrils flared. "You," I said, pointing at him, "should've warned me." His subtle hints earlier this morning did not count as an actual warning. Isaac looked at me warily but didn't say anything to defend himself.

I started walking, though I wasn't entirely sure which way was the right way. "Anyway, I need to go find your grandfather," I said anxiously.

"Didn't you meet with him already today?" Isaac asked tartly.

For one wild second, I wasn't sure what Isaac was talking about, and then I remembered our conversation last night, which now felt like a lifetime ago. "No, I haven't yet."

"Well, I'm sure if he wants to talk to you, he'll find you."

My blood curdled. Isaac's smug, over-confident tone was aggravating, but the fact that he thought of me as some maid called in to pick up the trash is what really pushed my buttons. But I'd just been in one fight and didn't have the energy to get into another. "He's probably in trouble." I grimaced. "Your grandfather may not be able to call for help."

"In trouble? What do you mean?" Isaac sounded alarmed.

I sighed. It was time to come clean about my midnight jaunt to Bull's house the night before. I told Isaac everything—well, almost everything—about the drone and the other intruders.

"You lied to me!"

"Yeah, so what? You lied to me first." I drew my fingers through my bloody hair. "Listen, I'm not the problem here!

Didn't you hear those guys? They know your sister is gone, Isaac. They think I'm responsible. They suspect your grandfather of helping her."

"That was an empty threat. I doubt Hexum would ever try to hurt Grandpa." Isaac dismissed my concerns with a wave of the hand. "They wouldn't dare. They need him too much."

"I wouldn't be so sure," I said, inspecting the damage to my hands. "Do you know where he is now?"

"Probably busy in his office," Isaac said. "I'll take you. It's not exactly within walking distance."

10

WE ARRIVED OUTSIDE BULL'S OFFICE twenty minutes later in Isaac's vintage hybrid JX Jeep Wrangler. This was the second vehicle I'd actually seen since arriving here, and I couldn't help but wonder why nobody else seemed to drive besides the Bull-Smiths.

Neither of us really spoke, and I was grateful for the silence. It gave me time to recalibrate and think through my next move. And also nurse my wounds. Luckily, the damage was minimal. Nothing was broken, and I didn't think I'd need any sealant to repair the bleeding either. Next time—and I was certain there would be a next time—I might not be so lucky.

But my more immediate concern was for Julius Bull. I hadn't heard from him since leaving his daughter's home and, though there were a lot of odd things about his behavior, I was confident that he was the sort of man who liked regular updates. No, he was the sort of man who *demanded* regular updates.

My intuition told me something was terribly wrong. That look in my attacker's eye was familiar; the bloodlust, anger, and contempt were always the same everywhere, regardless of caste, creed, and gender.

"This is the back entrance," Isaac announced as he pulled over. "What's your plan?"

My first plan hinged heavily on finding Bull and convincing

him and his family to get the hell out of dodge, and ideally, take me with them. My second plan (and the most optimistic of the two) was to meet with this Hexum and convince him I truly meant no harm, but that was probably a pipe dream.

"How many of them are there exactly? These Federate goons?" I rolled my window down and stared at the building we'd parked next to.

"Maybe forty or so," Isaac answered uneasily. "Why?"

"All right. I doubt they're all in there, but we should expect at least a handful," I said, pushing the heavy car door open. "Otherwise, we're in serious trouble."

"Hmm. I might have something to tip the balance in our favor," Isaac answered, jumping out of the driver's seat. "It's not as fancy as your wrist thing, but it'll do the job."

Isaac beckoned me to the tailgate and grabbed two shotguns. He handed me the one in his left hand. My insides immediately raged with disapproval and disgust. The Millennial War had seen the worst violence both on and off the battlefield. Even worse than the two World Wars that preceded it. After the war finally ended, so did the production and sale of arms around the world. The new world order declared a weapons armistice backed by nearly every country on the planet. Survivors of the war had wanted nothing more to do with weapons of that kind—in fact, the metal collected from countless gun components had been melted down to help build Peregrinus.

What didn't burn made it to history museums and antique collectors around the world, never to be seen in public again. Evidently, burning them down had not been enough to keep them out of dangerous hands. This one didn't look like an old firearm, though. It was well-maintained, but it was more than that—it looked like a new design, unlike anything I'd read about at the Academy. That could only mean that firearms were probably still being manufactured and sold illegally to the colonies and who knew where else.

It was mind-boggling to me that a weapon so outdated could have found a resurgence in this century especially when the standard police-issued T-Patch did the job just as well and was non-lethal.

On the other hand, I reminded myself, maybe it wasn't so surprising. After all, Corinth was founded on archaic colonial foundations, and it made sense (in a weird and twisted way) why they'd resorted to using weapons from a bygone era.

As I processed this wave of new emotions, I thought about how ironic it was that it was now my turn to be disgusted by Isaac. There was no way I was touching this thing, not even if my life depended on it.

"You do know that it's illegal in the United States for civilians to carry firearms?" I asked incredulously. "Even if they are antiques."

"Oh really? I had no idea," Isaac said innocently.

Like his grandfather, Isaac had a great poker face, but he wasn't fooling me. The sight of these weapons riled me up in ways even Hexum's men had not been able to. Weapons like this didn't belong on the streets, in homes, or in schools. And they certainly didn't belong in Corinth, where tensions were already running so high.

"You are not bringing them in there! I won't allow it, not around civilians. These weapons are primitive and dangerous—

even to you," I said sternly, just barely keeping my rage at bay. "Especially to you!"

"What makes you think I need your permission?" Isaac asked, completely unperturbed. "The Federates use these same weapons, and trust me, they don't give a damn about your disapproval. If you think I'm going up against them unarmed, you're crazy." Isaac stood his ground.

"Fine, fine. Have it your way." My opinion of civilians carrying weapons was unwelcome, and now was probably not the best time for this discussion. There were more pressing concerns on our plate, and the gun control issue would have to wait until after. How did anyone, especially in Corinth, even have access to such weapons anyway?

"Where did these even come from?" I asked.

"We make them here," he answered, stuffing his pockets with bullets.

"You what?"

"Yeah, we have a small manufacturing facility," Isaac explained. "It's pretty old and everything is falling apart, but we manage. Actually, Evie and I sometimes volunteer to help the manufacturing unit."

I uneasily watched him take back the weapon he had offered me. Now he had two shotguns and I had none. The more time I spent in Corinth, the more vulnerable I felt. Everywhere I looked, dangers of all levels seemed to be lurking and waiting to hit me in the face when I least expected it.

"Okay, then." I exhaled, starting toward Bull's office, but Isaac jogged over quickly and put his pale muscular hand out in front of me. "What?" I snapped.

"I don't think you want to go rushing in there." He was attempting to be friendly. "Especially looking the way you do."

Looking the way I do? I raised my eyebrows.

"I mean, the way you look right now," Isaac faltered. "All bloody and messed up. It might frighten people. But also, yes, the way you normally look."

There was no way I was going to dignify this with a response. I knew exactly what he meant. Embarrassed twice over, he now led me to the back of the building instead of bringing me through the main entrance. Under other circumstances with other people, I would've dismissed it as their way of easing me into a new environment. Baby steps, even. But this? This was Isaac's way of showing me my place. He was embarrassed to be seen with me. Probably even afraid, though on that part I couldn't begrudge him. I would be afraid to be caught hanging out with me if I lived here too.

Isaac pushed the back door open gingerly and poked his head through. A stillness had fallen over our immediate vicinity. The only sound I could hear was our two steady breaths. It was much too quiet here, different from the uncomfortable silence I'd encountered out in the city so far. This was the blanketing hush that took over after a violent storm had passed through.

"Something's not right," Isaac said as soon as we were both in.

I nodded in agreement.

We walked farther inside. It only took a millisecond to confirm our suspicions that something was indeed not right. Shattered glass littered the floor, and nearly all the furniture had been turned upside down. The exit doors across the hall from us were wide open, and the walls had been smashed in. I looked around but didn't see anybody, dead or alive, on the ground floor. I reactivated my T-Patch. The Federate Army had passed through here, and after my first encounter with them, I wasn't taking any chances. The crisp blue light came alive and enveloped my wrists.

Just let them try to come at me. This time I was more than ready for an attack. Standing beside me, Isaac looked enviously at my mechanism. I couldn't blame him. Sure, my T-Patch didn't have the range of Isaac's shotgun, but it didn't need reloading. It was much lighter and way deadlier *and* great for hand-to-hand combat. If you ask me, Isaac's shotgun was the equivalent of a club to my T-Patch.

"No signs of a struggle," I noted, mostly to myself, as we made our way to the elevators that went up to Bull's office. "This seems to be just plain old vandalism."

"Well, yeah," Isaac said. "Hexum would never hurt any of the, um, fertile people."

Of course your grandfather only has able-bodied people in his office, I wanted to say, but I bit my tongue. "Get behind me and don't shoot until I say so," I told Isaac when the doors opened, but Isaac only rolled his eyes in response.

We saw it as soon as the elevator doors slid open. At the end of the corridor was an unmoving male body lying on the floor. He had lost one of his shoes, and the top half of his body was hidden behind the adjacent wall.

"Oh, God!" Isaac whispered.

We slowly made our way up the corridor. I kicked the foot still wearing a shoe tentatively to make sure he really was an unconscious victim and not a foe lying in wait. I wouldn't put it past the Federates to pull a fast one.

"Who is this?" I asked, kneeling beside the unconscious man. He was a tall, sickly thin man, probably younger than he looked, with a white goatee that did, in fact, bear a striking resemblance to a goat.

"That's Ivan. He's grandpa's second-in-command." Isaac reached down to feel a pulse. "I think he's still alive!"

I needed to be sure. I activated my Auge and set it to diagnostic mode. My eyes studied Ivan's unconscious body, and the MRI and ultrasound function of the Auge deduced, just as Isaac had, that he was still alive.

"He just took a bad blow to the head, but nothing's broken, and there's no internal bleeding either," I informed him, methodically searching for other injuries. "He'll live."

Isaac looked up at me in surprise. His blue eyes met my glowing bionic ones. "Oh," was all he said.

We stepped over Ivan's unconscious body and walked toward the door at the end of the corridor. Judging from the fancy wood paneling and artwork, this was probably Bull's office. As we got closer, we saw bloody footprints on the carpet leaving Bull's office but none entering. Isaac's face was sheet white.

He pushed open the door slowly, and I followed close behind. The amount of technology Bull had in here was astounding. It was so much more extravagant than his home office. The walls around him were adorned with large Holo Screens and quantum computers that would have looked more fitting in a situation room. Some of them were shattered and others seemed barely functional. One of them intermittently flashed *1,487*—this Holo Screen   faced Bull's desk directly on the other side of the room. Another flashed *All Systems Disconnected.*

The place had been ransacked. The cabinets were broken, and glass and paper covered the hardwood floor.

"We're too late," Isaac gasped.

Behind the large desk, Bull lay on the floor. My mind involuntarily focused on the small details—the shocking white pupils, the blood-stained lips, the dark green tie.

Isaac was right—we were too late.

Bull's face was a death mask, pale and bony. His salt-and-pepper hair barely covered his half-open bloody scalp, his eyes were sunken, and his cheekbones protruded sharply out of his pallid skin. Bull's features had petrified.

But it was nothing compared to the damage the rest of his body had taken. Bull's chest had been cracked open. A single incision had been made from the top of his chest to the very bottom of his stomach. The skin around his body had been pulled open, exposing his insides.

"Oh my God..." Isaac's voice trailed off. "Are those his...? Oh, God."

"His intestines? Yeah."

Bull had, literally, spilled his guts. The stench from the blood and the contents of his stomach was unbearable, but I had to get close enough to use my Auge's X-ray function. I saw that a bullet pierced Bull through the left shoulder. Some of his ribs were broken, too, and his left shoulder dislocated.

"He was tortured, wasn't he?" Isaac sounded aghast.

I nodded. "Yes. This was personal," I said, inspecting the body methodically and consciously keeping my emotions at bay. Scenes like this were the norm in my line of work, and I needed to have a thick skin and stay detached. It's the only way I knew to avoid PTSD. "They made sure he suffered. His death was slow and painful, and he was helpless to fight back."

"Was he alive when they... you know?"

"I think so, yes."

"It has to be Hexum," Isaac said, gripping his knuckles so tightly that they appeared ghastly white. "No one else could have done this."

I was inclined to agree with Isaac's hypothesis. Since studying the other crime scene photos, it would certainly fit the Federate Army's MO. Hexum had the most to gain from Bull's death.

Isaac stood up unsteadily, picked up a wastebasket that was lying under the table, and rushed to the other corner of the room. He stared at the wall for a few seconds before he knelt down and hurled into the wastebasket.

Instinctively, I took a few steps back. While my peers experienced violent reactions at the sight of spilled guts, I could coolly inspect a crime scene. The sight of someone throwing up, on the other hand, sent my head into a tailspin.

Watching Isaac barf into the wastebasket, my heart went out to him. There was no right thing to say to someone who had just lost a loved one. When my brother died, people were always trying to comfort me by saying things like "he's in a better place," "it'll get better," or, my all-time favorite, "it was just meant to be."

I know they meant to console me, but nobody seemed to understand that their words were meaningless to me. Aric and Vir's deaths ripped open a hole in my heart, and I refused to accept it was *meant to be*.

Just like their deaths, Bull's death was going to have a

profound effect on his family. But it was going to completely change Isaac. Finding Bull in this awful state was his misfortune, and he didn't deserve this. I should have shielded him from this. I should have expected the worst and done everything I could to spare someone else the trauma I'd had to live with.

"You were right," Isaac admitted when he was done. "I can't believe it. I just can't."

Isaac looked stunned. I stood there, unable to do anything. "I'm so sorry, Isaac."

"They killed my grandfather," Isaac repeated. "After all these years, after everything he's done for them." Isaac's eyes narrowed as he turned to face me. His anger turned into a full-blown panic attack. "My family," he said, his voice rife with alarm. "Oh my God, my parents! Christ, my family is in danger!" He started to grab fistfuls of his hair in panic. "My parents. Florence. Oh God, we have to find them before it's too late!"

I'd seen people panic like this before. Combined with shock, it was impossible to get them to listen or reason. So I did the only thing I knew would snap him out of it. I stepped forward and slapped him across the face as hard as I could.

Isaac blinked several times like he was trying to wake up after a long slumber.

"You can't help anyone if you're hysterical," I said, looking him in the eye.

"You slapped me," he said blankly, touching his red cheek.

I grabbed Isaac by the elbow and began walking toward the stairs. "Yes, I did, and I'll do it again if you can't get it together," I said. "Now, let's go find your family."

11

"**I HAVE TO REPORT THIS TO THE OREGON** authorities," I said urgently as we rushed out of the building. My virtual assistant had taken the liberty of compiling my notes and event logs from the last day and a half. At my request, it relayed everything from Bull's death to the missing people and the Federate Army to my friend Iyer, the only person I still trusted from my old unit. They'd know what to do once they saw it. Seconds after the files were sent out, I received a *failure to send* notification.

That's strange.

That had never happened before. Fear crept through my veins like ice. Since arriving in Corinth, I had no idea what was happening on the outside. I hoped to God it wasn't another Cyber Blitz. Without any connection to the outside world, I felt incredibly alone. There was no one I could rely on in Corinth. Nobody I trusted. Everyone seemed to have their own agenda, and I was trapped in the midst of it. And now the only man who could get me out of this was dead.

I couldn't help but wonder how Bull's untimely death might affect my career. I doubted anything I had done since coming here would be construed as helpful. The whole affair made me appear particularly incompetent. I swore out loud, cursing my damn luck. Of all the private investigators in the country, Bull had come to me.

I remembered what Bull said when we first met about the few people in government who knew the colonies even existed. A lightbulb flashed in my mind's eye. Bull must've pulled some strings with Vera's mother, the deputy governor of California, to find out how I was related to Vir and pull my personal info. I bet she recognized my name instantly and thought it would be a hoot to get me into Corinth. Once again, Rahul Vera was having the last laugh at my expense.

Beside me, Isaac seemed to be lost in his own thoughts. The image of his grandfather, bloody and mutilated, was probably etched in his brain. I knew from personal experience there wasn't enough alcohol in the world to get rid of that memory.

"We were never close," Isaac said when we walked out of the building. "Never." Isaac shook his head. "He was a selfish old man, and sometimes I really hated him. But this isn't how I wanted to remember him. How could this happen?"

I knew that much about Bull already. He really was a selfish old man. I hated that he'd only thought to bring in an investigator when it affected his political career. And even then, Bull had given no consideration to my safety. I was disposable. A second-class citizen. My life just didn't have the same value as the people's here.

However, I couldn't say I completely blamed him for keeping me in the dark. When we lost Aric, I would've done anything—*anything*—to get him back. In the days leading up to the funeral, I spent days and nights begging and bargaining with whatever higher power was responsible to send him back to us. I guess when you love someone enough, you're willing to sacrifice the whole damn world to save them.

"I don't know, Isaac," I sighed. "I wish your grandfather had warned me about Hexum. I need to figure out why they think I'm involved. That I helped."

Isaac was only half-listening, though. When we got into his Jeep, he pulled the seatbelt over his shoulders and turned to face me. "Look, I know I've been a dick to you, and you have no reason to agree to this," Isaac said in a rush. "But I need your help. I can't protect my family from Hexum by myself."

I frowned. Now he wanted my help? "I barely got out of that fight in one piece."

"That's true." He nodded. "But if we band together, we might have a better chance of getting through this alive."

I considered him. This was a total 180 from his attitude so far. Like his grandfather, Isaac had been sullen and unfriendly. I had no reason to trust him, and vice versa. On the other hand, we did seem to have a common enemy.

"You haven't actually asked me anything yet," I pointed out.

Isaac swore loudly. "Fine!" he said hotly. "Fine. Will you please help me?"

Under normal circumstances, I might have been tempted to say no. But there was nothing normal about Corinth. The fact was, I needed Isaac's help as much as he needed mine. There was no way he was equipped or even able to take on Hexum's men by himself, and the last thing I wanted was his family's blood on my hands.

"Yes," I answered and stuck my right palm out.

OUR FIRST STOP WAS ISAAC'S HOME TO pick up Evie. We drove in silence, lost in our own miserable thoughts. I kept trying to connect to the outside world, but even my T-Patch couldn't put me through to anyone. Frustrated, I cursed under my breath. My Auge was an extension of me. It had been my constant companion since I was seven years old, and without it, I felt disabled and disconnected. Maybe I had underestimated the blow I had taken at the library. Maybe something short-circuited during the fight. Was that even possible? I had never heard of an Auge malfunctioning. They were supposed to be indestructible.

"Hexum and his men …they've been waiting for an opportunity." Isaac gritted his teeth. "And Cara just gave it to them on a silver platter."

Cara may have caused a domino effect, but I sincerely doubted that she was responsible for her grandfather's death. Hexum and his men were obviously bloodthirsty and violent, but it was my arrival and not Cara's departure that had been the last straw.

"No, it wasn't her fault." I felt a strange sense of responsibility for the girl. "Your grandfather miscalculated the effect my presence would have on your community. I know he hoped I would fly under the radar, but the chances of that were always pretty low."

Isaac let out a string of expletives. His concern for his family was justified, though. Hexum had found a weak spot in the Bull-Smiths' armor, and the question was how he planned to use it against them. Whatever he had planned, I was sure, would overshadow the pain he'd put Bull through.

We arrived at Isaac and Evie's place faster than I expected. The Cape Cod–style house was much smaller than the Bull-Smiths' ostentatious home. Unlike the other rundown homes on this street that were painted in traditional shades of brown and beige, Isaac's front door was bright turquoise.

"Wait here," Isaac said as he dismounted the Jeep.

Waiting outside in the middle of a cul-de-sac where I could be easily spotted by my attackers was the last thing I wanted to do. It occurred to me that Isaac might want a moment of privacy with his wife, but I knew better. Even now, he was letting me know where my place was. And that was outside his home.

Rebecca hadn't wanted me in her home any more than Isaac wanted me in his. Isaac, just like everyone else in his family, wanted my help as long as I stayed within the confines of their small-mindedness. I didn't care that someone didn't want me in their home. Certainly, I didn't expect everyone I'd ever met to have me over for a cuppa. But what annoyed the hell out of my being here was the reason why. It wasn't because I was rude or unfriendly and not because I had poor hygiene or told bad jokes. These people didn't want me in their homes and their restaurants because they thought of me as some sort of vermin. Even when Isaac invited me to stay in the loft last night, I knew it wasn't out of the goodness of his heart. He was a calculating bastard; he just wanted to keep a close eye on me.

I glared at Isaac and jumped out of the Jeep. I had

intended to hang outside for a few minutes to try my T-Patch again, but now I was reeling with anger. Isaac hurried inside to find Evie before I could say anything to him.

Frustrated, I tried to get the T-Patch to connect again. But it was no use. The words *call failed* flashed in my Auge. "Goddammit!" I swore loudly and hurried toward the front door. Isaac and his bigotry be damned.

The front door swung open immediately after the first knock. Evie stood on the other side, her face full of surprise and confusion.

"What the hell is going on?" she demanded, gesturing for me to come inside. I instantly recognized the most prominent aspects of Isaac's loft, like the black-and-white framed pictures and the bright furniture, in their living room. "Isaac's upstairs getting a few things. Has something happened? He looked upset." Although she spoke softly, the authoritative tone in her voice was unmistakable.

Sharing bad news to unsuspecting family members came with my job description but, in this case, I didn't think it was my place to tell her. "Yeah, it hasn't been a very good day," I warned her instead. "I'm sure Isaac will want to tell you himself."

Before she could ask anything else, Isaac hurried into the living room carrying an empty backpack. His face turned white with anger when he saw me standing in his living room, but he didn't say anything about it. "Grab whatever you can," he instructed Evie instead. "Quickly!"

Evie ignored his instructions. "Isaac, what's going on? What's happening?" she asked, looking back and forth between me and her husband. "Hey, talk to me!"

"My grandfather is dead," he announced bluntly.

"Dead? What do you mean he's dead? How?"

"It was Hexum." His voice broke. "They murdered him. Probably sometime this morning. We were just there ...it's terrible. We found Ivan, too, unconscious but alive. The whole office is a mess. God, there was so much blood!"

"Where's Ivan now?" she asked, looking toward the front door as if half expecting him to walk through it.

"We didn't bring him with us," I said. "Ivan's safe though. We moved him to an empty room. He'll wake up with some pain, but at least it'll be somewhere, um, clean and safe."

Evie then listened carefully as Isaac described briefly how we had found his grandfather in his office. The only part he left out was his convulsive reaction.

Evie's eyes widened and she gasped. "Oh, Isaac, I'm so sorry. They really are monsters!" Tears welled in her eyes. "Do you know why?"

Isaac clenched his fist and, for the first time since we'd arrived, looked at her directly. Bubbling just underneath the surface was a violent version of Isaac that I hadn't seen yet. Evie didn't recoil though. She stared back at him with equal contempt.

It was disheartening to see anyone struggle in their marriage, especially when they were this young. "They know Cara's gone," I chimed in, hoping to alleviate some of the tension. "You saw how they accused me of aiding and abetting your sister-in-law's escape." I pointed at the damage they'd done to my face.

Evie looked away from Isaac and turned to face me instead. Her eyes darkened, and any shred of emotion erased entirely from her face. She wasn't easy to read, but I could tell that she was not the sort of woman who was often caught off-balance. "Why would they think you were involved?"

"I'm not white and I'm an outsider. Anyway, they didn't seem the smartest bunch."

"Those fucking eunuchs!" Isaac slammed his fists against the coffee table. "What could they possibly have to gain from killing him? He's done so much for them!"

"Control," Evie responded shrewdly. "It's a power move. They've probably been waiting a long time for your grandfather to make a mistake, and now he's paid the price for it."

Isaac looked accusingly at me. Evie sat down beside him and wrapped her arm around his shoulder, but he shrugged it off. Apparently, whatever they were fighting about couldn't take a backseat to Bull's death. Evie's face turned bright red as she pulled her arm away. "They've always hated your grandfather," she said. "He used them to do his dirty work. He probably thought they were all brawn and no brain, but he underestimated them like he does everyone else. They couldn't go after him when he was so omnipotent, so completely faultless, but after Cara... they just saw an old man who couldn't even keep his family in line."

"In other words, Hexum has taken control of the city," I said, folding my arms against my chest.

"Exactly." She nodded. "They've gotten difficult to manage these last few years, and now that Grandfather's out of the picture, the city is theirs for the taking."

This was even worse than I thought. "Do the other six colonies have such an equivalent?" I asked, unable to picture the possibility of more thugs like the men who attacked me walking freely around the country.

"It's hard to say. I've never seen anything that would indicate such extreme tribalism in the other colonies. But, of course, we only visit them a couple of times a year and... um, procreation is pretty much the only thing anyone wants to talk about," Evie answered.

Was that why they were fighting? Did Isaac want the pitter-patter of little feet running around their home? I thought back to what Evie said about procreation in the library. In the colonies, having children was more than just about building a family; it was about succeeding in their mission to grow as a species. It was surprising that Evie and Isaac didn't have any children, now that I thought about it. The colonies were all about growing their population—the arranged marriages, the chalkboards with the population count, the segregation of the infertile people. Everything they did here was to benefit their growth as a people. And yet Bull's only male heir was without any offspring himself.

"But if they do exist, I doubt they're as extreme as Hexum's men," she said after a moment's thought. "Why? What are you thinking?"

"I'm thinking you're right," I said. "But if the other colonies have similar groups, then they might all be in cahoots with each other. And this might be a coordinated attack on your entire colony."

"I doubt it." Evie shook her head, dismissing my hypothesis. "Julius did not allow communication devices in the city. Except, of course, for the smart intercoms," she pointed out. "But nobody, not even the Federate Army, has personal communication devices.

And, you know, conspiring to overthrow the entire council would be tough with just their walkie-talkies."

The idea of the Federate Army using prehistoric technology was laughable. There was a joke in there somewhere, but I decided this probably wasn't the best time to explore it.

"Okay, that's it," Isaac said more urgently than before. He stood up and grabbed his backpack. "We're leaving. Now. We need to get out of here for a while. Until things calm down."

"You really think they would come after us?" Evie questioned. "I mean, what could they possibly achieve from killing us? We're still in our prime baby-making years... I don't think they'd discount that."

"Isaac is right," I said. "I don't think it's safe for your family here. Is there somewhere you can all go? Somewhere far enough away that the Federates won't find you?"

"Hmm," she contemplated. "Yeah—my parents live in the Arizona colony. They'll be happy to have us, and we can stay there for as long as we need."

Going from one trouble-riddled colony to another potentially dangerous one wasn't the best idea, but I already knew the Bull-Smiths would rather die than live anywhere that wasn't one of their colonies.

While Evie and Isaac scrambled to pack everything they needed for Arizona, I cleaned myself up. Drained from this day already, I took up Evie's offer to help myself to some lunch in their kitchen. Her warm, welcoming attitude was in stark contrast to everybody else's in Corinth. *Maybe there's hope for these people after all.* As soon as the thought crossed my mind, I felt a twinge of guilt. I was generalizing an entire town based on my interaction with a few bad apples. Who was being biased now?

Annoyed with myself, I digested everything else I'd learned so far. Evie's insight had opened up new possibilities and new threats. If she was right about Hexum taking over, then I would need to find a way to intervene. It was the right thing to do. Despite their unfriendliness, I couldn't leave the colonists to fend for themselves.

And from the looks of it, the Bull-Smiths were going to need my help—even though I wasn't sure they deserved it—getting safely out of Corinth.

But the question was, how were we supposed to get to Arizona? The closest Hyperloop station was all the way in Salem, and I doubted there was a direct connection to whatever remote corner of Arizona Evie hailed from.

If only my Auge was still functional. All of this would be so much easier. I kicked myself for not having the Auge pinpoint my exact location when Bull first brought me here and also for not having an emergency contact. I felt like I was living through my own little Cyber Blitz.

I groaned loudly. Why hadn't I thought of it sooner? During the Blitz, the terrorists had used GPS dampening technology to nullify all incoming and outgoing communication. Could that be what was happening here? GPS dampeners would explain how the colonies maintained their anonymity and why nobody (except maybe Bull) had any communication devices.

Bull must've set it up, his own personal invisibility cloak, against satellites. I had to admit it was very smart. From the sky, Corinth and the other colonies wouldn't appear to be anything more than farmland or national parks. Was that how Bull ensured nobody here had access to technology? That would be the only thing that made sense.

If I could find the source of the GPS block, then I could call for help. Back in Bull's office, one of the Holo Screen s had flashed *All Systems Disconnected*—that must've been it! I bet that when the Federate Army ransacked Bull's office, they took the GPS dampener with them and switched on the Auge cloak, knowing that it would effectively paralyze me and end any chance I had of calling for help.

I cursed again.

The sudden activity outside the kitchen window snapped me out of my trance. The streets of Corinth were not usually busy. Besides the library plaza, I had hardly seen anybody outside their homes or on the streets. And yet, in the last few minutes, I had seen over a dozen people sprinting down the lane.

I sincerely hoped they weren't clearing the path for the Federate Army. I wasn't sure I could handle a second round with them today.

But the commotion was getting louder, and more and more people seemed to be running toward something. Alarmed by the growing commotion, Isaac and Evie ran to the front door to see what the excitement was all about. I followed them outside, mentally preparing myself for another attack, but whatever was happening, it wasn't here.

"What is going on?" Evie asked. "Where are all these people running?"

There was a familiar scent in the air—a mixture of warm charcoal and fuel. The air was thick and heavy with black smoke.

"Fire!"

It wasn't too far away, and it was growing more ferocious by the second.

"Somebody's house is on fire," I said grimly.

WITHIN MINUTES, ISAAC AND EVIE LOADED their Jeep with everything they needed. Evie rode shotgun this time, and I was forced to sit in the backseat with their backpacks.

In the distance, a whirlwind of thick black smoke rose into the clear blue sky. Isaac rolled the windows up and activated the chemical, biological, radiological, and nuclear (CBRN) defense controls (that was the norm for vehicles built over the last couple hundred years) to keep the searing stench and toxicity of the fire from polluting the air inside the Jeep.

"Does Corinth have a fire department?" I asked.

"Not a proper one," Evie murmured. "Just some volunteers and a couple of trucks."

Isaac sped through the city driving aggressively, ignoring stop signs and taking sharp turns. The closer we got to Isaac's childhood home, the more palpable the tension became in the car.

The three of us already knew what to expect. We just didn't know how bad the damage would be until we got there.

The iconic, pristine, all-white home of Jonathan Smith and Rebecca Bull-Smith was ablaze. Through the large windows, plumes of thick black smoke escaped, and the roof had caved in on one side. My stomach felt like a bag of hot coal. I couldn't bring myself to ask Isaac who was usually home at this time. Maybe Florence was still at school and maybe Jonathan and Rebecca were out for a stroll or running errands. I hoped they were because the alternative was unimaginable.

In the front seat, Isaac choked back tears as he watched his childhood home wither and crumble. Evie caressed her husband's shoulder (this time he let her), comforting him in silence. Isaac was going to need every bit of support in the coming hours. Including mine.

A small group of men did their best to contain the aggressive flames, but it was hopeless. The fire was out of control, and these men did not appear to have the experience or the strength to fight this. It wouldn't have mattered at this point anyway. The house was too far gone to be salvaged. The beams tumbled like matchsticks on the inside, causing echoes to rumble through the ground. And every few minutes small explosions sent glass hurtling across the driveway.

The Federate Army must've used an accelerant of some kind to speed up the process. What should have taken several hours would now be completed in less than two. They knew exactly what they were doing. This was not a warning gone awry; this was a deliberate punishment meant to serve as a message for anyone who dared to defy Hexum.

There was no chance of getting closer to the house. Throngs of bystanders had gathered to watch, none lifting a finger to help, spilling into the adjoining streets. Isaac, Evie, and I jumped out of the Jeep and made our way toward the burning house, desperately scanning the crowd for Isaac's family.

The bystanders parted to let us through. Once again,

I sensed the feeling of being watched and studied. None of these faces seemed familiar from earlier this morning, but it was disconcerting to be surrounded, nonetheless.

"Is that him?" a raspy female voice reached my ears. "Is he the chinky?"

"Christ Almighty!" someone else—a young male this time—shuddered. "He is a fugly one!"

I tried to ignore the whispers and keep focused on the problem at hand, but it was nearly impossible to shake the intense feeling of being watched.

"Ignore those idiots. They're not going to attack you without Hexum's permission," Evie said reassuringly.

Isaac spotted his mother first. Rebecca's face, ghost-like and in shock, stared up at her beloved home going up in flames, hardly aware of anyone else around her. Florence stood next to her mother, covered in soot and weeping uncontrollably. As far as I could tell, neither was hurt, save for some minor cuts and bruises.

"Mom? Florence? Are you okay?" Isaac asked as soon as we reached them. "Mom?" He shook her shoulders "Mom, where's Dad?"

Rebecca opened her mouth, but no words came out. Instead, she let out a long, painful wail—an almost inhuman cry—as she collapsed into her son's arms.

The three of us turned our heads simultaneously to face the burning house. "No!" Isaac shook his head. "No!" He wrapped his arms around Rebecca and whispered through his teeth. He looked at his sister, Florence, as though expecting her to dispute his assumptions, but she only shook her head.

Isaac released his mother and rushed toward the burning

building, but he never made it past the makeshift border the firemen had set up. Two bulky firefighters stopped him in his tracks and dragged him, kicking and screaming, toward their fire truck. "Don't be stupid, man! We're not going to let you go in there," one of the firemen said. "There's nothing anyone can do now!"

For the second time today, we were too late. Isaac fell to his knees and cried. In spite of the cacophony, it felt as though the world had gone dangerously quiet. The ashes, the fire, and the sound of rubble and debris seemed eerie and distant. I had the odd sensation of floating, weightless like a balloon, as the flames licked the skies.

"We have to get out of here," I warned, trying to shepherd Rebecca and Florence away from the hordes of spectators. The heat from the flames was becoming unbearable. The thick, toxic smoke was spreading quickly, making it harder for the bystanders to breathe. "Now."

"No," Rebecca said numbly. "I'm not leaving." She shook her head. "Not without my husband."

In any other situation, I would have dealt with a grief-stricken family member with more patience and empathy, but none of us had the luxury of time today. We needed to get out of here quickly before things got much, much worse.

My eyes scanned the crowd around us.

For just a second, a prominent face wearing a gleeful smile passed through the crowds. It was all the time I needed to identify my attacker with the mismatched eyes. The venom in those eyes sent a cold shudder through me. Those Federate animals weren't done with Julius Bull's family—and I feared they had us all right where they wanted. In front of a crowd, heartsick and too helpless to fight back.

"Rebecca, I'm sorry." I reached for her arm but stopped. I knew better. "But your husband is dead. And if we don't leave now, we're going to be next!" Forget it—I grabbed her by the shoulder.

Just like it did with Florence, the touch of my hand against her skin set her off. The grief was swiftly replaced by revulsion, and she glowered at me. "Get your dirty hands off me!" Rebecca shrugged off my grip. "Don't you touch me!"

Beside me, Evie had taken Florence by the arm and was also raring to go. "Rebecca! Stop it," Evie screamed, aghast by her mother-in-law's extreme reaction. "He's just trying to help!"

"Okay, we really don't have time to stand here and pick apart your prejudices." I was starting to feel exasperated. "We are leaving. NOW!" Rebecca was heavier than I expected, but despite her protests, I managed to throw her over my shoulder.

"Let me down!" she screeched. "Let me down now!" She tried to wriggle free from my hold.

The crowd was watching us intently—their eyes full of revulsion and loathing—but they were, surprisingly, keeping their distance. I had expected, after the incident at the library, some sort of public intervention or whatever their version of a citizen's arrest looked like, but they seemed determined to not get involved. Maybe they were as afraid of Bull as they were of Hexum.

Florence and Evie led the way out. Tear-stricken, Florence kept turning back every few seconds to see that we were still behind her. I didn't have to imagine what she was feeling right now, seeing her mother so helpless and pathetic, losing her father to a fire that destroyed the only home she had ever known. Her heart was shattered into a million little pieces, just as mine had been in the aftermath of both Aric and Vir's deaths.

Isaac's composure faltered when he saw me carrying his mother like a sack of potatoes. A range of emotions shuttered through his face in just a few microseconds—surprise, disbelief, confusion, and finally, anger.

"What the hell is going on?" he demanded.

I dropped Rebecca unceremoniously back on her feet. "We have to get out of here." I wheezed heavily to regain control over my breathing. "We've got to leave immediately!"

"What are you talking about?" Isaac asked, waving at his mother to be quiet. "We can't leave! My father is in there!"

"That's exactly what I've been saying," Rebecca yelled. "Then this moron dragged us away!" She pointed at me accusingly.

This wasn't getting us anywhere. I looked to Evie for support.

"Isaac," Evie said softly. "I'm sorry, but your father is dead. Nobody could have survived that. You know it's too late." Evie stepped in front of me. "I saw them. Hexum's men. They're here, and I don't think they're done with us."

The surviving members of Jonathan Smith's family turned to look at their house one last time before it completely burned to ashes. They must have known she was right, even if they could not bring themselves to admit it. I knew that feeling, of course. As soon as you said it out loud, it became the truth, and right now the truth was unbearable.

"No," Rebecca cried. "He just can't be dead!" She shook her head, violently sobbing. "Not like this!"

"Rebecca, I really am sorry for your loss. Truly. But the longer we're out here in the open, the higher the chances are of another attack," I reasoned. "We need to get somewhere safe, somewhere we can regroup."

"My father," Rebecca suggested without hesitation. "We'll go to my father. He'll end them all!"

Evie, Isaac, and I looked at each other. We had momentarily forgotten that Julius Bull was still dead in his office.

"Oh, Mom..." Isaac whispered, taking Rebecca's hands in his. "There's something I need to tell you."

12

BLACK FUMES CLOUDED THE AIR around us. My eyes welled up from the irritation of the smoke particulates, and the heat from the fumes had driven the hordes further back—though not enough to escape their death stares. But the Bull-Smiths and I stayed right where we were, watching as Isaac broke the news about Bull to his mother.

At first, I wasn't sure if Rebecca had heard anything Isaac said. She was startlingly calm as he described the state of Bull's office and the condition in which we found him.

"Your mother's in shock," I noted, as the hysterics from a few moments ago were replaced by a cold, vacant expression.

"Mom, did you hear what I just said? About Grandpa? He's... dead. In his office."

Rebecca Bull-Smith blinked in acknowledgment but didn't say anything at all. A few feet away, Florence was inconsolable. Evie had the teenager wrapped in her arms while she mourned her father and grandfather. Both women had been handed more tragedies in this one day than most people faced in a lifetime, and I couldn't shake the feeling that it wasn't over.

"We have to go now, okay?" Isaac spoke to his mother as if she were a small child. Having only seen Isaac angry and irritable, this soft, nurturing side of him came as a surprise. Judging from the hurt look on Evie's face, this was new to her as well.

Isaac lifted Rebecca's arm over his shoulder and proceeded back to the Jeep. As they shuffled past me, Isaac met my eyes and mouthed a quick thanks. The gesture was so unexpected that it took me a couple of seconds to register it, but I managed to nod in return before it got awkward.

We walked close together, with me in the rearguard position. My senses were on high alert. I constantly surveilled the crowds for potential threats, Argus-eyed and ready for battle if it came down to it. I couldn't see any of the men who had attacked me earlier, but I was confident I hadn't imagined that leering face in the crowd.

"What are we going to do now?" Florence began sobbing as soon as we reached Isaac's Jeep.

"We're going to leave Corinth for a bit," Evie answered. She and Florence were trailing close behind Rebecca and Isaac. If Rebecca had an opinion about this, she wasn't sharing. "We'll go to Arizona. Stay with my family."

I walked over to the driver's side of the car and leaned against the hood. "How exactly are you going to get there?" I asked, frowning at Evie and Isaac. "The closest Hyperloop is in Salem. We could drive there, but I'm willing to bet that the Federates have locked down the only way in and out of the city."

"That's a safe bet," Evie said, walking over to the trunk. "But we don't need to drive to get to Arizona."

"No?"

"No, we'll fly, like we always do," Evie said.

I couldn't help but shake my head. *Right, of course you will.* Their obstinate attitude toward modern technology was even more baffling than before.

On the one hand, they embraced AI-operated cars and jets but, on the other, they completely shunned communication devices.

I peered over the Jeep to see if the chopper Bull had brought me to Corinth was still on the helipad across from Jonathan and Rebecca's burning home. But the helipad was empty. Bull must've had it moved somewhere after I left the house last night.

"But... but the airfield is on the other side of the city," Florence stammered.

Isaac put his hands over his sister's shoulder to reassure her. "It's okay. We'll drive. It's not too far from here."

Rebecca crouched down on the asphalt and put her head in her arms. Isaac released Florence, and they kneeled next to their mother. Florence put her head against Rebecca's knees while he wrapped his arms around the two women. They held each other tight and grieved for everything and everyone they had lost today. It was a tender moment. I looked away to give the family a moment of privacy while they consoled each other.

Florence released herself from the group hug first. "If we're driving, I want to ride shotgun," she said in a petulant tone. "'Cause we're not all"—she looked at me sullenly—"going to fit."

I frowned back at her. What was it going to take for these people to get over this mentality? Florence's father and grandfather had just died, her house had burned to nothing, and her mother was practically catatonic, and all she could think of right now was my brown skin coming into close contact with hers. God knows I said a lot of stupid things to my friends and family members in the aftermath of Aric's death, but I never let my grief cause anyone else hurt or pain. That was my burden to bear.

Besides Florence's personal discomfort, fitting five people in the Jeep would be a tight squeeze, and I couldn't see Rebecca allowing herself to be crammed into the backseat with me either. Aside from the space, traveling in Isaac's four-wheel drive posed another problem.

"We should go by foot," I said, walking over to the trunk. Evie was repacking their backpacks with a couple of guns, knives, and some canisters I hadn't seen before. "They'll be expecting us, and the Jeep is too conspicuous."

Isaac looked unwilling to part with his Jeep, but Evie was already nodding in agreement. "He's right, Isaac," Evie sighed heavily. "We have to break away from our usual patterns. Hexum will expect us to drive there, but we have a better chance of making it to the jet if we sneak in as quietly as possible."

So the five of us set off for the airfield. We had only made it a few blocks when a thundering snap stopped us in our tracks, leaving us completely petrified.

"Where do you think you're going?" a familiar voice called out to us.

"Everybody, stay calm," I whispered softly so only the four Bull-Smiths could hear. Florence whimpered next to me, but nobody dared to move a muscle.

Isaac, Evie, and I had agreed that taking the longer route to the airfield was the best course of action. It had seemed like the smart thing to do a few minutes ago, but now I was no longer convinced we'd made the right decision.

Hexum's men had in all likelihood never lost sight of us since we left the house. If I'd been in their shoes, this is exactly what I'd do too—catch up to us before we disappeared into the cityscape. From my last encounter with them, I knew that exacting corporal punishment in private wasn't their style. They'd want to finish us off here in front of terrified witnesses.

We turned around slowly to face the Federate Army. There were at least seven men, including the three that attacked me earlier. I recognized the large man with odd-colored eyes immediately. I was happy to see that he had a shiny bruise on his chin from our first meeting. Feeling a rush of bravado, I winked at him.

On either side of Clayton were two large animals, barely restrained by their leashes, glowering at us. The cockiness from a few seconds ago disappeared. Seeing the animals—if they could even be called that—in such close proximity made my blood run cold.

"Oh no," Florence whimpered. "They have hellhounds with them."

"Shit," Isaac said, his concern evident.

"Shit indeed," I agreed.

13

EVIE CLEARED HER THROAT SOFTLY. "Nobody make any sudden movements," she ordered, her voice brittle.

Isaac nodded and stepped forward slowly, placing the shotgun he'd brought on the ground to indicate he wasn't a threat.

Clayton raised his eyebrows at the gesture, but the tension in his shoulders didn't ease. "I asked you a question," he said.

"We're going to my place, Clayton," Isaac answered politely. "Unless you've burned that down too?"

"What, without your precious Jeep?" Clayton snarled.

"Yeah, the battery died. It happens from time to time." He shrugged.

Clayton just folded his arms and stared at us. He didn't believe Isaac for a second, and he let it show by relaxing his grip on one of the mutt's long leashes. The creature on his left leaped forward the instant the leash loosened. Its slow growl sent an involuntary shiver through my bones.

"I asked you a question," Clayton repeated. "Where are you going?"

Isaac responded with a question of his own. "Why did you kill them—my father, my grandfather? My father was innocent! He never did anything to you! Not once did he stand in your way. Why would you hurt him?"

"Aw, you know we'd never hurt a fertile man!" Clayton tilted his head with a *tsk tsk* sound. "Your daddy was just in the wrong place at the wrong time." Clayton mocked a frown. His callous tone elicited snickers from his mates. "But you know," he shrugged, "collateral damage and all that."

That did it. Rebecca snapped out of her trance. "You bastard!" she screamed at the men. "How could you? After everything my family did for you!"

"Your old man did nothing but lie!" Clayton reciprocated her animosity. "Just look at that dog he brought into our city." He pointed his fat fingers at me. "And let's not forget about your precious daughter. That's right! We know she took off."

"Mom, no, come back!" Florence screamed, but Rebecca was rushing forward to face Clayton all by herself. Her usual swanky uptown behavior had been replaced by a profoundly barbaric presence.

"You ungrateful swine!" she yelled. "If it weren't for my father, you'd still be working the fields like the animal that you are!" Rebecca spat on the ground. "Don't you stand there and pretend you're better than us!"

Rebecca's verbal assault gave me a chance to look for an escape route. I looked up at the buildings around us and saw people moving away from the windows. Our only option was the street on the right that Clayton and his men had left unrestricted. But outrunning those beasts was going to be a challenge, if not impossible.

"I have a plan," Evie whispered, barely moving her lips. "We're only two blocks away from the library. Isaac, do you think you can aim for the mutt on your left?"

He silently nodded.

The shouting match between Rebecca and Clayton was becoming savage and unrestrained. Years of built-up animosity and mistrust between both parties spilled onto the streets— unwittingly providing us the perfect cover for a quiet conversation.

"Okay, Florence, you see the grey canisters on the side of my backpack?" Evie turned her backpack more for Florence to see.

Florence searched the backpack until she found the little tubes. "Yeah," she nodded.

"Take one out slowly," Evie instructed. Florence let go of Evie's hand and took a couple of steps behind her. From the Federates' perspective, all they saw was a scared teenager too afraid to face them hiding behind her family.

"Well done, Florence!" Evie whispered in approval. The teenager skillfully picked up a canister without drawing attention. "Now here's what I want everyone to do: Florence, you deploy the canister—try to aim for the men on either side—and Isaac, you shoot."

"But what about the other hellhound?" Florence's voice broke.

"Oh, I've got that bitch covered," Evie murmured. "Jimmy, you grab Rebecca and run like hell! Everyone, head for the alley behind the library. Understood?"

It wasn't the task I would've picked for myself, but we were outnumbered, outgunned, and out of options. Evie's plan felt like a Hail Mary. But it was better than having another go with Clayton and his fiendish creatures. We silently agreed and took our positions.

"Oh, you'll answer for your crimes, I can promise you!" Rebecca was still yelling at Clayton. "When I tell the council what you've done, they'll hang you like a dog! A dog, Clayton!"

Clayton pretended to shudder, eliciting a round of laughter from his friends. "Isn't she hilarious?" he laughed. "And my Pop always said women had no sense of humor."

This is it! I readied myself. The Federates had let their guard down and were completely unaware that something was happening right in front of their eyes.

The hellhounds seemed to have sensed the sudden shift in energy. Their bodies tensed, and their noses lifted up in the air. Could they smell the adrenaline and trepidation emitting from the other side of the aisle? Whatever made up their genetic code was evidently part predator. The animals could sense a chase coming. They stood in attack mode, waiting for us to make a run for it.

Clayton and his men were too busy laughing at Rebecca's threats to notice the mutts were on their feet, growling.

"NOW!" Evie screamed.

The laughter stopped abruptly. Clayton and his men looked at us with surprise and confusion. Their animals had begun struggling against the leash, and they tried desperately to restrain them. Equally surprised, Rebecca swung around as if she had forgotten her family was with her.

And then everything happened all at once. Everyone moved in unison. Rebecca froze when she saw me reach for her with lightning speed and pull her away from the line of fire. Isaac reached for the ground and grabbed his shotgun. He fired at the hellish creature to his left. Evie pulled out a smaller caliber handgun and shot at Clayton and his men.

The Federate Army was taken aback by the sudden assault. Evie and Isaac's bullets hit them before they even had the chance to react. Rebecca screamed. One of the hellhounds escaped from its master's hold and headed right for us, but Evie expertly fired a bullet into its skull. Clayton's other hybrid mutt wasn't any luckier than its brother. It took a clean shot through the foreleg and another to its shoulder.

That was the first time I'd ever seen guns in action in real life. The sheer violence of it was breathtaking and completely paralyzing—the crack of the bullets leaving the guns was infinitely more terrifying than anything I'd ever witnessed before.

Meanwhile, Florence flung the canisters with so much force that one of them exploded in the air. Luckily, it was closer to them than to us. The other one exploded at Clayton's feet and released a hiss of black smoke right in his face.

"What the hell!" Clayton screamed. "What's happening?"

I smiled for the first time since I'd gotten here as Clayton and his lackeys disappeared from view.

The intensity of the smoke bomb was surprising. I had seen only them used during war games, but they were never this intense. Thick acrid fumes surrounded Clayton and his men until we couldn't see them anymore. All we could hear was heavy wheezing and painful screams. It was hard to tell if the guttural cries belonged to the men or the lone animal.

Even from this distance, the fumes made my lungs feel heavy and congested. Clayton and his goons were going to feel a lot worse than they did now. Soon the stinging under their skin would morph into bright-red, pus-filled boils, and the irritation in their lungs would feel like sandpaper.

When they got out of the gaseous bubble—if they got out—they would need to be properly decontaminated or risk being scarred for the rest of their lives. Evie's smoke canister was much more than a diversion. It was a dirty bomb.

I wanted to ask where she had gotten this, but the smoke was much too intense and there was too much chaos at the moment. I shielded my nose and mouth with my palm and looked around to see if everyone was okay. The Bull-Smiths were just as transfixed by the smoke bomb, which was growing darker and more acrid by the second, creating a thick curtain between them and us.

Standing there beside them, I couldn't quite shake off the feeling that I had chosen to side with the lesser of two evils in Corinth.

14

"GO, GO, GO!" EVIE SCREAMED AS THE Federates fired at random. I pulled Rebecca by the arm forcefully and followed Evie as she led us through Corinth.

Despite the excess violence, Evie's plan had been a tour de force—Clayton and his men had been completely incapacitated, and we had gotten away with nothing more than a few teary eyes and a slight ringing in our ears.

Adrenaline powered my body. I had not expected to survive a second encounter with the Federates, but somehow Evie's vision had come together seamlessly. We were lucky to be alive. Well, lucky the Bull-Smiths packed so much firepower, I should say. Where the hell had they gotten that stuff from, anyway?

Those smoke bombs were not homemade. They couldn't be. It was too concentrated, much too powerful to have been put together in somebody's basement.

"Jesus Christ!" Isaac exclaimed when we came to a halt.

We were already a few blocks away from the epicenter of the fight, but the Federate Army's superabundant firing still rumbled through the quiet town.

"Everyone okay?" I asked, searching everyone for possible injuries in between breaths.

"I can't believe we made it!" Florence exclaimed. Even Rebecca nodded with surprise.

"That was a… really great idea, Evie." Isaac patted his wife's shoulder like she was one of his bros. Normally such a gesture would come across as a sign of approval, but the lack of affection made it seem more awkward than anything.

Clearly, Evie thought so, too, because she shirked from his touch and stepped a couple of feet away. Strange how they didn't behave like most married couples. They were orbiting each other's space but that was it. They weren't a unit.

Did Cara see their unhappiness as plainly as I did? Was this marriage the reason Cara decided not to go through with hers? It might well have been. Evie and Isaac were hardly the poster children for arranged marriages in the colonies, and neither were Rebecca and Jonathan, from what I saw yesterday. If Cara was around and always watching their squabbles, I wouldn't be surprised if it put her off marriage completely.

"I don't think they followed us," Evie said with a note of relief.

If I hadn't known where Evie was bringing us, I would not have recognized this as part of the library. We were on the other side of the main entrance where I had met the Federate Army. It looked like a private entrance that wasn't in use any longer.

"Follow us?" Isaac said. "Evie, they couldn't even stand up straight!"

"That won't stop them from trying," Rebecca warned. The run here had winded her so much that she was wheezing as badly as the men we left behind, and the words came out in a struggle. For a woman her age and size, she was desperately out of shape.

"Are you okay?" I asked cautiously, moving close to her. "You might want to sit down for a minute."

Florence was only an adolescent, but she was just as winded as her mother. She clutched her belly and coughed loudly. Both mother and daughter seemed like they had run a marathon and not sprinted across a couple of blocks.

"She can rest later," Evie said impatiently. "We should keep moving."

Isaac ignored that and walked over to his mother and put his arm around her shoulders. "Mom, you okay?" he asked.

"Oh, she's fine." Evie waved her hands in the air. My surprise at her callous tone must've shown because she responded by explaining, "In the colonies, the women aren't allowed to do any sort of laborious physical activities that might adversely affect their fertility or their ability to give birth."

Evie crossed her arms around her chest and looked at her mother-in-law with pity. "We're expected at all times to care for our 'birthing vessels'"—she used air quotes comically—"so exercise is doing the bare minimum. What's important is that we start taking prenatal vitamins as soon as we begin menstruating, bathing two times a day to stay clean for the men ...you get the gist."

Isaac coughed. "Evie's being sarcastic. As always. It's not that stringent."

I cringed. Birthing vessels? No exercise? It was no wonder that Rebecca was always in such a foul mood. I was starting to see what Cara meant in her letter about being treated like a baby-making machine. A woman's worth was irrevocably tied to the efficiency of her womb, which they clearly knew nothing about, seeing as how their medical advice was actually counterproductive. Maybe if they let the women go jogging once in a while...

My eyes fell on Evie's flat belly. She and Isaac were definitely an anomaly in Corinth, all things considered.

"Come on, Mom." Isaac helped Rebecca up. "It's time to go."

She stood up unsteadily and nodded. We were out of danger for the moment. But the significance of the losses they'd suffered today had only just begun to register. Evie was right. The Federates had, at least for the moment, been disabled, but this was probably Corinth's version of kicking a hornet's nest. Hexum and his army would almost certainly regroup and come back more prepared than before.

Hopefully, we would be long gone before they got the chance to strike.

Everyone besides Evie studied our surroundings carefully while she led us deeper into the alley. The fountain on the other side of the library could be heard splashing somewhere behind the dead end. The smell of chlorine was a nice change from the flames and smoke.

"What is this place?" Florence asked, taking slow deep breaths. She looked faint and nauseous.

I smiled at Florence encouragingly. In all the chaos, it was easy to forget that this young girl had just witnessed her father's death. Just like I carried the guilt and anger of losing Aric, she would do the same with her father. And her grandfather. I resisted the urge to pat her shoulders and offer my condolences. The Bull-Smiths had made their feelings about my touching them very clear.

Evie walked down the narrow passageway and stopped in

front of a reinforced steel door secured by a keypad on her left. "It's a... um, kinda like a getaway," she answered without making eye contact with anybody. "It's my safe house."

A safe house?

Isaac raised his eyebrows. Rebecca and Florence looked puzzled. Even though Evie had been the easiest person in the Bull-Smith family to talk to, she was something of an enigma. She clearly didn't share any of their prejudices, though she seemed to hate Hexum just as much as they did. Only I wasn't yet sure if it was for the same reasons.

"Why do you need a safe house?" Rebecca demanded.

"To get away from you." Evie's answer came swiftly.

I suppressed a smile. That answer told me at least three things about Evie—she savored her privacy, she didn't like being questioned, and she really didn't like her mother-in-law. Though that last one was true for most married women.

Rebecca was about to respond when the distant sound of a whip snapping reached us. Hexum was already starting to re-rally his forces, and soon they would comb through every inch of the city to find us.

"Let's just get inside," I urged.

"Why are you even here?" Rebecca turned her attention to me. Her anger had transferred from Evie to me now. "You're the reason they're after us!"

"Not now, Mom," Isaac intervened. But Rebecca wasn't having it. And to my surprise, Isaac added, "I asked him to be here, okay? Can we discuss this later?"

Evie entered the passcode quickly and pushed the innocuous-looking door open as soon as it buzzed. When she stepped inside, the entrance lights came on automatically and revealed a narrow staircase that led somewhere deep beneath the library.

Once again, I stayed behind until everyone was inside and made one final sweep of the artery—still no sign of the Federate Army. I stepped inside and pulled the steel door back in its place. Just before it clicked shut, a successive blast of booms broke through the air.

Thankfully, the barrier repressed the ambient sounds. The surviving members of the Bull-Smith family and I followed Evie noiselessly down to a sub-basement at least two or three levels below the library.

Florence was the first one to break the silence. "I didn't even know there was a basement down here."

"It's not a basement," I corrected. Judging from the steel bones and general structure of this subterranean space, I knew that it had probably been used as a bomb shelter during the War. Sequestered from the activity upstairs, nothing short of a dozen nuclear bombs could penetrate this space. "It's an abandoned fallout shelter."

This one wasn't as sophisticated or luxurious as the one in my grandparents' old house in Fremont, but it was pretty similar in design. It was roughly the same size, about eight-hundred square feet, but this shelter even had a secondary escape route and a nice-sized water closet. And the kitchenette appeared to have been stocked recently.

Evie offered us some refreshments and first aid kits. Large jugs of water, some military-grade Meals Ready to Eat, spare clothes, blankets, and pillows were scattered throughout the space. Almost as if somebody had left in a hurry.

The sight of the water burned my lips and throat. So much had happened today that I had barely eaten or drunk anything at all. I rushed to the kitchenette and helped myself to a whole jug.

While I quenched my thirst, Florence and Rebecca sat down next to each other and began tending to their cuts and bruises. Isaac dropped his backpack on the floor and sat down on a three-legged wooden chair next to them. He was itching for answers; it was written all over his face. After Aric had died, questions upon questions had eaten at me from the inside out: why him? Who would do this? How could this be? So I knew that look very well. I often saw it staring back at me in the mirror.

"What happened, Mom?" Isaac asked.

Rebecca sighed loudly. "You know, it was the oddest thing." She shook her head. "We're never home at that time. Never. Florence is usually at school, I'd be at Grandpa's office, and your father at the greenhouse. But today we were all home at the same time."

Her eyes welled up, and fat tears rolled down her face. In the space of a few hours, Rebecca had gone from being a devoted wife and daughter to a homeless widow and orphan. "What are the chances of that?" she cried.

Very low, I wanted to say, but I bit my tongue. I'd rather Rebecca realize the fire was engineered all on her own. "What made you all stay home today?"

Rebecca chewed on her upper lip. "We got a call from Ivan this morning. He said Daddy wanted to meet Jonathan and me at home to talk about something important, but..." Her voice broke. "Florence, why did you come home so early?"

Florence tilted her head side to side. "I don't know. Marte was executed at Hexum's rally today, and I just wanted to be home alone." She broke down in her mother's arms. "Daddy went back inside to get me. It's my fault he's gone."

"Oh honey, no it's not. We barely escaped and if it hadn't been for Jonathan..." Rebecca sobbed uncontrollably.

"I jumped out of the living room window, but I think a beam fell," Florence sobbed. "I'm not sure."

The image of Jonathan's kind face fighting his way through the rubble flashed before my eyes. Jonathan deserved better. He may have been Bull's right-hand man, but I don't think he bought into the propaganda like the rest of the family. He was too affable and approachable, and all of this would probably be easier if Jonathan had survived. I sighed. This day had gone so hellishly wrong for the Bull-Smiths.

"Oh, Flor." Evie sat down beside Florence to comfort her. "I'm so sorry."

We had all tracked in soot into Evie's bunker, but none more than Florence and Rebecca. Their hair was gray with ash and their faces almost as dark as mine from grit. Thin white lines where tears had streamed down were the only parts of their skin really visible.

I placed two glasses of water in front of them and took a seat across the table. "I'm terribly sorry for your loss," I said. "What the Federates did today is unforgivable."

Rebecca's tears instantly stopped, and her eyes turned to slits. "You should be sorry! It's your fault my family is under attack," she screeched.

Well, that didn't take long. Just as I expected, the finger-pointing landed in my direction. "Actually, Rebecca, I would argue it was your father's fault," I said coolly. I may have been raised to never speak ill of the dead (or living), but I'd had enough of the Bull-Smiths and their racial agenda. I was not going to let Rebecca turn me into the fall guy for her father's miscalculation, nor was I going to just sit there and take it anymore. "He knew damn well that bringing me here would cause more harm than good. And if he didn't, then maybe he wasn't the political genius you think he was."

Evie's jaw dropped. So did Florence's. And Isaac just looked flabbergasted. "Your father willfully misled me when he brought me here," I went on. "You should have told me about Hexum and the Federate Army, Rebecca! If not for my sake, then Cara's." The words spilled out of me. "I've had two attempts on my life in the last six hours, and I'm pretty sure now that Cara didn't just run away. She escaped. She escaped this madness and this prison. And I hope to God she got away safely."

It was harsh, but it needed to be said. The time for delicacy and diplomacy was long gone. Moreover, my mission to find Cara had altered. When I first arrived at Corinth, I was tasked to find her and bring her back home, but now I was set on surviving. I needed to be in one piece if I was expected to find the girl.

Isaac linked his fingers with his mother's and pulled her attention away from me. "Mom, I asked him to help us," he said guiltily.

"Your grandfather already did that," Rebecca replied.

"I asked him to help us get out of here safely," Isaac clarified.

Florence was the first of the three women to react. "What?"

Isaac nodded solemnly. "We can't fight Hexum or his men alone," he said. "You know that."

Rebecca stood up suddenly and walked toward the kitchen, one hand on her chest. "You're just like your grandfather, you know that?" she said, her back still facing us. "I never understood why he wanted to bring in this mongrel! I say we trade his life for ours." She turned around and pointed her long, white fingers at me. "It might be the only way to salvage this with Hexum. He might just forgive us if we give him a One Worlder."

Suddenly an image of me strapped to a gurney and a bright white light blinding me as someone with a scalpel tore into my chest popped into my mind's eye. If Hexum ever got his hands on me, I would be worse than dead. I would be on the receiving end of his madness. Instinctively, I turned to see if the rest of the family agreed with her. Evie's jaw dropped in disbelief. Isaac kept a poker face, while Florence was nodding in agreement with her mother.

My mouth turned sour. "There's no need for that," I said sharply. "You're welcome to try and hawk me to Hexum, Rebecca, but you would do well to remember that I'm the only person in this city who wants to—and can—help you. Also, Hexum might want me, but he wants you a whole lot more."

The energy in the room shifted dramatically. Long gone were the relief and adrenaline. Anger and suspicion were now rearing their ugly heads. I leaned forward and calmly took a sip of water, deliberately making eye contact with everyone.

"He's already killed two members of your family today

and burned down your house. Do you really think he's done hunting you? You were probably the target. If you were at your father's office like you were supposed to be, do you think they would have just let you walk away after they killed him?"

"He's right, Mom." Isaac nodded. "You know that. Can you please put aside your feelings about…" He looked at me uncomfortably. "Everything? I can't risk losing you and Florence now."

I was half expecting Rebecca to give me the boot when she finally said, "Fine. But I don't like it."

Translation: I don't like you.

That was fine with me. The day Rebecca outgrew her small-mindedness would be the day hell froze over.

"Fine," I said. "And if we are doing this together, I want to be clear that the next time you speak to me in a way that I find unacceptable, I will leave you and walk the other way. Are we clear?" This part would be hard to do, but Rebecca didn't need to know I was bluffing. Without my Auge and T-Patch, I was stranded in Corinth. I needed the Bull-Smiths as much as they needed me.

"Fine," she said again in a clipped tone. "And if we get caught, you're on your own. I won't vouch for you. I won't risk my family for someone like you."

That was surprisingly upfront, albeit not unexpected. Bull had washed his hands of me the second we landed. I had no reason to think his daughter would be different. Isaac, on the other hand, was dispelling my first impression of him. A small part of me felt sorry and hopeful for Isaac. Underneath all that anger and bravado was a man still trying to figure out who and what he wanted to be.

With that agreement in place, the room relaxed a bit. Evie

handed Rebecca and Florence fresh clothes and showed them the bathroom where they could freshen up and change.

Meanwhile, Isaac and I walked around quietly studying the bomb shelter with interest. The setup was very much similar to Evie and Isaac's home, from the placement of the pillows on the divan to the neatly organized kitchenette and even the choice of fruits and vegetables I found in the refrigerator.

"This place doesn't look very abandoned to me," Rebecca carped as soon as she joined us again in the common room. "How did you even know it was here, Clarissa?"

Evie looked uncomfortable under the spotlight. She had barely said a word, but I had a feeling that was about to change. We were all wondering the same thing—about this bunker, about Evie, and about the secrets she kept from her husband and his family.

This bunker was more than a getaway. It was a safe haven. Not just to Evie but other people as well, judging from the array of clothes, shoes, and personal items lying around.

When I had first met her, she was an enigma. But now my impression of her solidified. Evie was an outsider amongst the Bull-Smiths. Isaac either ignored her or was livid at her. Rebecca rarely spoke to her. When she did, it was always cold and without any eye contact. Florence, on the other hand, appeared to be on neutral ground with her sister-in-law.

Right now, Rebecca was staring at Evie with contempt. I took my seat on one of the three-legged stools and sipped a cup of warm green tea that Evie had just made. Florence settled down beside her brother, and they both watched the uncomfortable exchange between Evie and Rebecca.

When Evie didn't respond immediately, Rebecca drew her hair out of her face and said, "Excuse me, am I invisible? I asked you a question, Clarissa."

It was the sort of tone that could instantly antagonize someone. Evie's face flushed with fury and embarrassment. She crossed her arms and glared at Rebecca.

Florence leaned closer to her brother and away from her mother's line of fire.

"Her name is Evie, Mom," Isaac said, trying to feebly deflect.

"I don't give a burgundy flying fuck if she's called Jesus fucking Christ," Rebecca screeched. "Now answer me, dammit!"

Florence and Isaac cringed hard when they heard their mother swear. I did too. Clearly, Rebecca's carefully crafted upper-class veneer was falling apart, and her children were seeing the real person beneath it for the first time.

"Nearly every government building constructed after the asteroid storm of '75 has an underground bunker," Evie said matter-of-factly.

"That's not what I asked, Clarissa." Rebecca jutted her jaw out imperiously. "How did you know this place was here?"

Rebecca narrowed her eyes at Evie. The rest of us watched uncomfortably as the tension in the room became palpable.

I cut Rebecca off and asked Evie, "It was you, wasn't it?"

"Her what?" Rebecca looked confused, and her head turned back and forth like she was at a tennis match.

Evie blinked, but it was Isaac's reaction that piqued my interest. The blood drained from his face, and his breathing became shallow.

Isaac knew exactly what I meant, and he swore continuously under his breath. "You knew, didn't you?" I asked him.

Isaac let go of Florence's hand and stood up abruptly and began pacing. "Goddammit it to hell!" he swore again. "I told you he would figure it out sooner or later. You're not as smart as you think!"

Rebecca shook a fist in frustration. "Excuse me, but what is going on?"

"Did you know my brother?" I asked, my voice thick with grief.

"What's happening?" Florence choked back tears.

"Just tell them already," Isaac said with a sigh.

Evie took a deep breath and turned to face her mother-in-law first. "Rebecca, I'm really sorry for telling you like this. I never, in a million years, imagined it would happen but..." She pressed her lips together. "It was me. I was the one who helped Cara escape. I've been helping others, too, ever since I got here."

It was the *aha* moment I'd been grasping at since I arrived in Corinth. Hearing Evie say the words reinforced all of my theories. She was the mysterious person I'd been looking for. And it was all the more ironic, considering the family she had married into.

"And yes, Jimmy, I knew Vir. He was one of my best friends," Evie revealed. "I'm so sorry for your loss."

I let out a heavy breath that I didn't even realize I was holding back. Evie's confession sent a flurry of emotions through the small den. Shocked, Florence covered her mouth with her hands while her mother gasped loudly behind me. Isaac's features were inscrutable when he met my eyes.

There was so much I wanted to know about my brother,

about the night he died, but I couldn't bring myself to ask Evie outright. I wasn't ready yet. I was afraid the answer would be too final. As long as I had hope, I could go on. I could survive and fight, but there was no way to hide from the truth now.

"He'd been helping you, hadn't he? Since the beginning?" I asked instead, mentally calculating when she first arrived here and when dissent started to grow.

"Yes," she said, shifting her weight from one foot to another.

"Helping you with what? How would you even know his brother?" Rebecca cried.

"It's a long story." Evie sighed and sat down on Isaac's recently vacated spot. Florence shifted uneasily in her seat.

"Who's helping you?" Rebecca demanded again.

"On the inside—nobody," Evie said quickly, but I wasn't convinced she was telling the truth.

For all intents and purposes, she was an undercover agent who was much too intelligent and careful not to have prepared plausible answers in the event she was ever found out. Colleagues from the force who spent years embedded in the field would often recount how they would play and replay their speeches in their head before going to sleep each night. It helped them prepare for worst-case scenarios. It seemed like Evie had done the same—and now she was in her worst-case scenario calmly spitting out lies. Knowing that should have made me distrust her, but the strange thing was I didn't. Something about the way she talked about my brother told me she wasn't lying. There was affection and respect when she said his name, and that was enough for me.

"You've known this whole time, Isaac?" Rebecca bit her lip. "How could you?"

Isaac shook his head sadly. "Not the whole time, Mother," he said. "It's only been a few days."

"Days?" Rebecca rasped. "You've known for days?"

"After Cara left?" Florence surmised.

Evie nodded. "Yes. I told him so he wouldn't worry."

So that explained why he wasn't invested in finding Cara. Isaac already knew she was long gone. At the Hercules, I had mistaken his blasé attitude for indifference when, in fact, it was conviction that I would never find her in Corinth.

"This whole time I've been blaming Cara and this"—she pointed at me, trying desperately to find a polite word to describe me—"*man* here when I should've been blaming you! You did this to my family. You filled Cara's head with this poison!"

A cannonball would have done less damage to Rebecca's pride. Florence's thin eyebrows disappeared into her forehead, and Isaac, slack-jawed and as upset as the rest of the family, dropped into the chair next to her. Evie had surprised them beyond their wildest imagination.

Even I had to admit that when I first suspected someone on the inside of helping kids escape, I had not imagined it would be a woman. Maybe it was the ingrained sexism of our forefathers, but I had automatically assumed that the unidentified person in the drone video was a man. To her credit, Evie used her femininity as the perfect cover for rebellion. Her husband, her in-laws, and the whole goddamn town had underestimated her—and she had let them.

Rebecca flew at Evie in a wild rage. "You bitch! Where is she? Where is my daughter?"

Unruffled by the sudden attack, Evie parried her punch and caught Rebecca's arm in a painful twist. Her form was impressive.

"I know you're upset." Evie gritted her teeth. "I would be too. But don't you ever— and I mean *ever*—raise your hand at me again. As for your daughter's current whereabouts, I'll never tell you."

The rest of us were on our feet—Florence yelped, taking wide steps away from the women.

"Evie, let her go!" Isaac rushed to help his mother.

As the one closest to them both, I put myself between them and tried to dispel the fight.

Evie let Rebecca fall to her knees and stepped away from us.

"This is all your fault! You did this to my family!" Rebecca cried.

Isaac wrapped his arms around her and tried to pull her back. "My father, my husband, my daughter ...they're all gone because of you! Our home is in ashes!" Rebecca sobbed.

Evie wiped away her own tears. "I really am sorry for your loss. I never intended for anyone to get hurt." She looked directly at Isaac and Florence when she spoke. "But this is exactly why it was important to get your sister and everyone else out. Why we all need to get out of this town. Hexum and his men are keeping us prisoners here! Doesn't it bother you that they treat us like we're nothing more than human incubators? They're so wrapped up in their 'cause' to survive that they don't even see that they're killing us. This place is toxic, and we deserve more than this."

Corinth *was* toxic, and it was refreshing to hear it from someone else. It was encouraging too. If Evie and the members of her underground rebellion felt this way, then surely there must be more people who were of the same mind.

Rebecca had heard enough. "There is nothing more important than our survival!" she stuttered. "Look at how his people"—Rebecca pointed her index finger at me, her eyes red with rage—"have ruined our beautiful country and this planet! You are so ungrateful for the things the colonies have given you. After everything we've done for you. I welcomed you into my home, treated you like a daughter!"

Evie glared back. "You treated me and every other woman in this city like an animal!" Evie's eyes narrowed. "Has it ever occurred to you that not every woman here wants this?" She crossed her arms. "You've taken away so much from us, from me, from your daughters. How can you live with yourself knowing that you forced your son to marry an absolute stranger? I know you believe there's some cause to fight for here, but so do I and so do other people," she spat. "You took away our choices, our freedoms, and you really wonder why your brother and daughter abandoned your ways?"

Her brother? So Cara wasn't the first member of this family to dissent. This was an interesting piece of information that might come in handy at some point. Clearly, Florence and Isaac thought so too—they looked at each other and their mother in surprise.

Rebecca looked unfazed. Evie's words had had no effect on her. "How on Earth did you even manage it? How did you bypass the patrols?"

Evie cleared her throat. "The patrols change their routes every month," she explained. "I could usually figure out their routine after a few days, and they rarely deviate, so that was easy."

"What was the hard part, then?" I heard myself say.

"Hiking through the mountains and getting to the other side in one piece," Evie said. "It's harsh terrain, and the nights are pretty brutal, but it's a testament to how badly they wanted to get out of here."

Florence cleared her throat. "How did you sneak out without anybody noticing?"

Evie hesitated. Her eyes shifted from Florence to Isaac and back. "Well, I only went on the nights your brother slept in his loft above the Hercules."

"You mean the nights you were supposed to be helping out at the clinic," Isaac scoffed.

"But how did you get Cara and the other kids out without being tracked?" I asked before they began arguing.

Evie gave me a conspiratorial smile. "By taking the microchip out," she said. "Everyone in the seven colonies is tagged almost as soon as we're born"—she pointed to a tiny incision on her left shoulder—"but it's pretty easy to take out. And we do it a few weeks before the kids are scheduled to leave too."

"Isn't anyone tracking them?"

"Oh, I'm sure Julius was, but I had the kids carry it with them after it was removed and go about their usual routines. And when it was time to go, they'd just leave it somewhere in their homes."

Smart, I thought. By sticking to their established routines, the runaways could ward off unwanted attention while preparing to leave Corinth. That's why Bull never saw Cara's dissidence coming.

"But how did you avoid eyewitnesses? The Federate Army must have a routine patrol or guards posted around the city," I asked her.

"They do." Evie nodded. "But you know ...it takes a village. And there are people, even within Hexum's circle, who want to do right by the kids, their family members, and neighbors."

I grimaced. It was hard to believe anybody in Corinth wanted to do anything right. Or maybe they just did the right thing for them, even if it meant standing back and watching those unlucky kids who were caught and dragged back to be sacrificed. Did these people, the ones in Hexum's group, think the lives of their family members were more valuable than others? Than mine? It seemed to me they wanted to reap all the benefits of being part of One World without even trying to honor the principles that come with it.

Rebecca shook her head sadly. "Why would you betray your own people?"

"First of all, I didn't betray anybody. I helped those kids when no one else would. And I would do it all again. It was Hexum that killed your family, not me," Evie retorted. "And second, I am not one of you."

"What does that even mean?" Rebecca sounded exasperated. "Of course you are."

My lips curved in anticipation. This was the moment I'd been waiting for.

"No, Rebecca," Evie said politely. "I am of One World."

Evie's admission bounced violently off the steel walls. Confusion first spread on Isaac's face, then disbelief, and finally comprehension. I could see the questions forming in his eyes, but he just sat there motionless, in shock. Rebecca and Florence looked dumbstruck by the admission, not entirely sure if she meant to be literal or theatrical.

For the people here who'd never met anyone outside their own race, Evie's strong almond-shaped eyes, high cheekbones, and thick brown hair were probably just quirks, but to me, they were anything but. That, plus the clue about Peregrinus in Cara's diary and this underground bunker, was enough for me to verify what Evie had just said.

Evie let the words sink in. Her whole body emanated relief and liberation at saying those words out loud.

Isaac clutched his chest. "What?"

"I'm not one of you. I am part Asian and Middle Eastern," she said proudly. "I just happen to look a lot like you. It happens sometimes."

"How?" Rebecca demanded. If she was tempted to have another go at Evie, she exercised great restraint. "I know your parents, and they most certainly aren't Asian or A-rab." Her pronunciation of the word Arab made me want to gag. "Why, their descendants can be traced back to twentieth century Texas. Do you think you were chosen to join this family for your brains?"

After talking to Isaac and Florence, I had surmised that the education system was lacking in Corinth. The colonies had essentially adopted the old Nazi education model of glorifying their Caucasian race while labeling the rest of us as inferior and incapable to create race-conscious, obedient, and self-sacrificing citizens. So it made sense that the people here were out of touch with current affairs and technologically backward, and it didn't surprise me that Rebecca didn't understand the basic concept of genes and how traits were passed down from parent to child.

Evie laughed. "You think you know everything, but my father—my biological father—was of Asian descent."

Rebecca gasped. "Your *what*?"

Evie had shocked us into silence. Florence clapped her hands over her mouth, and her eyes kept darting from one person to another. None of the others knew how to respond. Isaac looked shell-shocked. I was completely riveted by her story.

"My real father. He was a soldier tasked with border patrol back when the government used to help our colony a lot more," Evie continued. "And my mom had, of course, never met anyone like him before. They fell madly in love, and she was going to elope with him, but he died. We don't know how."

Evie had our full and undivided attention. "My mom was very young when she became pregnant with me, and she knew her family would never allow it. She decided she wanted to leave the colonies, start a new life somewhere else, but my father, the one who raised me, stepped in. It was a risk. They couldn't have known what I'd look like after I was born, but my mom couldn't bear the idea of an abortion," she went on. "Anyway, they had grown up together. He was kind, decent, and desperately in love with her, and he convinced her to stay. So they got married and raised me together."

Comprehension slowly dawned on Rebecca. "He's infertile, isn't he?"

"Yes, I think so," Evie confirmed.

Isaac began laughing out loud, startling everyone in the room. It started as a soft chuckle but quickly turned into a hysterical outburst. "I'm sorry," he said, trying to control himself. "It's not funny. It's just so goddamn ironic."

It was ironic. Rebecca and Jonathan wanted nothing more than for their children to marry someone with the perfect heritage. The bloodline must be kept pure if the colonies were to survive, and Evie, by their twisted definition, was the exact opposite of everything they believed in.

Pin-drop silence filled the room. Isaac's chest heaved up and down, his fists curled. "Who sent you here?" he demanded. "Wait, did you only marry me so you could get close to my grandfather, to spy on the council?"

The rest of us stood eerily still. The answer was painfully obvious, but sometimes you needed to hear out loud for it to hit home.

Evie's eyes welled up, but she stood tall and proud. "Yes."

Isaac looked like he'd been sucker punched. I felt for him. If I were in his shoes, I would be devastated too.

15

IF IT HADN'T BEEN FOR THE OLD-TIMEY analog clock, I would've never guessed it was only just after eight p.m. So much had happened today it felt like we'd been here for a week when in reality it had only been a couple of hours since Evie dropped her bombshell news. We had all remained in the common room, sitting in awkward, sullen silence since then.

"We're all alone now," Rebecca said, teary-eyed. I could practically hear my mother just then. I could see her pain in Rebecca's eyes and knew full well the desperation, the urgent need to go back in time and change everything. Rebecca's body was here in the safe house with us, but her mind was frantically imagining all the ways she could have saved her family, just like my mother had after learning two of her sons had passed.

It had taken nearly a year for me to truly accept that Aric was gone. When it did happen, it felt like someone had lifted the blinds and the light was finally seeping in. I wondered when I would feel the same way about Vir. If Rebecca and my mom would ever be able to find closure or if they would spend their remaining days replaying their losses over and over again until their last breath.

"That's not true, Mom." Florence rested her head in her mother's lap. Her eyes were bloodshot and her face puffy from crying. "We still have each other."

It was a private family moment, and I was sure they didn't

want me there any more than I wanted to be. I quietly removed myself to the kitchenette where I could watch them from behind the counter, ready to intervene if necessary. The hush barely lasted a few minutes. A faint howl pierced the strained silence, forcing us all to look up at the ceiling. Evie and I stood up at once and ran to check the entrance and make sure it was sealed on our end. My body was on hyper-alert.

"Oh my God—" Florence started to say, but Evie gestured to her to be quiet.

"They must be right on top of us," Evie whispered to me.

I nodded in agreement, hoping that they were on the other side of the library and not in the tunnel we hid in after our last encounter with Hexum's men. I watched the door like a hawk, waiting for rapid gunfire to break through. But nothing happened. After holding our breaths for twenty minutes or so, we decided the danger had passed. At least for now. Just because they were gone now didn't mean they couldn't come back.

Rebecca was the first one of us to break the silence. She sat up straight and rubbed her temples. "How could you keep this from us, Isaac?" she asked.

"I told you already, Mom," Isaac said, fidgeting with his hands. "All I knew was that she"—he nodded at Evie—"helped Cara escape. That was it."

"You should have told us," Rebecca maintained. "Your father and I had a right to know."

I glanced at Evie who, like me, had moved away from their line of sight. She was perched on a stool away from the divan, watching the scene unfold intently.

This must've been what they'd been arguing about. It

must've come as a painful revelation for him to learn about Evie's extracurricular activities. I would hate to be blindsided by my partner, though in this case, I thought Evie had done the right thing.

"You're right," Isaac admitted. "I'm sorry."

Florence stared at her big brother bitterly. "Cara would never tell me who was helping her," she said, turning her attention to Evie. "She trusted you more than she trusted me."

"You need to tell us everything, Evie." Isaac sounded drained. Listening to Evie had been emotionally fatiguing, but she had barely scratched the surface.

"What more do you need to know, Isaac?" Rebecca scoffed. "She violated this family, our trust."

My mind flitted back to our conversation about arranged marriages yesterday. Jonathan and Rebecca had made it abundantly clear that their children had no say in their choice of spouse. Just as it was in Cara's case, Rebecca must've been instrumental in finding the right partner for her son.

"If only you had exercised more authority in your marriage," Rebecca said, clearly disappointed, "this chink might not have run amok, raising an underground to defect against our colonies!" Rebecca made a harrumph sound. "I knew we should have sent her packing after the first year. But now I thank God you have no children!"

Evie's silhouette moved further back into the shadows. She shook her head as she leaned against the wall. This must've been a regular topic of conversation in the Bull-Smith household, considering hers and Isaac's exasperated reaction.

Isaac breathed heavily. "I will say this one last time,

Mother," he sighed. "I am done letting you make decisions for me, you hear me? You asked me to marry Evie and I did. Now we are staying married until we decide otherwise. We decide. Us. She and I. Okay?"

Good for you, I thought. I was surprised to see this firm and decisive side of him. This sudden change in his attitude toward his wife was probably the late realization that he had married a badass who personified everything he wasn't. After years of taking her for granted, maybe it finally hit Isaac that he was not only going to have to start treating her better but also actually work on being better for her.

"You can't be serious!" Rebecca sputtered, clearly thinking the same thing I was. "No son of mine is going to stay married to this yellow bitch, you hear me? She does not belong in this family."

"I am serious," Isaac retorted. "This isn't up to you. Not anymore."

It was refreshing to see this side of Isaac, but I couldn't help but wonder if it made a difference to Evie in the long run. There was no doubt that Isaac's feelings for her were genuine, but the fact remained that she only married him to infiltrate Corinth. What relationship could survive that?

"Don't be ridiculous," Rebecca pleaded. "Think about your sister. You're ruining her prospects of finding a suitable husband by keeping some One World bastard. Why would you do such a thing?"

"Because she's my wife!" Isaac yelled. "And because... I love her."

"You will learn to love somebody else," Rebecca said coldly.

"He might," Evie said from the shadows. "But if and when that happens, it will be his choice. Not yours."

Rebecca bared her pearly white teeth. "So much confidence for someone so barren," she mocked her daughter-in-law. "How can you hold onto a man when you can't even do the one thing you were created for? You might as well be dead if you can't bear children!"

"Oh, Mom!" Isaac groaned. "Just stop. Please."

Evie's soft chuckle filled the small room. "God, you really are the worst." She rolled her eyes. "I'm not barren. I'm on birth control! Do you really think I would bring an innocent life into this madness?"

"What's birth control?" Florence piped in.

"Nothing!" Isaac and Rebecca yelled simultaneously.

I cleared my throat loudly. It was time for a change in topic. I'd learned more than I should have about any couple and figured now was as good a time as any for a segue. "Are you Raptor?" I asked Evie.

Evie leaned out of the shadows and looked at me with surprise. "Where did you hear that name?"

I fished out the little diary from my jacket pocket and held it up for everyone to see. "In Cara's journal." I handed it to Isaac. Florence and Rebecca scooted closer to him as he flipped through the pages. "Are you?"

Evie nodded. "Yes, I am."

"This is gibberish," Florence said, taking the book in her hands. "It doesn't mean anything."

"No, it's coded," I replied. "It's called shorthand."

Evie made no move to inspect Cara's diary, but she

watched closely as the Bull-Smiths passed it from one person to the next.

"She doesn't mention you by name," I went on. "But there's a drawing of Peregrinus in there, and I wondered if she learned that from you."

"Not from me, no." Evie shook her head. "A fellow cohort taught us how to use shorthand, but I had no idea she was keeping a diary."

I was eager to hear her side of the story. There was so much about Vir and his connection to the colonies that didn't make sense to me. Not to mention Hexum and his army of goons. Evie's story was probably crucial to understanding this subculture, as well as finding Cara and the other runaways and knowing for certain they were safe and looked after. Florence, Rebecca, and Isaac looked up from Cara's diary and waited for Evie to answer my question.

"Okay. Maybe I should start from the beginning." Evie hesitated. "I never liked living in the colonies, you know. Actually, I hated it. I wanted to see the world, climb mountains, meet new people, and my parents... well, you can probably imagine how they took it. They were so afraid I would get into trouble. They decided to tell me about my real father around the same time our marriage was being discussed. God, I was just sixteen then!"

Evie shuddered, acutely aware of the scrutiny she was under. "They thought it might help ground me. Reduce the risk of being found out if I knew the truth. That I would be afraid like they were. And they were always afraid someone would find out, but when your grandfather brought up the idea of us marrying, they were thrilled. Being a part of your family would shield any doubts about my ethnicity. I guess they were right—people only see what they want to see."

The Bull-Smiths looked ruffled by this. Clearly, they had never thought of her as anything other than one of their own, and it was only now that they knew her origins that some of her physical aspects popped out as foreign.

"Anyway, I didn't want to be married—the whole idea was terrifying to me. Plus, I was hellbent on finding out more about my biological father, so I left," she went on. "I ran away from my colony without so much as a sweater. It was the stupidest thing I ever did. I didn't have a plan. I had no idea where I was going; I just knew I had to get there. That's why our wedding was delayed." She gave Isaac a meaningful look. "I just remember walking. Sleeping where I could, mostly under abandoned highways or bridges. I don't know how long I went on like that. Probably weeks. But it happened one day, sheer luck. I actually thought it was a mirage at first, but there it was—a military convoy driving down the highway." She laughed at the memory.

I raised my eyebrows. "Wait, you hitchhiked with the army?"

"I sure did!" Evie nodded proudly.

Her face lit up from the memory, and her hands became animated as she began describing her experience. "I haven't thought about that day in a long time." She scratched her head. "Gosh, I can almost smell the stale dust in the air! When I first saw the convoy shimmering in the heat, I thought I was dreaming. The first thing I said to them when they pulled over was 'water,' and then I fainted."

We listened intently while Evie told us about the condition

the soldiers found her in. "I was really fortunate they had a medic onboard; after days out in the wilderness, I was terribly dehydrated and had so many blisters on my feet the skin was practically falling off."

Florence shuddered and touched her own feet gingerly. Evie then told us about how they administered first aid in the back of the truck, intravenously giving her fluids and medication until they got back at the base.

Among the soldiers she met that day was Orion. "He wasn't Commander yet, but he certainly acted like one." Evie smiled fondly. "There was no mission too dangerous or task so impossible that Orion couldn't handle it. Sometimes even single-handedly. He was the sort of man soldiers could blindly follow into battle. I certainly did."

Rebecca looked over at Isaac and raised her eyebrows, but he simply looked away and gestured for Evie to continue with her story.

"Anyway, I later found out that they picked me up in the west desert area of Utah."

"Utah?" I asked. "But that's probably the most isolated place in the country! How did you get so far with so little?"

Evie smiled happily. "Sheer willpower. I think it was the fear of going back to the colonies that kept me going."

"Incredible," I said admiringly. "So what happened when they took you back to their base?"

"Well, they didn't know what to do with me," she admitted. "After they brought me back to their base and treated me, I tried to find out what happened to my father, but they wouldn't even tell me if he had served."

"You didn't have the clearance," I surmised.

Evie nodded. "That, and I didn't even know his name. My mother would never tell me. All I had to go on was the approximate time and place he met my mom."

"What happened then?" Florence asked eagerly. "Did you go back home?"

"No, I didn't want to go back to the colonies. I decided to join the army instead. Orion took me under his wing. Trained me, taught me how to fight, how to think, how to be strong. It was the best time of my life." She smiled fondly at the memory. "Not because I finally fit in somewhere, but because I finally fit in with myself."

"Then why come back?" Isaac frowned.

"A few months after, we started to get reports of these weird deaths along your borders. I knew from the general location that it must have been Corinth," she said, tucking her hair behind her ears. "Orion was able to find out about the Federate Army and their relationship with your grandfather. It raised more than a few red flags."

It was hard to hear about Evie's old life without experiencing a range of conflicting emotions. On the one hand, I admired her strength and willpower for leaving her parents and venturing out into the great beyond, but on the other, I was astounded that she decided to come back. Although I liked to think I would make the same choices if I'd been in her shoes, I wasn't sure what I would really do. Anybody else would have stayed as far away from the colonies as possible.

"So, how does my brother fit into all of this?"

"I met Vir right after I joined the army. He was a couple of years older than me, and he'd already been with the unit for a short while."

"My brother wasn't in the army," I countered. "Vir was an anthropologist. He didn't—"

"Vir was recruited right out of college. His work was highly sensitive, and he wasn't allowed to talk about it," she said, apologetically. "He really wanted to, trust me."

I felt sick. "Was he even an anthropologist, or was that just a cover?"

"He was, yes. Vir's insight into subcultures is what kickstarted the army's interest in Corinth to begin with."

"So, it was the army that covered up his death then?" I scoffed.

Evie nodded. "I'm really sorry. Your brother was so brilliant. Everyone loved him. I loved him. Watching him die was the hardest thing in the world. If it wasn't for him, none of these kids would've ever left Corinth." Pride and anger and jealousy mixed together uncomfortably.

I could barely contain my emotions. My brother, my baby brother, had accomplished so much. He had made more of a difference in this world than most people could in their lifetime. But I couldn't help but think how little he must've thought of me over the years. While I was washing out of the force, he had covertly joined the army and had been helping the colonies' young people dissent safely.

"You were sent here to spy on us," Isaac concluded.

"No, I volunteered." She measured her words carefully. "I chose to come here. Nobody forced me."

Rebecca sneered. "Volunteered? Volunteered! You mean you used us, all of us."

"How could you not tell me?" Isaac demanded. "I don't

understand how you could keep this a secret."

"I didn't trust you," Evie said honestly. "I didn't in the beginning. You can't be mad at me for that." She put her hands on her hips. "You're Bull's grandson. I had to be certain!"

Evie left her spot and walked over to where Isaac sat. She kneeled beside him and cupped his face in her palm. "I may have come here to build an underground resistance, but you must know that I stayed for you and your sisters," she said softly, ignoring Rebecca's protests. "Your friendship kept me going. Trust me, there were days when I wanted to throw in the towel, but Cara was such a mess. I couldn't leave her or you alone here."

"You don't love me, do you?" he asked, unable to look her in the eye. "Did we really have a marriage, or did you just show me what I wanted to see?"

"I do love you, very much. But"—she hesitated—"I would be lying if I said I was *in love* with you. Our marriage wasn't the fairytale love either of us imagined, but you are my best friend here, and I don't say that lightly."

Evie had only been in Corinth five years, but it was clear she had developed feelings for her "family" despite her mission. She had taken the time to nurture a trusting relationship with Cara, she had risked her life to help all those kids, and she had invested in her relationships. Underneath all that anger, rejection, and disappointment was love. Maybe not the romantic love Isaac was expecting, but a different, deeper one. That much was evident when I overheard them arguing at the Hercules. People who didn't care for each other didn't fight the way Isaac and Evie did.

"God, my mother is right. You used me."

"You know that's not true. If our relationship was meaningless to me, you'd win every argument." She managed a small smile. But Isaac shook his head and looked away. "You remember how it was in the beginning? How we were around each other in the early days, always walking on eggshells, sleeping in different rooms, trying to accommodate the other's feelings and routines. We used to be so polite and proper in those first few months that all we ever said was *thank you*, *excuse me*, and *sorry*."

"Did you love him? His brother?" Isaac demanded, pointing at me.

Tears rolled down her face. Evie looked at me when she answered. "Yes, I do. I love Vir. He was my... we were..." She began sobbing, unable to say the words out loud.

I wanted to cry too. Vir had been in love, and most importantly, he had been *loved*. There was no doubt about it. I wanted more for them. I wished they could've had a chance to be a normal couple, for me to have met Evie at a family gathering, to see them together. My chest contracted painfully.

"Thank you for telling me." It was all I could manage without breaking down.

"How could you?" Isaac yelled. "How could you be with me, sleep in my bed and have sex with me, and love someone else at the same time? What sort of a woman does that?"

Rebecca glowered. "A whore! You see, Isaac, I was right about her. She used you, she used all of us."

Florence shuddered. "Mom, please," she reproached her mother.

But Evie ignored Rebecca's potshot. "I know it seems awful right now, but Isaac, you of all people must understand. You hate everything about the colonies." Evie looked pleadingly at her husband. "I couldn't just sit back and let Hexum kill innocent people. I did what I had to do."

My ears perked at this little tidbit. Besides his disdain for Hexum, Isaac hadn't said or done anything to indicate that he hated the colonies. If anything, I had thought he was an ardent supporter, considering the way he treated me and Evie and the way he talked about the colonies.

"What's this?" Rebecca croaked. "Isaac doesn't hate the colonies. This is his home."

Isaac looked like a deer caught in the headlights. "Well, hate is a bit of a strong word." He could barely look his mother in the eyes. "I dislike some things about it."

"Like what?" Florence leaned in.

"I guess it's mostly Hexum," he admitted. "And maybe the fact that we can't ever leave, and that all anyone can ever talk about is having babies and marriages."

Rebecca looked gobsmacked. "That's... a lot of things," she managed to say. "I never knew. You should have come to me with your doubts, Isaac."

"Did you ever think about running away like Cara?" Florence inquired.

This question had crossed my mind more than once. My initial feeling had been that it was Isaac's sense of loyalty to his family that kept him here. As the oldest sibling in the family, he had probably been groomed by his parents and grandfather to set an example not only for his sisters but also for the people of Corinth. The Bull-Smiths were the de facto first family of the seven colonies, and Isaac was the heir apparent. But now I wasn't so sure.

When Isaac didn't answer, Rebecca nudged him with her elbow. "Tell your sister you would never consider such a thing, Isaac."

Isaac turned to face his mother and sister. His face was gaunt and tired, and there were deep lines on his forehead that hadn't been there this morning. "I can't, Mom," he stammered. "I didn't just think about leaving. I actually tried."

I felt my eyebrows pinch sharply together. The three women reeled from the shock. Evie grabbed Isaac and gawked at him. "What?" Her voice came out hollow.

"You're not the only one keeping secrets." Isaac sniffed. "Did you ever hear about what happened to Tommy Carlson?"

I nodded. Carlson's name was on the list of kids who'd run away. Except unlike the other teenagers who'd never been found or heard from again, Carlson had been caught less than a mile from his parents' home the night he'd tried to make a run for it. When the Federates captured Tommy, they dragged him back to the town square instead of bringing him home to his parents. An emergency town meeting had been called at two a.m., where they had stripped the boy naked and flogged him for his insolence.

"We were friends," he sighed. "Best friends, actually. The night that the Federates caught him, I was there," Isaac said, like he had memorized the words. "I didn't want to marry you." He turned his face away from Evie. "Or anybody. Tommy and I decided to leave together rather than go through with an arranged marriage. It was his dissent that really inspired the others to leave."

"But they found you?" I asked, moving closer to the Bull-Smiths.

Rebecca looked aghast at her son's confession. She wrapped a protective arm around Florence as if she were trying to shield her from the truth.

Isaac rubbed his eyes. "We ran as fast as we could and we were so close, but when I turned around, he was gone." His voice trembled. "I don't even know when we got separated, but the second I realized, I went back to look for him. I just couldn't leave without him."

I knew what had happened next. Tommy Carlson became a cautionary tale for anyone who dared try to leave Corinth.

"They screamed horrible things at him, just terrible things. Words I'd never heard before. 'What makes you think you can escape your responsibilities? When the rest of us are dying here?'" Isaac choked on tears. "His back was covered in lashes, and he screamed for help. Nobody stood up for him, though. Not his parents." Isaac shook. "Not even me."

He wept into his palms. When he raised his head, his eyes were bloodshot, and he breathed heavily. "A week later, Tommy died. He was my best friend in the whole world, and I left him to die!" Isaac held back more tears.

Evie gasped. "Oh, Isaac, it wasn't your fault what happened to Tommy. It's just this goddamn town. It's your grandfather and the Federates. What happened to Tommy is on them. Nothing you could've done would've changed what happened. Tommy wouldn't have wanted you to die with him."

Isaac shook his head. He was reliving that night all over again. I could see it in his eyes. Tommy's death had frightened him, and that's why he had stayed. Isaac knew, just like everyone else, that his choices were sorely limited. He could either stay and be part of the colony or he could try to leave the boundary and face the consequences that came with it. But by choosing to stay, he had fallen in the eyes of his sister. Isaac probably knew, somewhere deep down in his heart, that he had disappointed Cara when he agreed to go through with an arranged marriage. He was her older brother, he had set the example, and she felt forced to follow in his footsteps.

"That's why you went through with our wedding," Evie said, her voice barely above a whisper.

Isaac stood up abruptly and walked to the kitchenette where nobody could see his face. "Yes."

Rebecca stood and followed him. She took his hand and forced him to look at her. "History keeps repeating itself! First my brother, then my daughter," she spluttered angrily. "And now you? It's like a bad joke! How could you just leave us? How could Cara? After everything we've done for her!"

"If by 'everything' you mean forcing her to have an arranged marriage, live an isolated life, be a baby-making machine... yeah, how very selfish."

Isaac had no time to react. Rebecca leaned forward and struck her long bony fingers against Isaac's face. The sound resonated harshly. "You disappoint me," she spat. She whirled around to face Evie. Rebecca raised her hand again, this time to point it directly at Evie. "Do you have any idea the danger you've put us in? If anybody had found out about your ...*heritage*, shall we call it? We would all be dead." Rebecca shuddered.

"Oh, bullshit! You had no idea, and I practically lived with you," Evie countered. "And my 'heritage' has nothing to do with the Federate Army coming after you. They've always hated your father. Don't you put that on me."

They glared at each other with unfiltered animosity. The air was practically crackling with bitterness and dismay. Even to me, the safe house was starting to feel claustrophobic. At first, I'd been relieved the spotlight had shifted from me to Evie, but watching Rebecca tear into her was much worse. She had risked her life every single day to help kids overcome their fear and find a safe haven outside these repressive walls. Evie deserved better than this.

"Tell me about Orion?" I asked Evie, hoping to steer the conversation away from Rebecca.

Taken aback by the sudden change in topic, Evie blinked and then said, "He's my commanding officer. He leads the rescue ops across the colonies."

"Is that who Cara left with?"

"Yes."

Orion. I didn't know that name, but the name was all I needed. It would be an excellent place to start when we got out of here. I didn't bother asking Evie where Cara was. Evie was determined to keep that information to herself, and I knew that it would be useless to try.

"Was Cara alone the night she left with your team?" I inquired.

Evie sighed loudly. "No, there were three other kids who went with her."

"What?" Isaac asked sharply.

"She wasn't alone," Evie said. "And that's all I'll say. None of the other parents have come forward. I'm sure they won't, either, and I won't risk their safety."

"It's a small town. Sooner or later, someone is going to notice," I said.

"It's true, but Hexum has bigger fish to fry right now."

"Okay, then," I said. "Any chance this Orion is going to come to rescue us?"

Evie bit her lower lip. "I don't know," she admitted. "I'm not sure if my message went through."

There was something in her eyes I hadn't noticed before—an Auge. So that was how she had bypassed Bull's communication blockade all these years and was able to stay in touch with this Orion person. And now the fact that she hadn't been able to connect with him only reinforced my theory that Hexum had, indeed, activated Bull's GPS dampening system and set up a firewall.

With so much animosity building up toward her, I figured Evie might want to keep that little tidbit about the Auge to herself, at least for the moment, so I didn't say any more on the subject. "We can't stay here forever," I said instead. "The Federate Army will probably start door-to-door searches soon. And we should try to get to the airfield before they find us."

"But how are we going to get there?" Isaac asked. "We left the Jeep back at"—he swallowed—"the house."

"We'll take the other way out," Evie proposed, pointing to a second door that I hadn't noticed before. "The passages are like an artery; they lead to different points in the city. The closest one to the airfield is two miles from here, and then it's going to be another mile by foot when we're topside."

Everyone turned to face the door simultaneously. It felt

oddly intimidating and uninviting. It quite literally was a gateway to the unknown.

"Why can't we just stay here?" Florence whined. "We're safer here, aren't we?"

Isaac shook his head sadly. "The safe house is pretty cozy," he admitted, "but staying here long-term isn't an option. We're going to run out of food and water at some point. And the Federates will come looking for us."

"Your brother is right," I concurred. "We have a better shot of survival if we stay on the move."

Rebecca cleared her throat loudly and raised her eyebrows at Isaac.

"What, Mom?" Isaac turned to his mom.

"What do you mean 'what'? I am not going anywhere with that half-breed," she said with a snarl. It wasn't immediately clear if she was referring to me or Evie. "And you can't seriously be thinking of bringing him to another colony—look at the damage his presence did to this one."

You can't be serious. We had just gone over how much they needed my help, and Rebecca was going back on her word before I could even get started.

Normally, I would never raise my voice to make a point, and certainly never at a woman, but I had had enough of Rebecca Bull-Smith and her warped rationale. "You know what, lady? I don't want to be here either! The only reason I am is because of your daughter and my brother. You think I volunteered for this job? No! I did your father a favor! Spare me the attitude!"

As I spoke, it dawned on me that Rebecca wasn't saying she didn't want my help anymore. What she meant was that once I had brought them to the airfield, how I got back to San Francisco was my problem. That was even worse. Much worse. She would have me face down the Federate Army by myself and potentially even offer me up as a bait.

Rebecca's face contorted in anger. She stood up abruptly and walked over to me, her eyes slit-like. I stared at her unblinkingly. From her body language, I presumed she wanted to strike me just as she tried to do to Evie, but I remained steady. But Rebecca didn't raise her hands at me. Our faces were so close that I could see fine lines around her face and thin veins popping out of her forehead. Without warning, she spat at me.

I heard Evie gasp loudly and saw Isaac jump to his feet and Florence cover her mouth in shock from my peripheral vision.

It was only saliva, but it felt like acid. The glob of spit bore into my skin like a red-hot piece of coal. I wiped it off of my face and collected myself. I stood slowly and stared Rebecca down. From this vantage point, she looked tiny in comparison to me. I would never raise my hand against a woman, but I would be lying if I said it didn't cross my mind. Rebecca didn't back down, though. She waited, almost defiantly, for me to retaliate.

"Rebecca!" Evie rebuked her mother-in-law. "How could you do that?"

"How could I not?" Rebecca cried. "Do you think I'm going to let some brownie piece of shit talk to me like that?"

Before I knew it, Isaac stepped in front of us and dragged his mother away to the other side of the room. "That's enough, Mom," he scolded her. "It's been a hard day for everyone, and you're making it worse. Jimmy didn't deserve that."

"Oh yes, he did," she insisted wildly. It was clear the deaths of her husband and father were finally hitting home. "I'm telling you now: I am not going anywhere with that creature! You can't make me!"

But Isaac responded without missing a beat, "You're very welcome to stay behind, Mom."

Confounded by her son's response, tears instantly rolled down Rebecca's face. Within a matter of seconds, she went from angry to weepy, and then she collapsed like a sack of potatoes on the floor, passed out. Isaac picked up his mother's unconscious body and carried her to the bunk beds.

"I'm sorry about that," he said to me after tucking her in. Isaac sounded like he genuinely meant it, but my anger was nowhere close to subsiding. If anything, I was growing angrier by the second. On top of insulting me, Rebecca had delayed our plans to leave the safe house. There was no way we were going to lug an unconscious woman across town *and* try to stay under the radar, which already was a challenge. We would have to wait until tomorrow night to leave Corinth.

16

THE NEXT MORNING, I WOKE TO THE most unusual smell ever. My nose sniffed the air trying to decipher what it might be. The aroma was oddly rich and invigorating but also bitter and harsh.

I sat up and looked around the safe house. Everyone was still fast asleep, but it hadn't been an easy night. I kept expecting the Federate Army to barge in any second. Florence had had trouble too. When the lights were off and she thought the rest of us were out cold, she sobbed quietly into her pillow until she fell asleep. Isaac, on the other hand, fell into a deep sleep as soon as his head hit the pillow. I envied his ability to shut his mind off and recuperate for a solid eight hours. I wished Florence could've had this gift. She had taken over the bunk bed. Rebecca and Evie and Isaac had made themselves a makeshift mattress on the floor. And I had gotten the tiny couch all to myself.

Curious, I followed the scent to the kitchenette, where I saw Evie sitting on a stool eating breakfast.

"Morning," Evie said softly. "Want some coffee?"

Her hair was up in a messy bun, and her eyes had dark circles under them. And I thought I had had a hard time falling asleep.

Evie yawned as she brought a cup to her lips.

"Coffee?" I repeated blankly. Coffee was extinct, just like

cocoa. The only caffeinated beverages (besides tea—we still had that, luckily) were artificially infused.

"Yeah," Evie answered. "One of the only things I like about living here." She took a sip and let out a satisfied sigh. "But still not worth it."

I grinned. I didn't imagine anything would be worth sacrificing a life outside these walls for Corinth. I sat down on the stool across from her and poured myself a glass. "Is this stuff real?" I asked curiously, sniffing the dark liquid.

Evie nodded. "Uh-huh," she said, chewing on her slice of toast. "Imported from South America. I stole some from Julius' kitchen a few weeks ago."

I looked up from my cup and stared at her. "That was *you* the other night at his home office, wasn't it?" I asked. "You stole the drone?"

Evie's eyes widened. "How did you know about that?"

"I was hiding under the desk that night." I laughed as I explained what had happened. "All this time I've been thinking it was Hexum."

"Hexum wouldn't know a drone if it hit him in the face," she snorted. "Anyway, I couldn't risk Julius finding out about me. If he saw me and Cara with Vir on video, my cover would have been busted."

I nodded. "The video was pretty corrupted. There only a couple seconds' worth," I said, building up to my next question. "Evie, what exactly happened that night?"

She put her cup down and looked me in the eye. "I was wondering when you were going to ask," she whispered. "Everything was going according to plan that night. We were even ahead of schedule, and then we heard the hounds somewhere in the woods. I don't know if it was a coincidence or someone tipped them off. I really hope they just got lucky, but as soon as we heard them, we ran like hell." Her voice sounded far away. "Vir was already waiting for us at the rendezvous point, of course."

"Was he alone?"

"No, he's usually with a small team of two or three soldiers on motorbikes. It really depends on how many kids are leaving that day," she said. "But that night was the largest group I'd ever ferried out, so he'd brought a Humvee. We had just finished loading up the kids and saying goodbye when the Federate Army caught up to us."

I could almost picture it. The urgency and panic they must've felt. "What happened then?"

"They fired at us. Vir stayed back to make sure I was in the clear. He asked me to go back with them, but I . . ." She slammed her fists against the counter. "I was so stupid. If I had gone with them, he would still be alive. I tripped and fell like an idiot, and he ran back to help me up."

That was the part of the video I'd seen already.

"He saved me. He saw them throw an explosive at us, and he pushed me out of the way," Evie said, wiping away tears.

I took her hand in mine, hardly able to keep my own tears under control. True to his name, Vir—Sanskrit for brave—died a hero. As much as I wished he'd run for it, I knew he wouldn't have been able to live with himself knowing he could have saved someone. So, I guess, one way or another I was always going to lose him to Corinth.

"I'm sorry," I said, choking up. "For the both of us. For Vir." Cautiously, I lifted the cup to my lips and took a tiny sip. "Ugh," I groaned. The vile liquid swished around my mouth for only a few seconds before I spat it back into my cup. This was worse than petrol, and yet somehow it had been an addictive phenomenon back in the day.

Evie's face lit up with amusement. "It's not that bad." She laughed.

"Oh yes, it is," I insisted, pushing my cup away from me. "Where does this even come from? I thought coffee went extinct."

"It did," Evie said, handing me some toast and jam. "For 99.9 percent of the population, anyway. But I don't know where Julius got his goodies from. He went up to D.C. sometimes, so I always figured he got it from a supplier there."

I didn't know if it was the coffee or what Evie just said, but I was suddenly wide awake. My vision shifted back into focus and narrowed on Evie. "And here I thought the colonies were self-sufficient." I remembered what Isaac had told me about the farms and greenhouse they had here.

"Well, the colonies do grow their own produce and have healthy-sized farms, but most of the other stuff is from the government," she explained between bites. "I don't remember exactly when we started to get aid, but I think it was Isaac's great-grandfather who convinced the White House to send us food and medicine and other equipment."

My mind conjured an image of Bull sitting on my couch in San Francisco. When we first met, Bull had been careful to tell me how few people in government knew of the colonies' existence. That conversation seemed like a lifetime ago. "In exchange for what?" I asked.

"Nobody knows," Evie said. "But I think part of the deal was for us to be left alone. Total protection and zero interference from the outside world."

In my mind, I imagined Corinth cloaked under an invisible dome that nobody could penetrate or even discover. A ghost town in every way, shape, and form. When I had looked up the words *Corinth, Oregon*, before I left San Francisco two days ago, I had found nothing relevant. No mention of an isolated Caucasian colony. Nothing. This pact ensured that not even future technology could trace the city or its inhabitants. It was astounding the lengths Isaac's ancestors had gone to protect and nurture their heritage and culture.

"So the colonies weren't always this isolated?" I said, making myself a cup of tea.

"Not to this extent, no," Evie said, resting her elbows over the counter. "I think once the white population reached a point of no return, all hell broke loose."

We had covered this portion of history in high school. Extreme right conservatives had rallied all over the world, not just the United States. South America, Europe (including the U.K.), Russia, and even India had targeted ethnic minorities. Citizenship had meant nothing if you looked different from the white majority.

Unfortunately for the racist conservatives, this level of umbrage only had the opposite effect. The multiracial population was blossoming beyond anybody's wildest dreams. Was it at this point that Bull's ancestors had thrown in the towel?

Was it then that they decided to cocoon themselves away from the burgeoning metamorphosis? What would they think of the colonies now?

"I'm really sorry about last night," Evie said, interrupting my thoughts.

"Thanks," I said. My face burned from the memory of Rebecca's attack. Somehow that irked me so much more than the beating I'd taken from the Federates yesterday. "I'm sorry you had to go through that too."

Evie smiled warmly. "It was going to happen sooner or later," she said. "And it was always going to be this ugly."

I looked at her sympathetically. It was hard to forget just how young she was. Evie was barely twenty-five, and she had already done so much to be proud of.

"Evie, I've been wondering about these trackers you all have," I said, trying very hard to sound calm. "Could Hexum track us here? He's been in Bull's office."

Evie shook her head. "Hexum can't track us," she said. "Only Julius and his council members—there's one for each colony—can access the system. Don't worry. Hexum would need to get approval from all seven members to be added to the system to actually track us."

"Couldn't he just bully them to give him access?"

"Hexum doesn't have a hold on the other colonies yet. He will soon, but time is on our side. The colonies are spread all over the country, and he'd probably have to go to each one and meet with them in person."

Sweet relief washed over me. Hexum was already on the warpath, and I hated to think about what he would do with that kind of technology at his disposal. "I assume you've taken yours out already?"

Evie peeked into the living room to make sure Rebecca, Isaac, and Florence were still asleep. Aside from Isaac's snoring, Rebecca and Florence were essentially comatose under the sheets. "Years ago," Evie admitted. "Almost as soon as I got here. Actually, I left mine at home yesterday."

We agreed that Rebecca, Isaac, and Florence should have theirs removed and destroyed before we left the safe house. Hexum's hunger for power might not be confined to Corinth for very long, and it might be prudent to stay under the radar, literally.

Isaac's loud snore broke my reverie. Evie and I didn't have much longer before the rest of the group woke up. "Evie, when did your Auge stop functioning?" I whispered urgently.

Surprised, Evie blinked self-consciously. "Shortly before you and Isaac came home," she said after a moment's reflection. "You?"

"About the same time," I said, thinking back to yesterday. "Did you know that Bull had a tech dampening device?"

Evie shook her head. "Is it still in his office?"

"No, I don't think so," I said, explaining what Isaac and I had seen at Bull's office. "Hexum probably has it."

"So that's why nothing will work. Jesus effing Christ!" Evie fumed. "Hexum. That bastard probably did it to make sure you couldn't call for help. And cutting me off was a bonus. I hope to God Orion got my message."

I didn't know Orion, but I hoped to God he got our message too. The image of Bull dead and tortured in his office flooded my mind's eye. I felt a twinge of regret that I couldn't get to him in time. In retrospect, I could see how clever the Federate Army had been. They had divided their enemies and struck us both at nearly the exact same time. If they had come after me an hour or so before going after Bull in his office, he might still be alive today.

17

THE DAY PASSED MOSTLY IN SILENCE. The tension between Evie and Rebecca was still running high, but the two women found a way to avoid each other altogether.

Rebecca spent most of the day lying on her cot with her back turned while Evie packed. Isaac also kept his distance from his wife, though there were fleeting moments of affection between the two. He had, by no means, moved past the things he'd learned, but it was encouraging to see him try. Florence, on the other hand, was as aloof as her mother. She barely spoke two words, and when she did, they were directed at Isaac.

Around noon, Evie herded us all back to the common area. "Hexum is going to find this place sooner or later," Evie cut right to it. "And I just don't want him going through this stuff."

Her concern was valid, I thought. Evie had spent the majority of her time in this bomb shelter building a community, planning, and creating a safe haven for anyone who needed it. We burned and shredded anything and everything, including Cara's diary. It was too much of a risk to leave everything be while the Federate Army was still out there hunting us.

"Where's the drone?" I asked her.

"Almost forgot about that," she said, walking over to the

water closet. Curious, I followed her. "It's not the best hiding spot, but it's right here." She opened the cabinet door and pulled out the drone I'd found in Bull's office two nights before.

We decided to break the drone apart into smaller pieces and take the backup SD card out, instead of bringing the whole thing with us. Even if Hexum's men found it, they wouldn't know what to do with it.

"Does anybody else have access to this place?"

Evie nodded thoughtfully. "Just a handful of people who've been helping me reach out to the kids and, you know, educating them on what's possible. I doubt they'll come back here, though," she said, looking around the safe house. "We always knew this was a possibility. And we agreed if one of us was compromised, we would take the fall for the others."

"What'll happen to the kids now?" I asked. "How are they going to get out?"

Now that Bull was out of the way and Hexum had taken full control of the city, I presumed that restrictions were probably going to get a lot more restrictive if they hadn't already. I shuddered at the thought of the staged propaganda events and student indoctrination programs Hexum would roll out now.

"I don't know," she admitted.

For the first time later that afternoon, Isaac addressed Evie. "How did you convince the kids to leave?"

Evie looked around, surprised. "It started with Iris," she said. "Remember Iris Gruger?"

"Yeah," Florence answered first. "She was the girl who always sang at mass. Wasn't she a couple of years older than Cara?"

"That's the one. I met her at the clinic one day, and she

looked like hell. This was in the early days. I had just moved here and didn't really know where to start. But she came in and..." Evie's voice broke slightly. "And I knew I had to do something."

Smart. If the kids, particularly the girls, were checking in with their doctor each month, and if they were as unhappy about it as Cara, then there was no better place to start than the clinic. I would've done the same. Evie's eyes were starting to swell up from all the tears. "And then I started teaching at the school, which made it easier to reach out to kids like her. It took some convincing, though. Some kids were harder to reach than others. And then talking them through the plan itself was another challenge. But, thankfully, I wasn't alone."

"What about Marte?" Florence asked. "How did she get caught last night?"

"She wasn't one of ours," Evie said. "Marte probably assumed the others just took off on their own. Poor kid. I wish I had known she needed help."

Rebecca, I noticed, had pulled a pillow over her head and was resolutely ignoring our conversation.

"Did they know?" Isaac asked. "The kids, I mean."

"Know what?" Evie frowned.

"About you."

"Yes," Evie said softly. "They knew."

Isaac's face turned bright red, but he didn't say anything more. It took me a second to realize why Isaac felt the need to ask something so obvious and then it hit me—dozens of people knew Evie's most precious secret while he was absolutely clueless about the comings and goings of the person he lived with. I know it wasn't the same, and I didn't see Vir as much as

Isaac saw Evie, but I could empathize with him.

"What will Cara do now?" Florence asked.

"Well, as soon as the kids arrive safely at the base, they're placed in foster care. And only with families that are equipped to handle special cases, where at least one person is a doctor or a therapist. You know, to help them adjust and adapt. So, what Cara does after she's successfully adapted to the new environment is up to her. She can continue studying and maybe go to university or can join the armed forces or travel or paint or... well, you get the idea." Evie painted an irresistible picture of the future outside Corinth. "The opportunities are truly endless."

Florence studied her sister-in-law with interest. "What are the people like out there?"

"Peaceful, for the most part," I responded immediately.

"And very different," Evie responded. "The color of their skin doesn't have any control over their identity. Neither does their religion or sexuality or even gender. They're not divided anymore. You know they don't even have border control anymore? People are free to travel and come and go as they please."

"Kinda like in Europe in the twenty-first century?" Isaac asked.

"Yes, exactly like that," Evie told him. "Of course, national identities didn't disappear, but after the war, when they truly and completely became One World, having borders didn't even make sense anymore. Their only choice was to adopt true freedom of movement. I think the colonies are the only ones with border patrol. Isn't that ironic?"

She stopped and waited for everyone to catch up. "And life

moves a lot faster than it does in the colonies. I know you've all heard the rumors about their technology, but just you wait!" She shook her head. "It's like nothing you've ever imagined."

"Is it true they can travel to space for a holiday?" Florence asked eagerly.

"But we're not going out there," Isaac warned. "We're going to Arizona where we'll be safe."

I would've preferred for the Bull-Smiths to abandon the colonies altogether, but convincing them would be a long shot. "You might want to consider the possibility that Arizona isn't safe from Hexum either," I chimed in when Evie didn't say anything. "You may not have a choice but to find a new home outside the colonies."

"He's right," Evie said, backing me up. "Hexum might already have his army waiting for us there. We'll be careful going in, but there's no telling what's happened over there."

"And, you know, you might even like life outside the colonies." I smirked. "You wouldn't have to hide anymore. You'd be free to go anywhere you like, do whatever you want."

Despite herself, Florence's face perked up. I could see the cogs turning in her mind; maybe she was finally starting to imagine another way of life. I hoped she was. I hoped that they all, even Rebecca, were starting to see that life didn't have to be so damn hard and that they had more choices than they could dream of.

LATER IN THE AFTERNOON, EVIE AND I

convinced the Bull-Smiths to let her take the microchips out. Surprisingly, Rebecca didn't put up too much of a fight, though she insisted Isaac be the one to remove it and not Evie.

"Normally, I'd have liked to have done this at the clinic with, you know, actual instruments, but I guess this will have to do," Evie said, handing Isaac some clean napkins, a small knife, and some warm water. "We don't have any alcohol either, I'm afraid."

Isaac had both Rebecca and Florence bite down on his belt while he made a tiny incision over their shoulder blades. Both mother and daughter handled it better than I expected, though it might have been a lot less painful for Evie to have taken them out. When Isaac pulled the microchips out with tweezers, I destroyed them by stomping on them.

"I can't believe those kids let you cut them open." Isaac shuddered while she worked on taking his tracker out.

"Why?" Evie snapped. "You're doing it right now."

"I'm just saying, you know, it's a lot of trust to put in a woman."

"You'd be surprised, Isaac, the pain people will gladly accept if it means a chance at freedom," Evie said, slapping an adhesive pad over his tiny cut.

"What I can't believe is that Bull put tracking chips in humans," I interjected before they began arguing.

We waited until it was dark to open the door connecting the underground tunnels.

The tunnel uncoiled endlessly in front of us. It was narrow and cramped, just large enough for two people to walk shoulder-to-shoulder. When Evie pulled open the hatch leading to the secondary escape route, cold, stale air from the tunnels emptied out into the bomb shelter.

We peeked into the passage over each other's shoulders, second-guessing our decision to leave through this exit. At least it was well lit; the solar-powered lamps illuminated the gloomy shaft just like they did everything inside the library and the rest of the building.

Corinth's forefathers had had the foresight to add a tunnel system to the bomb shelter during the early days of the war, just in case its inhabitants ever became trapped. I remembered what Bull's VR assistant had said as we drove through Corinth: the city was lucky to escape material destruction.

As the person most familiar with the tunnels, Evie climbed in first, and the rest of us followed her with uncertainty. Once again, I was the last one through. The dark gray walls were ice-cold to the touch, and the ceiling was no higher than my six feet and two inches. The top of my brown hair swept the plaster on the roof as we began the next part of our journey.

"Ready?" I asked, before pulling the heavy metal door closed behind me. Everyone except Rebecca nodded back.

"Oh!" Rebecca's eyes widened. "Wait! I forgot something!" She squeezed through the small opening and returned a few moments later, her face flushed. She quietly walked to Florence's side without saying anything.

The door slammed shut easily but sent strong vibrations through the tunnel. This was quite literally the road less traveled in Corinth. I wondered how many dissidents, how many sad, hurting teenagers, had taken this route out of Corinth as a last resort.

I couldn't imagine the terror they must have felt, the sadness and fear they had to overcome as they left the only home they'd ever known. What would I have done had I been in their situation? Would I have been able to leave my family behind? I couldn't say.

The number of runaways in comparison to Corinth's population wasn't particularly high, but that didn't mean everyone wanted to stay. A new concern was starting to gnaw at me. What would happen to the others now that Evie was leaving? Who would help other people get safely out of here?

The answer rang out like a bell, loud and clear. I was coming back to Corinth one way or another. There was no way that I could live in a world where men like Hexum roamed free. My brother gave his life so others could live without fear of persecution and hate. Now it was up to me to complete his mission or die trying.

Ahead of me, the Bull-Smiths walked in silence. Isaac whispered something indistinct to Evie, who nodded back wordlessly.

THE PIECES OF THE EVIE PUZZLE WERE starting to fall into place. We had covered a lot of ground during our chat over breakfast this morning, but there was so much I wanted to know about her mission and her life before Corinth. "So, Evie, how did you find this place?" I asked.

There was a subtle echo in the tunnel—everything from our footsteps to our breathing bounced off the walls.

"It wasn't hard. Every colony built one back in the day and... I guess you forget about things when you stop using them."

Isaac listened to everything she said with rapt attention. After all these years of living under the same roof, he was discovering the person behind the persona.

"Can you believe that even after all this time," Evie's voice echoed through the tunnel, "I'm still discovering new paths down here because the artery is so expansive?"

Isaac was just as eager to have his questions answered. "How were you able to ferry so many people out without raising any suspicion?"

"Yes, I've been wondering that too," Rebecca spoke up. "How did you start?"

She sighed. "Teenagers are very resilient. You never know what's really going on underneath until they tell you," she said. "I never doubted the kids who came to me with their problems. And, as for raising suspicion, nobody ever thought of me as anything more than a woman."

She stopped walking and glanced at Rebecca before turning to me. "The women of the colonies are essentially drones," she said. "Corinth is stuck in the pre-Millennial era when inequality and sexism were commonplace."

"Not to worry, dear." Rebecca fake-smiled at Evie. "Of all the things one might accuse you of, it would never be of being a drone."

Florence walked quietly beside me. She had barely said

anything about the fire or her father. In fact, she was holding up very gracefully. Florence had lost more than anyone else. Together with her home, her grandfather, and her dad, she had lost her childhood. And now she had inherited the burden of fulfilling the family's honor. With Cara gone and Isaac married to a multiracial woman, Florence was Rebecca's last hope for redemption in the colonies.

However, I suspected that Florence had come dangerously close to letting her family down. She had, on at least two occasions, told me with as much conviction as her brother that I would never find Cara. What I had chalked up to teenage attitude had actually been prior knowledge of the situation.

Florence knew what Cara was planning all along, but her surprise at learning Evie was Raptor had been genuine. If Cara hadn't trusted Florence with Evie's secret, then we had both come to the same conclusion: Florence truly was a blueblood. She was a model citizen of Corinth.

And yet she had ended up on a path she never intended to be on.

"You know you'll probably see your sister again very soon," I said in a reassuring voice.

Florence looked up at me in surprise. "Yeah, maybe." She didn't sound convinced. She sounded vastly different from the person I'd talked to earlier. Florence had lost her gusto, and her innocence had been replaced by a quiet, worrisome attitude in the span of a few hours. After Aric died, my personality shifted as well. I wasn't carefree or careless anymore. I was fueled by anger and hate for a long time. Florence would be, too, but I sincerely hoped it wouldn't be for as long.

We continued down the passage without saying another word. It was a long and weary walk, and the fact that we were only just getting started on this journey felt emotionally and physically taxing. And yet all these teenagers had had the gumption to do it. They persevered and overcame their fears and physical limits to escape.

Knowing they were somewhere out there, far away from Corinth's racial bias and agenda, made the last two days worth it. Still, I was starting to feel nervous about leaving the safe house. In there, the only people I had to contend with were the Bull-Smiths, and they had been so wrapped up in their own drama and dealing with the deaths of Jonathan and Bull that they had nearly forgotten that our skin tones didn't match. But soon we'd be back up in the city again, and there was no telling who we might run into. Hexum had probably declared all of us personae non gratae, and I wouldn't be at all surprised if there were a bounty on my head.

For now, I focused on the tunnels ahead of us. They were unmarked, and it often felt like we were just going around in circles, but Evie assured us we were still on the correct path. We walked for over an hour until Evie came to a halt in front of a narrow metal ladder that led to a hatch door a few meters up.

"This is it," Evie announced.

The tall ladder was another reminder of how deep beneath the ground we really were. Evie turned around and looked at us expectantly as if waiting for a question or comment, but none came. I volunteered to go up first, but Evie insisted that she be the one to go up. She started to climb when Isaac stopped her and pulled back.

"Listen, before we go up there..." he whispered—unfortunately, he hadn't taken into account the fact that everything echoed loud and clear when he decided to have a word in private with her. "I just wanted to say..." Isaac hesitated.

"Yes?" Evie said expectantly.

"I love you." Isaac grabbed her hand and kissed it. "I just wanted you to know that. I know I've been a shitty 'husband'" he said, using air quotes, "but I just wanted you to hear it."

Evie's face turned bright red, and her right hand clutched her chest. This was the last thing she (or any of us) had expected him to say. "Thank you for saying that. Really, thank you." Conscious of everyone staring at them, Evie raised on her tiptoes and kissed Isaac on the forehead. "But you know that I don't love you the same way? I do love you very much, but just not romantically, and I don't want to lead you on anymore."

Tearfully, Isaac nodded. "Yeah, yeah I get that," he said. "I guess our *marriage* was only ever real to me."

"I am very sorry... for everything. But I have to be honest now that I can be." She then leaned in and whispered something only Isaac could hear. When she was done, Evie wiped away the tears streaming down her face.

And just like that, it was over. The secrets and lies that had built up over the years were all out in the open. They wouldn't have to walk on eggshells around each other anymore. Their marriage may have come to an end, but there was no doubt that their friendship would survive this.

Touched by this awkward-tender moment, I volunteered to go up first and scout the area for any threats while Evie and Isaac collected themselves. I pushed open the hatch just high enough to peek through; there was nothing but wilderness. Tall, willowy trees stood motionless in the deadly silence.

I climbed slowly out of the hatch and surveyed the area before allowing anyone else to join me. There was nothing I saw here that constituted a threat, but I was wary all the same.

The two-mile underground pathway had brought us to a heavily forested area in the middle of nowhere. It was only when my eyes adjusted to the darkness that I realized that only a handful of trees were still living. Rot and insects had seeped into their cambial layer, and shrubs were spreading out of control. Most others were dead or damaged from forest fires. Their charred bark and singed branches looked eerie in the darkness.

Although we were only a few miles away from the city center, it felt like we had walked into another world entirely. There was a stillness in the woods that felt dreamlike.

My eyes instinctively searched the skies. In big cities like San Francisco, a substratum of light and smog pollution effectively disconnected the heavens from us mere mortals. The only time I'd seen the Milky Way was during a family trip around the moon when Aric was still alive. But this was something else. The sky was incandescent and seemed like one uninterrupted entity with stars packed so closely together. Suddenly, I felt tiny and irrelevant, very aware of my short lifespan in comparison to these infinite gas giants.

A soft rustling sound behind me tore my attention away from the stunning night sky. I turned around, braced to find one of the Federate Army's creatures, only to find Rebecca awkwardly holding herself. She was acting stranger than usual, and I made a mental note to keep a closer eye on her.

"What now?" I asked once everyone was above ground.

Evie signaled for our attention and gestured for us to

come closer. It was highly plausible that the Federates could catch us by surprise, and after the deaths the Bull-Smiths had endured, letting our guard down wasn't an option.

We gravitated toward her and formed a close circle. I found myself uncomfortably sandwiched between Rebecca and Florence. "So, we've still got a couple of miles ahead of us," Evie whispered as softly as she could. "Keep your eyes open, and if you see or hear anything remotely dangerous, run. Just run as fast and as far as you can."

"I'm really scared," Florence moaned. She was studying the ground beneath her feet.

Isaac put his arm protectively around her shoulder. "I am too." He gave Florence a quick kiss on the temple.

"Don't worry, I have a plan," Evie answered reassuringly.

"Which is what, exactly?" Rebecca demanded.

We looked at Evie expectantly. Her Plan A had been to call for help, but with the GPS dampener in Hexum's hands, that was out of the question. Which meant she was on to Plan B.

"Hexum and the Federates will be expecting us to go for the family jet." She hesitated. "They've probably surrounded the hangar already, just sitting there waiting for us."

"So, we're not taking the jet?" Florence sounded surprised.

"No. I was thinking of something a little bit more innocuous—the chopper," she answered. "They won't be guarding it."

"How can you be sure?" I interjected.

"I can't." She breathed out heavily. "But if I were Hexum, I wouldn't waste manpower on patrolling the other side of the hangar, because he knows we rarely use it."

"That's hardly an advantage," I noted.

"Do you have a better idea?" she threw back at me.

I thought about it for a second and shook my head. Evie's plan was going to have to do.

"Well, if nothing else," Isaac said, rubbing his neck, "it just gives us a good head start."

I considered them both carefully. As a rule, I never went into a situation, especially one that was dangerous, with a low chance of success, without being prepared. Ideally, I would've liked to study the terrain and layout of this airfield before going in.

I could almost sense the danger we were walking into, but there was more danger in staying. The Bull-Smiths and I would be hunted like animals, and in a city so small, the options to stay low and hidden were severely limited.

"And who's going to fly that thing?" Rebecca asked.

Evie turned around, and their eyes met in the darkness. "It can fly itself, Rebecca," she said. "It's called autopilot."

18

IT WAS HARD TO BELIEVE THERE WAS ever a time when Corinth was considered one of the most stunning places in the world. But, according to Evie, every year thousands of people had visited its snow-capped mountains, swum in its emerald-green inland sea, and gotten engaged by the luscious lavender fields.

"Corinth was supposed to be so picturesque that it was impossible to take a bad photograph anywhere," she said softly.

Isaac, Rebecca, and Florence marched ahead in silence, except for the occasional grunt or complaint. The reality of the situation was probably starting to sink in—the Bull-Smiths had gone from being heavyweights to fugitives. And they were starting to realize that coming back to Corinth was never going to be an option. Evie had said it best before we left: if they wanted to survive, they had no choice but to keep moving forward.

She and I walked shoulder-to-shoulder, watching their silhouettes dragging along. I doubted Evie had joined me because she wanted company. Rebecca was growing anxious, and I figured Evie wanted to put some distance between herself and her mother-in-law.

"I have to admit," I whispered back, "when I think of Corinth, I don't think picturesque."

"Yeah, neither do I." She grinned back.

"Tell me about my brother."

"What do you want to know?"

"Anything, everything!" I said. Vir had kept so much of himself private because of his work, and I was starting to wonder if I ever really knew him. "I want to know who he was, who his friends were, his interests... I hate that my brother was a stranger."

Evie got that far-away look on her face again. "Vir is the smartest, bravest, and most thoughtful man I know. Knew. He hated keeping his job a secret from you and your parents, but those were the rules," she said. "I knew the moment I met him he was special. He talked about you and Aric all the time. Losing your brother had a bigger impact on him than he was willing to admit, but every decision, every choice he made always reflected that loss. I can only imagine how hard this must be for you."

"It is," I said. "God, I miss him and Aric. But it helps to know that he had someone he could talk to. That he wasn't alone. It must've been hard leaving him behind and coming here."

"More than you can imagine, but we both knew this mission was more important than either one of us. I think, for Vir, after what happened to Aric, he couldn't live with himself knowing other children were suffering. It would've been harder to live with ourselves knowing we didn't do anything to help."

A familiar ache tugged against my chest. Aric had cast a long shadow over both our lives. He would be proud, I hoped, of both Vir and I and the choices we had made in our lives. "You don't have to answer this, but I'm just curious how you made it work. You know..."

"With me being married to someone else?" Evie finished my sentence. "With a lot of trust. And the promise of the future. We had things to look forward to when all this was over. I'll admit there were days when it felt impossibly hard, but thank goodness for my Auge."

My eyes stung. Vir and Evie were proof that love could survive the harshest conditions. I'd never loved anyone half as much as Vir and Evie had loved each other. They had endured distance and deception. A part of me was envious. Was I even capable of falling in love? I didn't know. The losses kept piling up, and it was getting harder to see past the pain.

"I miss him so damn much."

"Me too."

WITHOUT THE AUGE, MY NATURAL SENSES had come alive. My hearing had grown sharper and my eyes had adjusted to the darkness. Still, it would have been nice to know precisely what time it was and to check our surroundings for heat signatures.

Cold breath escaped Evie's lips. She was at a loss for words, and I was exhausted. My injuries from yesterday's attack were really starting to set in. We persisted in silence, each in our own thoughts.

It was an unusually cold July night. Thick fog blanketed the tree line and stretched deep into the foliage. The landscape changed so gradually that I didn't notice the difference at first. Tall trees receded to shrubs, and the scenery opened up, making it impossible to know where the vista started and the sky ended.

"We're here," Evie announced, walking back to the front.

The airfield was the size of a football field with a dome-shaped hangar on the far end. Without my Auge's scanning capability, there was no way of knowing who or what was lurking in the shadows.

The Bull-Smiths and I stayed as low as we could. I recognized the Huracan from my ride to Corinth. It looked even more dominating in the dark.

The only problem was that it was still a hundred yards away from us. Everything in between was open and exposed; without cover, we would need to run like hell.

"It's so far away!" Florence whined.

I silently agreed with her. The chopper was too far, and running that length was a terrible risk, but it was a small comfort to everyone besides Rebecca that Hexum would never hurt anyone of child-bearing age. Of course, it didn't matter that I was a healthy, young male because I was disqualified for the hue of my skin.

Rebecca put a reassuring hand on Florence's shoulder and squeezed it. Her pearly skin was flushed with bright red specks, and her swollen red eyes illuminated her blue irises.

"I don't see anyone." Isaac peeked through the bushes. Even though it was a frosty night, his shirt was moist with sweat and clung desperately to his back. I hoped to God he wasn't feeling an urgent need for a wastebasket again.

"I forgot to bring my damn binoculars," Evie berated herself.

"Maybe they're not here?" Florence asked hopefully.

"Oh, they're here," Evie answered with conviction.

Evie was right. Even I could smell it, that foul wet dog

smell. The Federate goons were here. Hiding somewhere in the shadows, watching and waiting.

There was only one course of action ahead of us. "We should split up," I suggested.

Florence shuddered involuntarily, and the rest of them looked at me in surprise. It was understandable, given everything that had happened the last couple of days, that they did not like the idea of separating, but to me, it was clear that that was the only way we could make it.

"No," Isaac said in a level tone. "I veto that idea. We are not going to separate."

"We have to," I said. "Five people running across a field will draw too much attention. If we separate into two groups and go around, we have a better chance of surviving."

"Isaac, you're not going to let monkey boy tell you what to do, are you?" Rebecca asked in a chiding tone.

I pretended not to hear her and waited for Isaac to answer instead. Ever since Evie had told us about her multiracial ethnicity, I'd been wondering if Isaac might turn over a new leaf and maybe even move past his bias. Behavioral change to that extent would be hard to master overnight, but if his feelings for his wife were genuine, I couldn't see it being that much of a challenge.

When he didn't immediately respond, Evie nudged him.

Isaac's head tilted from Evie's direction to mine and finally to Rebecca. "Mom, could you not talk about Jimmy like that?" he reproached Rebecca. "Evie is multiracial and I accept her. If you can't, that's your problem, but I won't allow it."

Evie beamed at him, but Rebecca looked as if she had been slapped in the face. I nodded appreciatively at Isaac.

"And no, we are not separating!" Isaac turned to me again. "That's not up for debate!"

Reluctantly, I acquiesced. That left us with only one option: run like hell. Like marathon runners, we crouched down and counted to five and let our feet barrel across the concrete ground.

The first thing I noticed was the cold air. Running against it was uncomfortable and made it hard to breathe.

I looked over my shoulder every few seconds, expecting to see hounds chasing us, but it was oddly quiet. No leather-clad men fired in our direction; no hungry, red-eyed mutts surrounded us. The only sound I could discern was my own heart beating wildly against my chest.

Where are they? I wondered. Could we have gotten lucky? Maybe they weren't here after all.

No, something was amiss, and I couldn't figure out what it was. We slowed down when we were less than fifty feet from the chopper. At this point, we were still in the clear when I heard a gun cocking close behind me. My body spun around immediately to find the source of the weapon.

From the corner of my eye, I saw Rebecca holding something small in her right hand and pointing it right at Evie. Time decelerated. Seconds expanded into infinity.

It was one of those bizarre moments where I could see in my mind's eye what was coming, and I pivoted forward to block her shot, but it was too late—Rebecca had already pulled the trigger. Florence screamed, midway through a 180-degree turn, her feet caught in a fall. Isaac and Evie turned away, trying to shield themselves from the assault.

There were two audible cracks in the air. One shot came

from Rebecca's smoking revolver, but the bullet meant for Evie missed and hit Florence in the shoulder instead. Suddenly, I realized this is why Rebecca went back into the safe house before we left. *Idiot woman.*

As for the second shot, I couldn't tell where it came from.

The mystery round went straight through Rebecca's right eye from the back of her head, shattering her scalp into pieces. Florence screamed again at the sight of the cranial fluid and brain matter that had splattered all over the ground. The bottom half of Rebecca's face was undamaged, and the ghost of her smile was frozen in place.

A third shot went through the air. I searched for the sniper, but all I could tell from the trajectory was that the shot had come from the woods behind us. Panic gripped my stomach. I was suddenly very aware of the nerves connecting my body and the blood rushing to my head. A small voice in my head screamed for me to run, but my body seemed rooted, desperate to find the shooter.

Rebecca's death was a harrowing sight. Seconds after her body fell on the tarmac, my legs buckled. I landed painfully on my side. The ache in my left leg was exquisite. The sniper had gotten a good shot; the bullet had hit bone and was lodged there. I tried to crawl away, but there was nowhere to hide, and there was very little I could do to stop the blood gushing out of my thigh.

The Federate Army, wherever they were, had learned from their mistake and outsmarted us this time. Instead of ambushing us on the tarmac and risking another teargas attack, they had debilitated their targets from afar.

A strange, inhuman noise distracted me momentarily from my discomfort. I looked up and saw a large animal charging at me with astonishing speed. Its bloodshot eyes gleamed with hunger.

Up close, the beast looked wild and muscular, almost like a jaguar or leopard. Powerful and terrifyingly fast. It would be here in less than a minute.

I turned to Florence, Evie, and Isaac and screamed, "Run!"

Isaac and Evie were helping Florence get back up on her feet when they realized the hellhounds were loose on the airfield. Isaac stepped forward to help me, but Evie held him back. Our eyes met, and I waved my hands at them. Florence needed Isaac to pick her up and carry her to the chopper. It was too late for Rebecca and me, but they still had a chance.

"Go!" I screamed. "Just go!"

The beast was attracted by the fresh blood seeping out of Rebecca's body. It glared at me, teeth dripping with saliva, readying itself for a big meal.

The hound was getting closer and closer by the second, and my body was going into shock. This was it. This was how it all ended for me. I would never marry or have a family, and I certainly would not live to be 110 like my grandpa—my life was going to end in this filthy town where I would only be remembered as *chinky*.

Behind me, Isaac had Florence over his shoulder, and he turned around to look at me one last time. Regret and shame surged over his face. I nodded at him in understanding, and he nodded back. For just one moment, we were simpatico. We had put aside our differences, and we were just two people expressing sadness. In another life, he and I might have been great friends, but for now, we quietly said goodbye to each other.

The weight of the beast crushed against my chest. Its sharp claws tore into my skin. I was delirious with pain. My scream sounded unreal and alien even to me. The animal was so close to my face I could see the inside of its mouth, its sharp cusped teeth and wet tongue, hungry for my blood. The stench of the creature was far more overpowering, though. My senses were overwhelmed, and my adrenaline capped out.

19

THERE WAS NO END TO THIS NIGHTMARE. No matter how hard I tried to wake myself up, I slipped further and further away from reality.

In the dream, someone had wrapped a tourniquet over my wounded thigh. Through the ripped pants and dried blood, I could see where the bullet had torn through the muscle and bone. When I tried to touch it, it became clear my arms were shackled behind my back. I was stuck in a dark abyss, cold and frightened, with no way out and no one to help me.

Wake up! Wake up! WAKE UP!

I gasped. My eyes fluttered open, and I fought my way out of the blankets, drenched in sweat. The relief of waking up in the safety of my apartment in San Francisco had an immediate remedying effect on my body; my overworked heart found a calm rhythm, and the cold sweats were gone.

It was just a dream. I laughed.

There was no Corinth or Bull, and there was no such thing as the colonies. It was all just a dream. I dropped my head gently back onto the pillow, closed my eyes, and smiled at my own overactive imagination.

Against the pin-drop silence was a noise that didn't belong in my bedroom, though—a deep cruel laugh. I could tell the voice was laughing at my pain. The recognition somehow multiplied the cackle. It was now seeping out of my mouth, the walls, the furniture... the cachinnation turned into a loud maniacal high-pitched scream.

I gasped again, more painfully this time. My eyes, bloodshot and swollen, flashed open—this time I really was awake. The screams were real, and they were coming from somewhere inside of my body.

It was real. All of it. The Federate Army had brought me back to an old church. Ancient, really. I wasn't expecting that— to be alive, that is—but their choice of headquarters didn't surprise me in the least.

A fresh bout of dread swept over me, gnawing against my insides like fingernails scratching against a wall. Death would have been preferable to my current predicament—the last thing I wanted was to be a prisoner to the Federate Army.

It was alarming how much trouble they had gone through to capture and then keep me alive. The sniper had aimed for my leg, not the heart or the head like they had with Rebecca.

They had meant to capture me alive, but why? I was hardly the catch Rebecca was. As Bull's only daughter, she brought more to the table than I ever could. Unless that was exactly why they killed her. From what I learned from Evie, the colonies had always had a member of the Bull family running the show. A dynasty rule that would have allowed Rebecca to take over had Hexum not challenged her father. Strategically, it made sense to off the person next in line. They were keeping me alive because they wanted something. Maybe they wanted to find Cara and eliminate Bull's entire line?

But the reason didn't matter, not now. I needed to get out.

But where was I exactly? I looked around desperately.

The ornamental floor tiles under my feet were bloodstained and dirty. Candle wax had built up a stratum of foundations, and the walls smelled distinctly wet and moldy. It was only when I searched the ceilings that I realized where exactly I was. A crucified figurine of one of the old gods, Christ, looked down at me in anguish.

When the Federate Army redecorated their new headquarters, they had kept very few of the original sacred objects and furnishings. Only the statues and pictures of Jesus, the Blessed Mother, and the saints remained in their original spots, along with the fourteen Stations of the Cross that circled the walls of the nave. But the pews, the altar, and other pieces of furniture had been broken apart and used for firewood. The chandeliers and most of the sacred objects were also gone. Instead, a miasma of dry stale blood, barbeque, and candle wax dominated the nave.

This scene was just like my nightmare: the Federate Army had confined me to a chair, cuffed my wrists against my back, secured the wounded leg with a tourniquet, and bound both legs together. Of all the times I wished my dreams would come true, this was not one of them.

I attempted to wring my wrists out of the metal cuffs, but it was useless; the handcuffs were fastened so tightly that I couldn't even dislocate my fingers from this angle.

That left me with only one option—escape on foot. If I could just unfasten the lasso around my ankles, limping (or maybe even crawling) out of here on my right leg should be possible.

There was no way to know the full extent of my injuries without a functioning Auge, and I was wary of damaging the muscle in my wounded leg any more than it already was. I tried to leverage my right leg to do the heavy lifting. First, I tried to stand up on my toes, but the weight of my body was too much for my bum leg to bear.

I took a deep cleansing breath and closed my eyes. It was a meditation technique trick I'd learned from my father as a child. The body is constantly talking to you; you just have to learn to listen.

Carefully, I let go of my inhibitions and listened to my body—I began, as always, with my feet and carefully migrated up to the rest of my body.

Body sensing told me there was no major damage besides the wounded leg and minor head injury, but I was terribly fatigued, dehydrated, and stressed. I tried to get up again, if only a few inches. Maybe the force of the fall might break the chair apart and free me. But my leg had met its limit.

"Dammit!" I cursed loudly.

"Don't even bother," a gruff voice advised me from the darkness.

Startled by the unexpected presence, I craned my neck to find the speaker. The voice was male and sounded familiar, but it didn't belong to Isaac—this was a slightly higher and more aggressive tone.

I looked around the chamber more carefully this time. The Federate Army had left me in the center of the room, facing the old altar area. Many years had passed since I had attended mass, but this church was unlike any I had ever been to.

The only source of light came in from the stained-glass

windows, but the moonlight was not strong enough to defeat the shadows. The voice, I was certain, had come from somewhere in front of me, but I looked over my shoulder to make sure there was no one stalking me from behind.

As if on cue, the sound of heavy metal chains scratched the moldy walls on my left. I could just about make out the silhouette of a tall muscular man standing against the wall in an odd posture: the way he had his arms over his head reminded me of the statue of the crucifixion.

"Who are you?" I called out.

The shadows released a large figure by just an iota. I gaped at the wretched creature—the man was stark naked, chained to heavy swinging cuffs on the wall, and his body was ravaged by grotesque boils and fresh bruises. He had been flagellated recently—his torso and back were covered with bloody gashes, and his feet were black from dirt and blood.

It was the eyes, however, despite their swelling and clots, that gave away the man's identity. I would have recognized those snake-like slits with dual-colored irises anywhere—I had seen them on two different occasions since arriving in Corinth, and both times he had tried to kill me.

Since arriving in Corinth, I'd experienced a whole spectrum of emotions, but I never expected to feel pity for my attacker, Clayton. This man had failed to capture me on two accounts, and now he was a pawn in Hexum's elaborate scheme to intimidate me. Hexum was going to have to try much harder than that to frighten me.

A scream echoed through the church, startling us both. It wasn't a voice that I recognized.

My head swirled with anger. Rebecca's savagery had doomed us all. If she hadn't stopped to fire at Evie, we might have all had a chance of making it to the chopper, and she might have even survived. I still didn't know if the Bull-Smiths had made it to safety. I hoped they did. The last thing I'd seen before I passed out was Isaac struggling to help his baby sister up, and Evie screaming for them to run. The fact that they weren't in the room was a good sign.

But if the Federate Army had captured the family, they might be keeping them somewhere else. After all, Isaac and Evie were of good child-rearing ages, Florence was quickly getting there, and the Federate Army valued that fertility more than anything else.

No, I told myself. *They made it out.*

The church door creaked open, and the shadow of a large man fell on the altar. My eyes tracked the shadow and watched it shrink until a corporeal being took its place.

The newcomer ignored both me and Clayton and settled into the throne-like chair at the altar. I strained my eyes to get a better look at him. The man was blonde, pudgy around the waist, and had blotchy red spots all over his face. He reeked of barbecue and alcohol.

Both Clayton and I watched him expectantly, hoping he was here for the other one, but the man seemed more focused on flicking his lighter on and off than anything else.

Minutes ticked by in tense silence until he transferred his attention to me. "You know, I've never met a colored person before. Tell me, do you tell each other apart?" A vile grin spread across his face.

At first sight, he looked completely unremarkable, but there was no doubt that this man was capable of great violence. Even his voice was barely above a whisper, but spine-chilling.

My mind only half-registered the intent behind his question. Somewhere deep within my body, fear and panic started to flood my bloodstream.

The man narrowed his eyes, the smile disappeared, and his features grew serious when I didn't answer. "Do you know who I am?"

Of course I did. Hexum was hard to forget, but I didn't answer. I knew better than to engage with the enemy. The Federates were in all likelihood going to torture me like they had Clayton, maybe even more brutally. But I had trained for this likelihood. They could break me in pieces, set those red-eyed monsters loose on me again, but I would not give them the satisfaction of cracking.

"Do you know who I am?" he repeated, enunciating every word slowly.

Aggravated by my pronounced silence, he stood up from his throne and made his way to Clayton's side of the nave. "No?" he asked, inspecting Clayton's chains. "Well, maybe Clayton can introduce us?" He patted Clayton on the face like a dog. "Tell him who I am, Clay."

Clayton's chains rattled loudly. "This is Leland Hexum, and he's the new leader of the seven colonies," he croaked immediately. "He has taken responsibility for all the souls here and those that are yet to be born."

"Why don't you tell him why you're here?"

Clayton gulped loudly. "I'm here because I failed." The big

lug's voice broke. "I failed to carry out orders. I failed to capture you." He nodded his chin toward me. "I failed at everything."

It was astonishing and painful to watch this giant of a man break down. But Hexum could not have looked happier. He smiled. Hexum was enjoying this. Taunting Clayton. Taunting me. The surge of superiority he clearly felt when he belittled the people around him.

Hexum turned to face me next. "Now you know who I am," he said. "And I, of course, know why you're here."

That was not a good sign. Whatever Hexum thought he knew could only mean that the reason they were keeping me alive now was ...for fun. The prospect of being tortured for pure entertainment, rather than acquiring information, was less acceptable (albeit equally terrifying). I didn't like it, but I knew that engaging with the enemy might be my only way out of this mess. All I had to do was keep Hexum talking and hope that would be enough to delay whatever torture he had planned for me.

"If you know why I'm here, then there's really no reason for us to be talking, is there?"

"Cute," Hexum said. "But we do have something to talk about. Tell me, *detective*"—he enunciated the word like it was a curse—"who else knows you're here?"

Cold sweat trailed down the length of my spine. "I'll answer your question if you answer mine," I offered.

Hexum didn't react one way or another. "Okay," he said, returning to his throne. "Who knows you're here?"

It was obvious why Hexum was asking. My death at the hands of the Federates, if proven, could start a chain reaction. The colonies might stand to lose whatever support they had from the government as retribution for the death of one of their own. Hexum couldn't afford to make enemies.

On the other hand, Hexum and his Army could easily dismiss my death as an accident. Maybe even pin it on Rebecca, call it the work of a deranged mother. It might just work.

"My partner, a couple of colleagues from the force, the governor of California and possibly of Oregon, and whoever else Bull told." I intentionally left Evie's team off the list.

Hexum simply nodded. "Your turn, then."

"I want to know where Isaac and his family are. I want to know if they made it out of this hellhole."

Hexum feigned nausea. "Why do you care so much about these people?" he asked. "You know you're the reason half that family is dead, don't you?"

"They're only dead because you killed them. You and your trigger-happy goons. I've seen the pictures. I know what you did to those poor kids."

Like a snake sheds its skin, Hexum shed his calm demeanor. He lunged from his throne and began pacing and hissing like an animal, exposing his sharp white teeth.

"Goons?" he screamed at me, "Goons? How unoriginal! Can you believe it, Clayton?"

In response, Clayton wordlessly slunk further into the shadows.

"How dare you!" Hexum spat.

"I just want to know where my friends are," I said. "I want to know if they're safe."

"'Where my friends are,'" Hexum mocked. "They're not your friends!"

Hexum crouched down so we were eye to eye. We were terribly close to each other, so close that I could see faint red lines in the blue of Hexum's irises. Those same eyes traveled down to my wound and back up again, taunting me for what he was about to do.

Instinctively, I clenched my jaw just before Hexum poked the gunshot wound, working his finger until a fresh stream of blood spilled out. I stifled a scream and forced myself to look Hexum in the eye while he did it. My brother died fighting this man and everything he stood for, and I'd be damned if I didn't do the same.

Hexum's cold breath brushed uncomfortably against my skin. "What I want to know is why you've been helping all of our precious children leave their homes, their families?"

Not this again. My head inclined away from Hexum's face. "I don't know why you think that when you know I just got here."

"Spare me the lies," Hexum said, suddenly grabbing a fistful of my hair. "I have always suspected that someone, some traitorous rat bastard, was helping people—no, encouraging them, forcing them—to defect! And right under my nose! Too many little boys and girls made it out of the city, and I think you are that someone who helped them."

Hexum pulled against my skull and jabbed me in the face with his free hand. A fresh jet of blood ran down my nose and dripped against the already bloodstained floor. "Where is she? Where did you take Cara Bull-Smith?"

"Why do you care?" I spat.

Hexum's face lit up in wonder. "Why do I care?" He

laughed. "Good God, are you chinkies all this stupid? Or is it just the black ones? I want to find Cara and all her little friends so that they can fulfill the commitment they made to our great colonies." Hexum looked at me with disgust. "And I will find them. Oh, I promise you I will. And when I do, they will deliver us healthy offspring."

Every time I heard the word *offspring* in this context, my whole body revolted. Having children should be a joyous occasion for any couple, and yet in Corinth, it was a brutal expectation. "Neither Cara nor any of the other kids committed to this," I said. "They should never have been asked to!"

"Cara committed when she was born!" Hexum's voice boomed through the empty nave. "Just like him"—he pointed at Clayton, who shifted uncomfortably in the darkness—"and just like me, just like everybody else. Every able-bodied man and woman must perform their duties."

"Like you have?" I smirked. Men like Hexum were few and far between, but egos like that were all cut from the same cloth. Behind his machismo and vindictive attitude, if I remembered anything from my college psych class, could only be an insecure narcissistic bully with extreme anxiety. I chose my next words carefully and hoped they would pay off. "If you can't produce any offspring, why should anybody else be forced to?"

Hexum's eyes ballooned with shock, but before he could retort or hit me again, I said, "Oh yeah, I know all about your... inadequacies." I nodded at his nether regions. "What does it feel like to be so powerless? To be unable to produce the one thing you fight so hard for?"

The righteous anger emanating from Hexum's body was blinding. With every kick and punch, I felt Hexum's aggression, built-up disappointment, and hatred. I represented everything he hated in this world: I could see it plainly in his eyes. Broken and brutalized as I was at this moment, my life represented the end of his.

My mind disconnected from my body and was so far gone I could barely hear a thing that Hexum screamed at me. I thought I heard the word *monster*, but it was hard to be certain.

When Hexum's hands and feet could no longer throw punches, he pulled out his trusty whip. The first crack flagellated the ground, sending minor shockwaves through the concrete.

Above us, the reflections from the stained-glass windows changed colors ever so subtly. Dawn was approaching, and a warm orange glow took over the chapel. Outside, a silhouette passed so quickly between the windows I thought I imagined it. The room felt hazy, and I could hardly keep my eyes open anymore. I had lost a lot of blood and hadn't slept all night. I was probably hallucinating. I struggled against the primal need to let my senses slip away and let my body shut down. I could already feel the fear and anxiety fading away. *It's not a bad way to go...*

Maybe Hexum noticed it, too, because he grabbed me by the collar and raised his palm again. Surprised by his reaction, my senses jolted awake, and I took advantage of the proximity between us to headbutt him as hard as I could.

At that precise moment, the windows above us shattered, sending shards of stained glass everywhere.

From the corner of my eye, I saw a cylindrical-shaped

projectile land at Clayton's feet. The smoke bomb dispersed throughout the nave, enveloping everything in darkness. Clayton screamed, but the chains kept him in place.

This was the moment I had been waiting for. When Hexum staggered to his feet, I gathered whatever little stamina I had left to lift the chair off the ground and body-slam it into Hexum's body.

It worked. The chair landed, with me still chained to it, on Hexum's chest.

"Get off of me!" he screamed.

Even with a wooden chair between us, I could feel Hexum writhing in pain, struggling to get free. Through the thick smoke, the church doors blasted open and several soldiers rushed in.

Hexum's chubby hands reached for my throat, desperately trying to throttle me. It was a struggle, but I managed to slam my head into his nose before Hexum could choke me to death.

Next to me, Clayton screamed obscenities, kicking the soldiers as they tried to approach him until someone shot him with a tranquilizer and then did the same to Hexum. That someone was a robust-looking man wearing heavy military gear and a night vision visor that did little to hide a thin scar that ran across the side of his face. He walked over to me and began untying me. I couldn't hear the words coming out of his mouth, but I got the impression they were meant to be reassuring.

"Are you Orion?" I asked, before succumbing to the heavy darkness bearing over my eyes.

20

I KNEW I WAS SAFE EVEN BEFORE I opened my eyes. I could feel it. My mind and body felt like mine again. Strong and healthy.

The sickly clean sterile smell of a hospital gave away my current location. Aware of nano-monitors attached to my chest and temples, my hand carefully reached for my wounded leg. The bullet was gone, and the doctors, whoever they were, had already rehabilitated the lacerated muscles. Chances were good that, by the end of the night, I would barely even have a scar to remember the trauma by.

The first thing I saw when I opened my eyes was a doctor checking the monitors I was attached to. She was a second-generation hybrid. Most of her face and skull, parts of her right arm, and both legs and hip were replaced with robotic parts. That kind of procedure was limited to the armed forces and for soldiers wounded in combat. That could only mean that I was in a military hospital.

The doctor's human eye met mine. "Ah, you're finally awake," she said. "I'm Captain Medin. We've been worried about you."

How long had I been here? Instinct kicked in, and I blinked in sequence to activate my Auge, but nothing happened. I tried again and again but still nothing. Panic sent my heart rate into a frenzy.

"Please try to stay calm." Captain Medin put her hand on my shoulder. "Your Auge was damaged. We had to take it out, but we'll get you a new one as soon as you're well enough to handle the procedure."

"Oh," I said faintly. "How long have I been here?"

"A week," she said sympathetically.

Knots grew in my stomach. A week. Corinth was a week ago.

"You've been in a medically induced coma," Captain Medin said.

"Where am I?" I asked.

"Military base in Nevada," a gruff male voice answered before the doctor could. I shifted in my bed to get a better look at the person who had just walked in. The man from the church was built like the human version of the Humvee: good-looking and brawny. "I'm Commander Orion. It's a pleasure to meet you, Detective Matoo."

So that's Orion. I looked over his shoulder, hoping I might see a familiar dark-haired woman with almond-shaped eyes following close behind him. But I was disappointed. Orion was alone.

Commander Orion looked very different without his helmet on, though no less threatening; his face was chiseled and bore a long sweeping scar along the right side of his face. My mind dimly registered the fact that Orion already knew my name. So this would be a one-sided introduction. Orion already knew everything he needed to know about me. Evie's SOS must've reached him after all.

I scooted up from the bed and tried to raise my right arm. Instead, I groaned in pain.

"No big movements, please. The nanites are still repairing your fractured ribs, and I don't want to have to put you back together again," Medin said, before leaving us alone.

After she left, Orion pulled up a seat beside my bed. "How do you feel?" he asked.

"Disoriented," I answered. "Dazed. Hungry."

"I'm not surprised," Orion scowled. "Hexum really dug into you."

That night in the church felt like a lifetime ago now. "Where are they?" I asked Orion.

"You tell me."

My heart sank. So, Isaac, Evie, and Florence were still in the wind? Hexum hadn't outright admitted to having them, and I hoped they had gotten away.

I looked at Orion, unsure where to start.

"Everything, and from the start, if you don't mind," Orion prompted. "In as much detail as possible."

And so, we got down to the crux of it. Every single incident, all of it, was still fresh in the crevasses of my mind.

I recounted everything from the first meeting with Bull in San Francisco to the interview with Cara's parents and even the dinner at the Hercules where I first met Isaac. As I got to the more excruciating details, my limbic system went into overdrive. Feelings of anxiety, anger, and sadness flooded my body, and I struggled to put into words the retribution the Federate Army had served Cara's family.

As I narrated the story of our escape, the ghastly image of Rebecca's shattered face flashed before my eyes. I had seen many dead bodies before, but I had never actually watched someone die. In retrospect, I should have expected Rebecca to get even with Evie. The signs were there, and I had missed them.

Orion listened without interrupting once. Deep lines burrowed into the space between his eyebrows. Every now and again he grunted or sighed.

"What about Evie's message? Did she say what her plan was?" I pressed my dehydrated lips together. Florence, Isaac, and Evie, if they were lucky, should have made it out of the city hours before Orion stormed into the old church.

But Orion shook his head. "After we got Evie's message, we began constantly monitoring all seven colonies," Orion explained curtly. His Auge was blinking so rapidly, he looked like he was having a seizure. Dimly, I wondered if that's what I looked like when I was communing with my digital assistant. "And no helicopter arrived in Arizona or anywhere else. Radar didn't pick up anything in the area, either."

"Was the chopper still there when you arrived?" I asked in a panicky voice.

"No."

So if the chopper wasn't in Corinth and it wasn't in Arizona—where on Earth were the surviving Bull-Smiths now? Did Evie bring them to another location? Somewhere she didn't want anyone to find her and her family? It seemed like something Evie would do.

In an ideal world, they could have decided to go somewhere far away from the colonies and start fresh. Or, in the worst-case scenario, the Federate Army had stopped them from leaving and moved the chopper somewhere else.

But that only raised more questions. If the chopper was

gone, then where did they go? Why didn't it show up on any of the radars?

"Maybe they wanted a fresh start?" Orion suggested. "Somewhere far away from all this stuff? Can't say I blame them."

"Maybe they landed safely somewhere? Hid it and then took off on foot?" I theorized.

It was optimistic but unlikely. Satellite searches would've picked up the abandoned helicopter, and too much time had passed already. It could be anywhere in the world right now.

Orion cursed loudly. "I failed Evie and your brother," he said. "She survived the harshest terrains and the worst people in this country to find a life she deserved. When she volunteered to go back to the colonies to help other kids like her ...I promised to find a way out for her. And I failed. I wish I had told her at least once how highly I thought of her."

Evie had earned the admiration and respect of everyone she met. Including me. "I'm sure she knew."

Orion considered me. "We need to discuss your brother, Vir."

"I already know everything. Evie filled me in," I said.

"Then I'm sure you understand why we couldn't tell your family how he really died." Orion leaned in. "Why they still can't know."

My parents deserved to know how their son really died. More importantly, why. They deserved to know that they had raised a brave, honorable man who stood up for everything they believed in, and when the moment had come, he hadn't blinked. They deserved to feel the same pride I felt when I thought about Vir.

Orion might have his rules, but my responsibility to my parents was much greater. They deserved to know they had raised a good, honorable man who risked his life for others. Besides, what would it say about me if I denied them the opportunity to take pride in their fallen son?

Orion watched me expectantly, waiting for some sort of acknowledgment, so I simply nodded. "Where's Cara? Did her friends make it out too?" I changed the subject. "Are they safe?"

"Yes, they're all fine," he said. "Cara and her friends are thriving and settling in well. It's going to take some adjusting, but I think they'll be fine."

A wave of relief washed over me. "I need to see her," I said. "I should be the one to tell her... about everything."

It was the right thing to do. Plus, I needed to see her in flesh and blood, talk to her, and make sure she really was okay. I owed Evie and Isaac that much.

There was another thing nagging me since I'd woken up. "Is he dead?"

"Who? Hexum?" Orion scoffed. "Of course not! I'd be lying if I said I wasn't tempted, but you know the rules: we don't hurt people. Even the horrible ones."

I did know the rules. But deep down, it sickened me, knowing someone as heinous as Hexum was alive out there, keeping people locked up, forcing them to breed for a cause that mattered only to him.

I would never be able to rest until I knew for certain Isaac, Evie, Florence, and all the citizens of the colonies were safe and liberated from Hexum's clutches. How could anyone go to bed at night knowing somebody else was hurting? I couldn't. Vir didn't.

Orion and I had only just met, but we looked at each other, aware that the other had come to the same conclusion.

"We're going to find them," I promised. "We'll start in Corinth and work our way out."

I said it with such resolve that I could almost imagine us combing through the Hvalsey Mountains, scouring the bottom of the dead lakes, and looking under every crack and crevice until Isaac, Evie, and Florence were found.

But going back to Corinth might also mean going to war against the Federate Army. And that was fine with me. It was time to liberate the colonies and snatch freedom away from the greedy, power-hungry hands that sought to squash it. It was time for a revolution. It was time to stand up to hatred and animosity and to the people who spread it.

Thank you for reading

CORINTH 2642 AD

Please consider posting a review to Goodreads or
Amazon so that other readers can find this title.

ACKNOWLEDGEMENTS

This book would not exist today without the constant support and encouragement from my husband Alexander. Thank you for reading every line, every page, every chapter, and every version of this book, and for always believing in me when I didn't believe in myself. I am so fortunate to have you and our sweet monster-puppy Apollo, who is more human than most of us will ever be. You make the impossible feel possible.

And to my chorus of supportive friends—Anja, Joris, Sanjana, and Tania—for reading early versions of this book. How can I ever thank you for all the handholding, feedback, and encouragement? (Maybe we'll start with cuddles and slobbery puppy kisses and go from there?)

To my editor extraordinaire and brilliant feminist Amy Tipton, whose detailed and thoughtful feedback transformed this book into something I am incredibly proud of. Thank you for pushing me, forcing me to confront the discrimination and prejudice around us, and for making me a better writer. This book would not be what it is without you.

And to the incredible team at GenZ. Thank you for believing in this book as much as I did. I feel immeasurable gratitude for the editorial team—Allison MacDonald, Jaret Czajkowski, Emily

Oliver, Lauren Johnson. And to Tracy Fernandez for bringing my vision for this cover to life. Thank you for all your hard work and devotion to this book.

ABOUT THE AUTHOR

BINDIYA SCHAEFER is a former defense and aerospace journalist and has written for top niche publications around the world. Before moving to San Francisco, she lived in Dubai, UAE, and Bangalore, India. When she's not writing, she's camping in the California wilderness (where she also writes) with her husband and baby-dog.

Corinth, 2642 AD is her debut novel.

ABOUT THE PUBLISHER

ZENITH PUBLISHING is a YA/NA imprint of GenZ Publishing, launched in 2019 and growing more every day. We believe in the importance of reading and writing in shaping the future. As such, we focus on publishing debut, emerging, or underrepresented authors whose voices are ready to be heard.

Find out more and submit your story: www.zenithpublishing.org

OTHER GENZ & ZENITH BOOKS

The Lion-Blade Saga by Preston Marshall

Aftermath by Meiling Colorado

Bloodline: Murmurs of Earth by Nick van der Leek

The Crusader by Nicholas Chimera

Fall, Rise, Repeat by Matthew Schneider

Marital Law by David Brown

CPSIA information can be obtained
at www.ICGtesting.com
Printed in the USA
FSHW011954140921
84771FS

9 781952 919534